The TABER File

S.J. Garrett

Other Titles by S.J. Garrett

CHRONICLE Series
Chronicle of Destiny
Chronicle of Summer

ETERNITY Series
Ghost Eyes

DESCENDANTS Series
Shadow on the Sea

3rd DISTRICT Series
The Shaughnessy File
The Carmichael File
The Dease File
The Lucino File

Stand-Alones
Until the Dawn Breaks

PROLOGUE

There was a place known as the 3rd District.

When viewed from a plane, it resembled a small triangle located in the edge of New York City, New York. From space, it could not be seen. It was not a landmark. It was not a place of great historical import. It was, for all intents and purposes, a backwater area in a bustling city of hundreds of thousands of people.

It was also the place where magic lived. If your life crossed the roads of 3rd District, it was said, then you would find true love and live happily ever. You would find a true faerie tale story.

This story is one of them.

Folder One
PSYCHE

CHAPTER ONE

(Ancient Greece; Roughly 2100 years ago)

Long before the world thought they were no more than myths and legends, there was a pantheon of gods and goddess that watched over the events within the land of Greece. There was Zeus, the Thunder Bearer and the king of the gods. His wife and sister was Hera, she who watched over women and marriage. Many of Zeus' brothers and sisters were in the pantheon as well, and so were many of his children. Each had a duty and role to fulfill. Most spent their days tormenting or pursuing mortals.

A part of the pantheon but not technically related to anyone within it was Aphrodite, the Goddess of Love and Beauty. She was married to Hephaestus, Hera's son, but fidelity was not precisely common among the gods. She had had many dalliances over her years, and her favored partner was Ares, the God of War. Such an unlikely union, Love and War, but it had produced a god who was arguably the busiest, most desired, and most mischievous: Eros, the God of Love and Desire.

Almost from the moment Eros was born, he used his gifts to make men and women, both mortal and god, fall in love. He would inflame their hearts with passion and he would take away desire where it was abused or not needed. Perhaps a bit ironically, the God of Desire was the only one who practiced monogamy. His mother represented polyamorous love, and he monogamous. They would inflame both equally as needed in the populous, but for their personal love lives, they had a distinct difference in preference. So, while Eros' consorts knew they may not keep him forever, but they *did* know that he was theirs for as long as he wanted them.

Even his fellow gods watched him with a bit of longing. He stood at a normal enough five-ten height for a god, and he truly epitomized perfect beauty. His golden hair curled around his sultry features, and his sky blue eyes would light with wonderful sparks whenever he felt the effects of his power. He wore a quiver of arrows on his trim hips, and a bow hooked over his shoulder where the string would cross his sculpted chest.

He was invariably putting out fires behind the other gods. Most had no concept of decorum or consent. If a mortal was assaulted by a god, he went out of his way to ensure that a future of happiness would follow. It just vexed him that he got the blame for the events happening in the first place. He didn't shoot arrows where they were unneeded; the pantheon was lusty enough without his help!

His chosen domain was hidden among the invisible clouds that supported the palace of the gods. Only his mother, father, and a few select other gods or goddesses knew how to find him. Everyone else had to call for him properly.

"Eros!"

The enraged shriek echoed through his halls as he lay perched on a cloud and watched the planet far below. He dropped his head into his hands on a groan. "By Zeus." He rolled over and sat up cross-legged to watch as his mother stormed into the area with suitable drama and flare that made her bright golden hair swirl around her shoulders and her skimpy peplos play peek-a-boo with her lush body. He merely propped his chin on his fist. "Now what has you in such a mood?"

Aphrodite scowled as she stopped in front him. She planted her hands on her hips. "My temples are being abandoned!"

He stared at her for a moment. "That is impossible. Why would they be abandoned?"

"The mortals are worshipping one of their own!" Her voice

climbed on every word, and she stamped a bare foot on the ground in punctuation. "They dare compare her to me! They dare say she is more beautiful than I!" She swung away on a frustrated growl. "Go take care of her for me! Avenge your mother's pride!"

He stifled a sigh. His mother's pride demanded that he find any female who might be her rival and make sure the mortal fell in love with someone ugly. He always did as she asked—it was best to keep her happy if only for his sanity—but he always made sure the lack of appeal was only on the outside. The maidens who had dared incur Aphrodite's wrath had ended up in happy relationships anyway.

Still, this was a bit new. It was usually just people comparing a woman to Aphrodite. That this mortal was being worshipped put it into a new field. She must have been truly spectacular. Curiosity filled him and he got to his feet. "I will see to her," he offered only. A few centuries of knowing his mother told him how to divert her, and he looked at her face intently for a moment. "You may wish to stop worrying over this issue so terribly. I think I see a wrinkle."

She yelped and rushed out quickly. He grinned a bit and picked up his bow and arrows in order to descend. It would not be hard to find his target. It was obvious everyone knew who she was and where she lived. At the least, he hoped she was enjoying the worship. It could be vexing sometimes.

Down on the land, among the mortals, the young woman named Psyche was indeed being worshipped though she tried her best to protest against it. She was not a goddess, after all, and she knew the whispered tales of what Aphrodite did to rivals. Her case was not aided by the jealousy of her sisters. Though lovely, they simply did not compare.

Some sort of strange perfection imbued her features in a way that meant any man or woman who looked upon her would find her beautiful. She was a fairly normal height of five-two, but she was deceptively delicate in her frame. She had a lovely figure only just settling into its true shape, and at eighteen, it was likely she might even become more beautiful later. Rich black eyes were framed by naturally dark lashes, and her smile could light a room.

What truly elevated her though, what truly made her stand out, was her hair. The thick mane tumbled down past her shoulders in a rich red hue. No one knew where it had come from. All of her family had brown hair. Some had initially accused her mother of dallying with a god, but Psyche had the little birthmark on her foot that came down through her father's family. She was not even a half-god, though many thought she ought to be.

Of course, her adoration wouldn't have been so prominent if she had not been as beautiful inside as she was outside. She was infallibly kind and gentle, could laugh at her own mistakes, and she was the first to offer a hand if you were in trouble. Her father had been trying to keep her from breaking her heart since she was a child.

Suitors had been knocking on the door for four years. Some had offered a great deal of money and goods for her hand, but her father had refused. He would prefer to keep her unwed and at home, where she could tend to things now that her mother had passed. She didn't mind that very much; she had no desire to marry for anything less than the love her parents had shared.

She did not realize that the rejected suitors might try to force their hand until one day while she was picking grapes off the vines. She heard a footstep and turned to see one of her neighbors approaching. She liked him well enough, but her shoulders tensed a bit. Her father had warned her to not be alone with any man. "What brings you here?" she asked. She tried to subtly put the basket in front of her body.

"I have come to ask for your hand." He took off his hat earnestly. "I will treat you well, Psyche. You can sit at home all day and never work again."

Where she could be put on display like a hunting trophy. Really, how foolish did he think she was? "I am flattered, but no. My father has already declined your offer, and I am doing the same."

Something cold and ugly filled his eyes. "You will change your mind when I am done with you." He grabbed her shoulders and jerked her closer until the basket crunched between them. He tried to kiss her, but she kept jerking her head out of the way. He released her shoulder to grab her chin, and her hand suddenly shot up.

Grapes smashed into his face and briefly blinded him. She tore free of his grip and went running away into the trees as fast as she could. She felt sick and humiliated. Her panting breaths were as much from tears as they were exertion. Her day was not set to improve, however. She forgot about the dip in the landscape and went tumbling down the side of the hill. She rapped her head hard enough on the ground along the way that she was unconscious before she skidded to a stop at the bottom.

Eros knelt in the nearby trees and notched an arrow in preparation. He started to pull back the string and then lowered it again as she still did not move. Something about her seemed to powerfully draw him. He put the arrow away and hooked his bow over his shoulder as he walked forward to kneel by her side.

His breath hitched in his chest as he truly saw her for the first time. Rival his mother? Somehow she had done the impossible by being *more* beautiful. The familiar claws of desire began to rake through his body though with a potency he had never felt before. He *ached* to claim those soft lips and taste that fragrant skin. He gently reached out with his power to see her heart, and his longing only grew more powerful. She was as beautiful inside as out.

He tenderly checked her for injury and found nothing severe. He eased the bump on the back of her head and wistfully looked again at her lips. She was too good, too beautiful, even for a god. Then again, if the other gods noticed her, they might not see her as anything except a new pursuit. It made a blend of jealousy and fury churn inside his heart.

Sensing himself getting in trouble, he tried to put her down in order to walk away. He jostled his quiver in the process and jabbed his arm with the point of an arrow. A violent surge of lust ripped past his self-control, carried on a nearly cataclysmic rush of emotion. He looked down sharply, expecting to see that he had accidentally induced himself to love, but the only arrow pointed upward was an instigator. All it did was remove inhibitions on existing emotion.

It was daunting to see and feel the sheer depth of his existing emotion for this creature he held. It seemed to have been there inside him all along. Was she the one that had been foretold to walk by his side? Her breath sighed out with the scent of strawberries, and he found he did not care. He had to know her taste. He covered her eyes with his free hand so she could not see who held her, and he bent his head to claim her lips with his.

A shudder moved through his body at the perfection of her. She stirred in his grip and sighed softly into his kiss. He took it for the invitation it was and deepened the embrace with a hungry thrust of his tongue. Her hand lifted blindly and found his shoulder. It slid up to get into his hair and she held him closer as she opened her mouth and let him teach her how to kiss him in return.

He savored the feel of the desire that throbbed through her body and tingled against his nerves deliciously. It was just another reason why he ensured his consorts enjoyed their dalliances; his power would not replenish without it. Somehow this one kiss with this one woman had managed to entirely refill him. What would making love to her be like?

Realizing he was rather dangerously close to finding out right then and there, he reluctantly released her and eased back. "I suppose I ought to apologize," he murmured thickly. "Do not make me apologize. I would not mean it."

"No need, I assure you. I am fairly sure that I was a willing

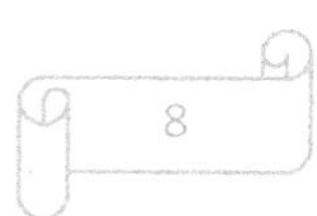

participant." She would have lifted her other hand but her muscles felt a bit as if they had melted. So *that* was what kissing was like. It was incredible. "Why do you cover my eyes? I do not know your voice so you must be a stranger." A hint of laughter filled her voice. "Do you think you are ugly? I think that would not matter at this point. I was happy to be kissed by you, no matter how you look."

"I do not wish you to see me." He could not resist taking another kiss from her swollen lips though he kept it light. "Count to twenty. You may open your eyes then. Your word, my lovely."

She sighed. "Very well." To prove she would keep her word, she lifted her hand to her eyes and covered his hand. It slipped away and she covered her own eyes as he tenderly placed her on the ground. She felt surprisingly cold without him holding her, and an equally strange sense of loneliness filled her. How could she miss him when she did not know him? She counted to twenty and removed her hand as she sat up and opened her eyes. There was no one around.

Heart pounding from a potent blend of love and desire and joy, Eros watched her get to her feet. Her eyes. Those beautiful eyes. Centuries before, the oracle of Delphi had found him lamenting being alone for once and not enjoying it. She had briefly entered a trace, and upon returning, told him that he would one day find his other half. His other half would be the source of his power and be the one who completed him. She would possess a power of her own that even the pantheon would have to bow down to. Most importantly, she would possess 'eyes as black as the velvet night that embraces lovers.'

He had not sensed active power inside Psyche, but perhaps she had not yet come into it. She was but a mortal age of eighteen. She had many years to mature. He would not wait for them. He would not wait to claim her as was his right. The problem of his mother remained, though; she would never approve of him having a dalliance with Psyche let alone wish to claim her as his mate.

He would have to possess Psyche in secrecy until he could

convince his mother to let him keep her. He would need to keep his identity hidden even from her for fear that she might rightfully wish to brag. It would be quite a claim to say you had enraptured the God of Love himself. She deserved that right, but not yet. Somehow he would have to make her fall in love with him though she could not know his face. He *could* have used an inducer on her, but he loathed the idea of it.

She was his other half. The only creature that completed him. She was already in love with him as he had already loved her. He would simply do whatever it took to ensure she gave him her heart as willingly as he would give her his.

His eyes narrowed slightly. As soon as he punished that foul beast that had tried to assault an unwilling woman, he would put his plans into motion. Psyche would be his wife before another week passed.

CHAPTER TWO

Psyche returned home in a bemused state. She could *still* feel the lips and taste of the man who had so brazenly kissed her. Delightful pleasure still rippled through her body though it had left behind something of a powerful longing to feel more. She felt slightly achy and frustrated somehow, though she did not know what was frustrating her.

She walked into her house on a sigh and sat the basket of grapes down in the kitchen. The unexpected sound of weeping made her frown. She followed the sound into the central room and found her father on the floor. He had his face buried in his hands as sobs shook his body. She rushed swiftly to his side. 'Father! What is wrong?"

He looked at her sadly. She was his most precious treasure. "My Psyche." He caught her face in his hands. "The temple oracle had a terrible vision. I went to her seeking advice for how to turn away your suitors. She told me that you are meant for no mortal man. No sooner did she see this vision than did a dark cloud pass over town. A voice spoke upon us all. You are to be given to a 'beast whose power makes Olympus shudder and that even the great Zeus himself must yield to.'"

"And if I refuse?" she whispered.

"The beast will rend our town full of despair and take away all that is loved." He pulled her into his arms and rocked her. "I would not ask it of you. We could leave the town to its own fate."

"No." She shook her head. "If this is what I am meant to do, then I will do it. My sacrifice will ensure the safety of those who live here." She thought longingly of the man who had held her. She had been hoping to seek him out and see if he would suit her. With her characteristic inner strength, she somehow reached for a smile. "I suppose I should make myself a wedding chiton."

The rush to wed her to the beast before it tore apart the town meant that many ceremonial aspects were foregone. Her sisters were very happy at the idea of ridding themselves of their so-called rival and were thus quite ready and able to help move the process along. One took upon the task of sewing the elaborate red chiton that Psyche would wear. The other fashioned the lovely veil that would hide her from her groom.

The day of the wedding, she was bathed and perfumed by her sisters and then dressed in her finery. Somehow she managed to withhold her fear and nerves as the process went on. Villagers turned out to see her leave, and many wailed and cried to the gods at the unfairness. It felt more like a funeral than a wedding day for Psyche.

Explicit instructions had been given. She was escorted beyond the town to a cliff where Zephyr, God of the Wind, would carry her to her new home. She was left alone to climb to the peak, and she had difficulty with the veil obscuring her sight. A pair of doves flew out of nowhere to aid, and they carried the veil just high enough to allow her to see. She did briefly wonder why messengers of the God of Love would help her, but finally decided it must surely be pity.

She reached the top of the cliff and found a glowing scroll hovering in the air. She gingerly reached out to take it and discovered that it was an agreement of some sort. A marriage agreement, in fact, though it did not refer to her future husband by name. They were called 'parties' instead. She could not even decipher his handwriting at the bottom; it looked more like a seal than a signature, and she had never seen the seal before. It almost resembled a heart. She skimmed over the agreement again and her eyes lingered on one line in particular. "'This agreement is a binding document that can and will be Enforced to the highest degree. This agreement is considered complete only on the basis of the signee's dreams coming true. If they do not find what they are seeking, this agreement is considered null and void."

Her dreams coming true? All she had ever dreamed of was finding someone to love and be loved by. To spend the rest of her life happy and serving the world to the best of her ability. It seemed like such an odd thing to find in an agreement that was sure to take away her dreams, but there was no going back. She lightly touched the blank space where her name was written, and her signature appeared. The scroll glowed and rolled itself up tightly, and she carefully held it tighter.

A gust of wind rippled her clothes. She looked up swiftly to discover a swirl in the air that must surely be Zephyr. Why he would aid, she did not try to guess. She stepped forward into the swirl and quickly closed her eyes as she felt her feet leave the land. Her heart pounded madly as she was carried for some distance before being gently deposited on soft grass. She opened her eyes swiftly and took in a breath of wonder.

A lush garden sat surrounded by thick trees. Lovely statues and fountains dotted the landscape, and the scent of peach trees was fragrant and wonderful. A pool for bathing had gently wafting steam curling into the air. A stone pathway led her through the glorious scenery until she discovered a beautiful palace awaiting her.

A warm power rushed over her as she stepped into the grand entry, and her veil flew back from her face. Across her mind, a strangely familiar male voice murmured, *You are my wife. I claim you as such. I have taken your veil; your innocence will be mine soon enough.*

She very nearly panicked and fled until the power curled around her tenderly and erased the fear. Somehow, she felt safe. She curled her hands together over her belly to combat lingering nerves as she moved slowly through the palace. There was much room to be had. She could do anything she wanted. There was a place for her to cook should she wish, and there was even a glorious pottery room where she could create the art she loved. It almost looked as if . . . as if she would survive whatever may come. It seemed as if she was expected to *live* there.

She stepped into the dining area and found it laid out with a suitable wedding feast, but nerves made her stomach too upset to eat anything. Again that power touched her and eased her emotions enough that she could consume even a bit. She seated herself at the lone place setting and hastily stifled a yelp as one of the statues along the wall seemed to come to life. Her wide eyes watched in disbelief as the statue picked up a tray and came to serve her. She was to have servants? *Statues*?

After she ate enough to please her watchful statue-guardian, she escaped into the garden where she had felt so secure. She remained there fashioning lovely wreaths of olive branches and flowers until the sun sank. Nerves returned with a vengeance as she got to her feet and slowly returned to the palace. A statue of a nymph came to escort her and showed her to the decadent bedroom.

She found herself left alone inside with only a single candle providing light. The moonlight could not penetrate the thick curtains at all. Her heart flipped into her throat as the door opened behind her and then shut. A soft breath extinguished the candle and plunged the room into darkness. Tears welled in her eyes and slid down her cheeks as she waited painfully for whatever terrors may come from giving herself to a beast that the gods feared.

A tender arm curled around her waist even as a familiar hand closed over her eyes. The scent of peaches seemed to imprint itself in her lungs. An equally familiar voice murmured huskily in her ear, "Fear me not, my beloved Psyche. I would *never* hurt you. You are safe with me. You will never know pain. Only pleasure awaits you within my embrace."

Her breath hitched. "You? You are . . . are my husband?" Her lips trembled. "What are you?"

"Yours." His teeth nibbled at her ear and sent flickers of delight streaming through her blood. "I am yours. Now, always, forever. You will find no greater love than what I have for you, my beloved. I am feared by the gods, yes, but you alone have nothing to fear."

Somehow she believed him. The utter tenderness in the way he held her, the emotion in his beautiful voice, soothed her nerves entirely. "Why can I not see you?" she whispered. "Can you see me?"

"I see you perfectly. You cannot see me yet. You must trust me. Trust me to know what is best. Perhaps soon there will be a day where we share the light. For now, the darkness is ours. I will come to you at every sundown. You may do whatever you wish during the day. The statues will serve your every need."

"What if I have need for you?"

Eros' heart quivered with violent emotions barely held in cheek. "Someday," he rasped. "Someday soon." When I find a way to keep you safe. "Will you trust me, my Psyche?"

She drew a long breath. "I will trust you." In a smaller voice, she asked, "There will be no pain? My sisters said that . . . that lying with a man would make a woman bleed terribly, that she would feel as if she was ripped in two."

His considerable temper nearly made his hands shake. How *dare* anyone scare a virgin in that way before her wedding night? Psyche had already been fearful because of not knowing his identity, and her sisters had dared plant that seed as well? Perhaps removing her from their clutches had been the right course even without the need to hide her away. Candidly, he admitted, "There can indeed be some pain and bleeding for a virgin if her lover does not take care with her. There will be none for you. I will ensure it."

She reached up to remove his hand from her eyes. "I will trust you, my husband." His arm loosened and she turned around in his grip. Only the trembling in her fingers gave away her lingering nerves as she reached up to touch his face. He was much taller than she had expected; she could guess him to be about four or so inches bigger than the average man. It seemed important though she could not determine why.

His hands framed her face and he drew her up to her toes as he bent his head to kiss her. His lips were hard and hungry as they fed from hers, and drugging heat flooded her body. How natural it felt to want him. How beautiful. She eagerly pressed up to return the kiss as he had taught her. The ache had returned and was starting to spread. He broke the kiss and began to nuzzle and tease the surprisingly sensitive skin behind her ear. "More?" he asked huskily.

"More." She stood meekly as he stripped away her veil and unfastened the clips at her shoulders that held her chiton in place. It fell down around her waist but a few tugs on the cord made the entire thing drop to her feet and leave her naked.

His breath wedged as he stared at her perfection. He could see every detail in the darkness, and she was too impossibly beautiful to be a mortal. She was trembling again and he quickly eased the nerves with a touch of his power. There would be *no* fear between them. She would destroy him if she feared him. Once she learned what ecstasy was like for them, he would never need to worry about her fear again.

He caught her hands and brought them to where his own chiton was fastened. "Undress me. Touch me." He curled his hands around her small waist and imagined seeing it expand with his child. She would make people fall to their knees in the streets with her radiance. He had always taken care to protect his consorts from his seed, but he would not hold back from his wife. "I want children."

Her lips quivered as she slowly unfastened the pins and let the material fall. "I might like to be a mother." A burning curiosity, need, to touch and caress with her fingers what she could not see made her reach out and press her hands to his chest. He was surprisingly hot, thrillingly powerful, and seductively soft. She could trace the line of his muscles and her mind built an image of what he must surely look like. "What are you?" she whispered.

"The man who loves you as no other ever will." He dragged her off her feet for a kiss that made the air quiver around them with the potency of its power. "Lie with me." He scooped her up and turned to lower her to the soft bed.

She gave a little gasp as whatever silky material was on it seemed to tease her sensitive skin. "It feels like a cloud!"

"Do you like it?" He shed his chiton entirely and knelt beside her on the bed. He trailed fingers slowly down her inner arm and found the tender nerves hidden there. She shivered and it was not nearly enough. He wanted to hear her crying out. He very badly wanted to hear her call his name, but he would have to wait for such a thing. He hotly caressed with his lips where his fingers had been and savored her little whimper.

She could do nothing except feel. Each erotic caress only made her body grow steadily more desperate for more of the pleasure he wrought. He seemed quite determined to map her body with his mouth, and he uncovered sensitive places she had not imagined could exist. A pulsing throb of need ran from her aching breasts to between her legs. She wanted to feel his hands there.

A soft laugh teased her ears as his teeth scraped delicately along her ribs. "Tell me," he urged huskily. "Tell me what you want. I am yours to command." He felt the little ripple of shyness inside her and vowed to remove it. There was no shame in telling a lover where you liked to be touched. "Take my hand." He put his hand into hers. "Tell me what you need."

She very nearly released him but something eased her shyness as it had eased her nerves. She brought his hand up to cover her breast, and her back arched reflexively as pleasure replaced desperation. He tenderly squeezed and caressed until she twisted beneath him. His mouth closed hotly over one taut nipple and a moan escaped her gasp. He nearly purred in response. "I love how you sound when you want me."

He moved slowly down her body and draped one of her legs over his shoulder. He was waiting when he felt her nerves surge, and he eased them again. He gave her only a breath to prepare before he found her softest flesh with his lips and fingers. Little cries answered his every caress and he savored the rising force of her hunger. His arousal pulsed and throbbed in time to her heartbeat and demanded he be inside her soon. He ignored it in favor of his hunger to please her. He loved the before as much as he loved the after of making love.

He urged her higher and higher before gently sending her over the edge. Her cry of ecstasy was the sweetest sound he had ever heard. Power ripped through his body in an unstoppable surge that stunned him. He could not resist starting to caress her again. The extra sensitivity from her release meant that it took no time at all to have her crying out for him. He wrapped his arms around her waist and rolled over to brace her on top. "Touch me," he pleaded thickly. "I must feel your hands. Taste me."

She could not resist his plea or her own desire. She felt ravenous for him somehow. There was so much more to this beautiful act than she had imagined. She sent up a mental prayer of gratitude to Eros himself, and never realized that her husband heard it and was humbled. No nerves could overcome her curiosity. She followed his example and found herself slowly savoring the flavor of his skin.

His fingers curled around her wrist and drew her hand down to his arousal. He waited, spied her expected shyness, and banished it. Her fingers curled around him to learn his shape and feel, and the surge of her surprised delight mingled with his own pleasure in a way that had him groaning.

It was his turn for surprise when soft lips suddenly teased the tip of his length. He let her pet and taste him at her will; his body was her playground the same as hers was his. The rising throb of ecstasy warned him how close he was to release, but he did not care. He tangled his fingers in her hair and urged her on when it seemed she would let go. To his delight, she teased him huskily, "More?"

"More, beloved."

The rasp of his voice made her feel strangely powerful. She had the notion she might be in danger of becoming addicted to the way he made her feel, but she was not at all bothered by the idea. She resumed her hungry caresses until his hips twisted under her and he called her name hoarsely. He was wonderfully unashamed and free, and it erased whatever lingering nerves or shyness had been inside her. She *needed* to feel him inside her where he belonged.

For just a moment, she thought she saw a gleam of bright blue eyes in the darkness as if they had glowed in response to her emotions. His hands grabbed her shoulders and he dragged her back up his body until he could consume her in a nearly bruising kiss. He rolled over to pin her, and he dragged her legs up around his waist. "Take me," he whispered fiercely, "and I will take you."

He surged forward even as she twisted upward, and he seated himself to the hilt in that first lunge. Her eyes slowly widened until the pupils disappeared into the velvet darkness, and her lips parted on a trembling breath of wonder. She could hardly believe how wonderful it felt to have him so deep. Pain? Never.

He slowly drew away and laughed richly when she tried to stop him by tightening her grip. "I am not leaving." He thrust deep again and savored her cry of delight. "See?" He took her again, and then again. Each wrought another breathless sound from her swollen lips. He fought back his release as hard as he could until she suddenly arched beneath him and he felt the searing heat of her ecstasy through his body and over his aching flesh. Only then did he let himself bury deep and stay there as matching ecstasy ripped through his body in a way he had never before experienced. It boiled out of his very soul until it consumed every drop of his existence. Finally, he knew what it meant to find the true desire born of true love.

He collapsed into her embrace and she coiled her arms around his sweaty shoulders. Loved. She felt loved all the way to her soul. Physically, certainly, but emotionally as well. Her heart and soul felt as if they were soaking up his love for her. She could feel it inside him like a beautiful glowing light.

"You have exhausted me, my beloved," he murmured thickly into her hair. "I will need to rest a bit before I can love you again." He shifted his weight so that he was lying beside her. She did not move, and he sighed as he reached out to turn her onto her side where she could snuggle against him. "I wish to hold you. Hold me in return."

She let her arm creep across his chest as she settled her head onto his shoulder. "I am happy," she murmured. "I did not expect to be. I thought . . ."

"I know what you thought." He gave a little shrug. "It was the only way to claim you as quickly as I wanted. Others would stand in the way of our union." He tucked a hand under his head and held her with his other arm. His fingers smoothed absently over her skin. "I will not apologize for what I have done."

"I do not need an apology." She closed her eyes since there was nothing to see in the dark. "What do you do during the day?"

He smiled. "I help people. I am accused of causing trouble, but it is more true that I have to clean up behind my friends." He gave a gusty sigh. "They are always demanding that I do things for them, but they never ask me for anything I want to do."

"I imagine that annoys them."

"Oh, indeed. They do not dare press the issue, though. I can make their lives quite uncomfortable."

"A man who makes the gods tremble? I imagine so." She unconsciously rubbed her cheek against his skin. She loved the scent of peaches clinging to his body. "What do you like most, my husband?"

"You." He was rewarded with a soft giggle that enchanted him. "I am fond of music and dance. I am drawn to places where people are happy, I think. I love the scent of strawberries and the taste of wine." His voice softened. "I love watching the sunrise and sunset. The sound of children laughing. Lovers embracing in the night and whispering promises to the air. If there is war, I stay away. It erases all that I hold dear."

Her lips trembled as she hid her face for a moment. How was it possible she fall in love with him so quickly? There could be no other word for the emotion inside her heart. No other word for the way she wished to be by his side and ease him if he was weary. It seemed as if there was a burden on his shoulders that she ought to be sharing though she did not know how.

His fingers stilled their stroking of her arm. A low sound of joy and wonder caught in his chest as he turned and gathered her into his arms for a powerful hug. It almost seemed as if he would never let go again. "My beloved," he whispered thickly into her hair. "Do you truly love me, my Psyche? I have given you no reason. I have asked for your blind trust."

"You have given me you." She cupped his cheek. "When you kissed me that first time, I had the thought that I might find you and see if you would suit me. I am happy enough to be here with you."

He found her lips with his and sank into the kiss as if it was the only thing in the world that he needed in order to survive. "I will touch you again," he warned huskily against her lips. His hands began to slowly stroke over her skin. "I have much to teach you. You may rest later."

She merely tugged him closer and contentedly surrendered to his embrace. She would take whatever he could give her and hope that the day came soon when they would share the light and she could have him by her side always. There was nothing else she could ever want but that simple thing.

CHAPTER THREE

A month passed in blissful serenity. Summer began to chill into autumn as Persephone returned to Hades' embrace in the Underworld, and Psyche continued to cherish every day of her new life. The days were spent with art and music and reading—she had been surprised one day by a wonderful supply of books—and her nights were filled with her husband.

He came to her after dark every evening, and he stayed by her side until the first light of dawn. She would wake alone in bed and battle back her painful loneliness by holding onto his pillow where his scent remained. Each passing day ensnared her more fully. He would never tell her details of what he did, but he would talk of himself. He was a gentle, caring, and fiercely protective man who had a bit of a temper, tendency to seek revenge for being wronged, and a strangely appealing arrogant streak.

He was also tender and loving, and he was selfless in giving himself to her. He encouraged her budding sensuality and taught her how to burn in his arms. He let her have him at her will, and he showed her how to give pleasure as thoroughly as she received it. He breathed his love with nearly every caress. When she would speak of her love, he would tremble as if he had been given a priceless reward. There was almost nothing to mar her sheer bliss and happiness with her new life.

Nothing except her growing need to have no secrets left between her and her husband. She felt as if she was only being given half of a relationship, and though the half she had was glorious, it was simply not enough anymore. The very love that allowed her to trust him implicitly was the very thing that drove her craving to remove all barriers. She very nearly prayed to the God or Goddess of Love for intervention but something made her hesitate.

Her situation was not aided by her growing loneliness. She had no one to talk to during the days. She could converse with the statues but they could not converse back. She missed people and being around others. Missed interacting and socializing. If she could simply have someone to visit with for one day, she might be happy again.

Her husband was highly sensitive to her emotions. As they lay together in bed, his fingers combed through her hair. "Tell me what you wish. I shall get it if I can. I do not like this sadness inside your heart, my beloved."

She gave a little sigh. "I am lonely. I have no one to talk to while you are away from me. I would wish you there with me during the day, but I would settle as well for a visit from someone."

He pressed his lips to the top of her head. It killed him to not yet be able to claim her entirely. His mother had been so thrilled at Psyche's supposed marriage to a 'cavernous beast' that he had not yet found a way to clarify what he had done. "Who would you visit with if you could?"

"Hmm. My father or sisters perhaps. I miss them the most."

"Your sisters are vile creatures with no love in their hearts."

She smiled at the bite in his voice. "Perhaps they are, but I cannot help loving them myself. Maybe a bit of me is a little petty as well. I would like them to see how happy I am. They were not very good at hiding their glee at my fate to be sacrificed for the village."

"Shall I dress you as a queen, my lovely wife? Deck you in fine fabrics and jewels so that they are rendered breathless with their envy?"

It was certainly tempting. "I will settle for one of those little love marks you have left before. After they tried to scare me about my wedding night, it would serve them right to see that I am treated well."

"Well?" A hint of laughter filled his husky voice as he shifted to pin her to the bed. "Treated *well*? There are far better words for how I treat you." His mouth closed hotly over her neck. "You shall have your mark, my love. And you shall have your rightful revenge. I will arrange for Zephyr to bring them to you. When you tire of them, call to Zephyr and he will take them away."

"That you can command the God of the Wind is daunting, my husband," she teased huskily as she curled a leg over his.

"He owes me a favor or two," he countered modestly. He nipped at her skin. "Now where to place that mark you wished. There are so many delightful possibilities."

She truly did not know where he had marked her until she bathed the following morning. His lips had lingered in many places and she had been so consumed with her hunger for him that she hadn't been paying attention. Much to her bemusement, she found the little red mark hovering quite blatantly over the curve of her breast where her peplos could not cover it. The peplos itself was of a fine and glorious linen in brilliant hues of gold and red that flattered her coloring. She lingered over her makeup and hair, enjoying the pampering, and then finally went to the front of her home to await her sisters.

They arrived shortly thereafter and the looks of ripe jealousy on their faces as they beheld the palace could not be mistaken. She merely smiled. "Welcome to my home, Peisma, Zelas. Please come inside."

Peisma's eyes swept over her sister's wear and envy churned in her heart. Her gaze found the little mark, and her mouth went bitter. "You look well."

"I am treated quite . . . beautifully." She led them into the dining area and gestured to two seats. "Please do sit. I have wine and cheese to enjoy."

Zelas barely withheld a yelp as a statue left his station to approach and serve the wine. "Wh-what is this? Is this magic?"

"I suppose it is." Psyche nibbled on a piece of cheese. "My husband has great power. He has ensured I do not lack for anything. I spend my days making my pottery or reading of the books he has given me. I am thinking of taking up painting. I fear I best not garden. I believe I got scolded by a statue for almost killing something."

Both sisters nearly choked on their emotions. First she had been so beautiful as to command worship. Now she had found herself treated as a queen rather than devoured by a beast. There was an obvious happiness inside her that glowed through to the outside. "So who is your husband?" Peisma asked as politely as she could.

"A good man."

"How nice for you. What does he look like?" At the silence, she made a little scoffing noise. "Surely you can share at least that much with your own sisters."

"The truth is that I do not know. There is something that keeps him from being with me during the day. He is trying, but it is not easy. I know not his face. I know only his voice and touch. The way he feels." Her voice softened. "I love him more than anything. I would ask only to see him in the light, to remove all secrets."

Zelas leaned forward. "Oh, poor Psyche." False sympathy dripped from her tone. "Such a naïve girl. You must have a demon after all. Why else would anyone wish to hide himself from someone as beautiful as you?"

Her sister leapt onto what she was thinking. "You will simply have to see him in the light, Psyche. We will worry about you until you do. What if he is a foul and vile creature?" She clicked her tongue. "What would you know of the difference, being as pure as you are?"

Psyche refrained from mentioning the fact that she had quite thoroughly examined her husband's body with her lips and fingers and had found no sign that he was anything except human. Could there be things she did not feel? Certainly so, but she did not care.

"Your concern is quite touching, sisters." A hint of a bite to her tone and the snapping of sparks in her eyes were a warning that her temper stirred. "Do tell me what you would do if you were in my place."

"You must light a candle to see him." Peisma leaned over and lowered her voice. "Once you have confirmed what he is, you must take a dagger to him. Be sure to have it in your hand when you light the candle lest you must fight for your life."

It was a sickening suggestion that she might wish to kill her husband simply because he did not look a particular way. "Get out of my house." She got to her feet with regal grace. "You would make me murder the man I love." Her chin lifted. "Zephyr! My sisters are done here!"

Strangled yelps were about all that Zelas and Peisma could manage as the wind swept in and snatched them away. Psyche stormed away from the table in disgust and sought refuge in the garden bath. Her loneliness had not been assuaged. If anything, she felt even lonelier than normal. Her sisters had driven home the point that the only person who loved her was, in fact, her husband.

Desperate need welled inside her heart. She *needed* to have everything of him that she could. She wanted to love him with her eyes as thoroughly as she had with the rest of her senses. Every aspect of her self that there was, she wanted to share. The situation would have been so, so much easier if she had only been blind. She would not have had sight to share and therefore would not have craved it as terribly as she did. In fact, being blind meant he wouldn't have to hide from her at all.

Her resolve firmed as she thought about things. She could light a candle, peek at him, and be appeased until the time when they shared the light. Surely he would understand her need. It was not a lack of trust that drove her, but too much love.

The emotionally exhausting day had her actually falling asleep before he came to her that night. She woke to the feel of his hands and the taste of his kiss. He loved her with a tenderness that brought tears to her eyes and overflowed her very soul with emotion. She could only lay limply across his chest when it was done and listen to the unsteady beat of his heart even out. "I like how you wake me," she murmured in a voice still husky.

His arm coiled around her waist. "I could not resist." His other hand lifted to thread into her hair and smooth it back from her face. "They upset you."

"I should not be surprised, but I am," she admitted. "They are very jealous of me and tried to insist that you must be a demon of sorts. I threw them out. You are no demon." She rubbed her cheek against his skin. He used lotions that made his body a delightful pillow to rest upon. "I think I would have found horns and hooves by now if you were a demon."

"You may examine me again, very slowly, at any time you desire." He tugged her up for a lingering kiss. "I am merely a man that loves you." Wonder filled his voice as he murmured, "You are so beautiful to me. I could look at you forever."

It only made her wish all the more fiercely to be able to give him the same. To worship him with her eyes as she had with her hands. She let herself doze for a bit and woke around midnight. Her husband's arm was draped over her waist and she gingerly freed herself. He did not stir and his breathing did not change.

She crept over to the table where the candle sat and lit it as quietly as she could. She started to pick it up, and a hand reached past her. Her heart froze as she saw a brilliant glow enveloping the skin of her husband. Only gods glowed in such a manner. He snuffed the candle and plunged the room into darkness again.

A blend of pain and anger filled his voice as he asked, "What say you, wife? Why do you not trust me anymore?"

"I trust you!" she cried as she swung around. "I need more than what you have given me! I *need* to have everything! I want to worship you with my eyes as yours have done to me! Why do you hide from the woman who loves you as I do?"

"If you loved me," he countered harshly, "you would trust me to know what is right! Love is supposed to be blind, Psyche! It should not matter whether you see me or not!"

"You do not know how it feels!" she flung at him. A surge of power made her yelp and she threw her arms over her eyes as the palace creaked. When the power faded, she lowered her arms slowly to find herself in the middle of an empty meadow. She shivered violently for she was still naked, and a rush of power down her body clothed her in a plain peplos. It did not help much though it did ease some of the chill.

"Turn and look upon your husband," she was mocked softly. "As you so desperately wished."

She slowly turned around and found behind her a man that looked almost exactly as she had imagined him in her mind. He wore a chiton that did nothing to disguise his powerful frame. Gold hair clung to a face too beautiful to belong to a mortal. It was only when she spotted the bow and quiver he wore that understanding came. Her eyes slowly widened.

He caught her chin in his fingers. "I am Eros," he told her with a hint of bite. "You will never be loved by anyone as you are loved by me. I kept you in the dark for your own safety! My mother quite hates your very existence. She would not approve of our union. I sought for a way to keep you. Fool that I am, I will seek it still. For now, I wish not to see you for fear I may say something I regret! When you have repented what you have done, I will come for you."

"No!" She reached out desperately as he disappeared before her eyes, but though she caught a trace of pain in his eyes, it did not override the temper still there. She found herself alone, cold, and heartbroken in the middle of where her home had once stood. Wind coiled around her to return her to the cliff, and it was even colder and darker there.

A lamp appeared at her feet with a hint of a bluish glow. An unfamiliar female voice murmured across her ears, *Your lamp will not go out. It is my wedding gift to my nephew's wife. I am Artemis, young Psyche. I will watch you during the night. My twin brother*

Apollo shall watch you during the day.

It was a daunting thing, and a humbling one, that the celestial twins would seek to aid her when she had been the one to ruin everything. She sank down to her knees and carefully lit the lamp. It produced light enough to see, and she wrapped her arms around herself as she stared blindly at the murky distance.

Something began to stir deep inside her mind. An odd sort of clarity moved. Images flittered past her mind as if she was watching some sort of record of events. She could even see events that had not occurred yet though they were covered in a thick gray that obscured most of them from true sight.

Understanding bloomed as she looked at what had happened. She could even see things that she did not have a legitimate reason to know about, and they all told her something that she just somehow knew was fact: she was not the only one who had not had enough trust. Eros had not trusted *her*. He had not trusted her to keep his identity a secret. She could even guess at his reasoning, but she knew he was wrong. For one thing, who would she have had to brag to while living in their secluded palace? For another thing, for a chance to know the man she loved, to simply have him, she would have gladly said not a word.

He wanted her to repent. She would carry the guilt for the rest of her life, but she could at the least prove that she truly wanted him. Truly loved him. She needed to prove she was worthy of the God of Love, and she needed also to win over his mother Aphrodite. Perhaps doing the latter might even take care of the former. She would need to find her way to Aphrodite's temple and hope she was not smited the moment she stepped inside.

With the lamp to light her way, she made her way gingerly through the night and down from the cliffs. A snowy owl arrived to aid her, and he showed the way through the thickest portions. She could somehow sense the power inside the beast and knew he must belong to Artemis. How odd that she could sense the power of the gods now. Was that from being Eros' lover, or had it come with her strange awakening?

To her surprise, she happened upon a new house as she exited the woods. A light was on inside, and she was even more surprised to see her sisters. Had they moved into their own home? Perhaps they had given up on the hope of any man wanting them. She couldn't be surprised by it. Her sisters were lovely only on the outside. A stirring inside her heart made her wish to teach them a lesson, and she approached the door.

She knocked lightly, and it was opened by Zelas. The elder female's jaw dropped briefly as she beheld who stood on her step. "Psyche?" She grabbed her sister's wrist and hurried her into the house. "Peisma!" she called. As the other joined them, she scowled at Psyche. "Why are you here and not with your precious husband? Did you do as we told you and remove such a vile beast from your life?"

"In fact," Psyche retorted coolly, "I would seem to be having a fight with my husband. It happens to all couples, I suppose. He thinks I do not trust him, and I do not think he trusts me either. But I suppose it was an inevitable moment as he feels far more deeply than any other creature alive."

"A demon?" Peisma scoffed.

A hint of a smirk touched Psyche's lips. "A god. I would seem to be the bride of Eros, the God of Love himself. I laid eyes upon him but an hour ago. He has left me in order to keep his temper, and I am seeking Aphrodite's temple to prove my worth. She does not like me. That was the whole reason for the secrecy."

Ripe jealousy rose like bile inside both Peisma and Zelas. She had married the *God of Love*?! She had been chosen by one of the most powerful of all gods, the one that even Zeus answered to. How was it fair that she be given such a thing?! "He has rejected you?" Zelas asked with as much calm as she could.

"Not rejected." Not if she could repent and prove herself worthy, at least. "We are merely apart."

As far as her sisters were concerned, that meant that she had been thrown out. Zelas grabbed Psyche's arm and forced her toward the door. "You will not stay here!" she snapped. "We do not wish to incur the wrath of the Goddess of Love! Take yourself off somewhere else and hope your husband forgives you! We have no care for you to be here!"

Psyche said nothing as she was shoved outside. The door slammed behind her and she contemplated it for a few moments. Softly, she murmured, "Such a desire to consume flesh from those you deem as beneath you. Your teeth are as sharp as your tongues." She scooped up her lamp and walked away into the nearby woods.

Zelas and Peisma did not hear her nor would they have cared. They swiftly washed and perfumed themselves and then dressed in their finest clothing. They bickered madly as they rushed from their home and toward the cliff. The swirl of wind that was Zephyr was there, and it seemed to be waiting. "We offer ourselves in place of Psyche!" Peisma announced. "We are far better than she! We deserve to be Eros' brides! We will worship the ground he walks upon and cater to his every desire!"

They tried to throw themselves into the swirl of wind but it winked out. They found themselves instead flying off the side of the cliff, and both shrieked in terror as they plummeted into the sea below. Try as they might to swim to the surface, they were dragged deeper and deeper. An odd glow appeared before them and they only briefly got a glimpse of a rather furious man holding a trident before power blasted into them.

Poseidon watched in satisfaction as the two sisters became piranhas and swam away quickly. It was the least of what they had deserved. He turned his gaze up toward the surface and sighed sadly. He could not aid Psyche directly; the best he could do was give her the vengeance she deserved for her sisters' cruelty. It would be up to the other gods to help her win over Aphrodite from her unreasonable jealousy.

Psyche was strangely aware of what he had done as she walked through the woods. It almost seemed as if the images in her mind had been crossed out in a way that meant they had happened as she had seen. It was a small comfort.

The night was growing colder. She shivered violently as she forced herself to keep walking. A few fat drops of rain landed on her skin and she looked up just as the skies opened with painful, stinging cold rain. Soaked, miserable, and more heartbroken than before as she remembered her husband's wonderfully warm arms, she tried to crouch under a tree for any semblance of protection.

A soft rumble made her look up sharply to discover that a wolf had approached. It glowed in a way not dissimilar from the owl before though it was a different sort of power. It felt rich and earthy. The wolf caught a mouthful of Psyche's peplos and tugged gently. Knowing it for a sign, she got to her feet and followed the wolf as he led her swiftly through the woods, up a rocky hillside. A cave had been opened into the backside, and the wolf urged Psyche inside. It was dry and surprisingly warm in there.

A small fire lit itself from some abandoned bits of wood. She carefully reached out to warm her hands and then scooted closer in hopes of getting dry again. Sensing the presence of a goddess still, she asked softly, "Are you . . . Demeter?"

I am, young one.

"Why do you help me?"

Because I believe that you and Eros are meant to be together. He hid himself from the eyes of his mother, but he could not hide from the rest of us. I have cursed his name for ages for his making Hades fall in love with my daughter, and she with him, but that does not mean I do not care for him.

"He is furious with me," she whispered.

He is, but he will forgive you. Love always forgives, Psyche. I have waited many centuries to see that boy take his fall, and I think he could not have chosen a better pair of arms to fall into. There is something inside you that perfectly complements him. When you come into your own, you will be equals.

It made Psyche feel a little better though she could not so

easily convince herself that her husband might forgive her so quickly. She would have a great many things to do in order to repent. "Thank you," she said only.

Sleep, child. In the morning, my wolf will escort you to where Aphrodite's temple is located. Be prepared for her to treat you worse than even your sisters. She has no desire to accept you. When she learns of what has happened, she will take out her wounded vanity on you. If the tasks she gives you are too hard—and they will be hard indeed—call out to the other gods. They will offer whatever help they can.

She laid down on her side and curled up. The wolf moved closer and laid down as well to give extra warmth, and eventually she was able to fall asleep. It was not to be a restful sleep. Not any longer. Her dreams were no longer her own. Was it a gift or a curse? She honestly did not know. The one person she could ask was the one person who was too furious to see her.

How long would it take her to earn his love again?

CHAPTER FOUR

Word could travel quickly where the gods were concerned. Aphrodite may not have seen her son much over the last month, but she hadn't really cared. He was a grown man who could take care of himself. She had too many other things to deal with in the meantime.

She was busily preening in a mirror when Eris, the Goddess of Discord, strode arrogantly into the chambers. Aphrodite tolerated Eris' presence only reluctantly since she was sister to Ares. "What do you want?" she asked curtly. "I am busy."

"So has your son been," Eris countered slyly.

"Has he found himself another consort? He seemed more powerful when I saw him last. He does gain strength with each lover he takes. I do wish he had kept that lovely athlete. I would have liked sharing him."

"Oh, he has no consort. Your son is married."

Aphrodite shot to her feet so fast that her chair tipped over and clattered onto the floor. "What?!" She whipped around. "Who would he marry? He never indicated he had his eye on anyone! The other goddesses are with their same consorts or already married!"

"He took a mortal." Eris' eyes were viciously malevolent. She loved to rattle her brother's lover. She rose to the bait so nicely. Eros had been quite generous to give her this ammunition. "I think her name was . . . Psyche? Might be."

"WHAT?!" The shriek redoubled and echoed throughout the entire area, and even Eris winced. Aphrodite shoved past her

informant and rushed from the place. She would have Eros' *head* if he had dared marry that outrageous, unseemly, upstart! She went to the edge of her domain and bellowed, "EROS!"

He arrived only a few minutes later. "For the love of Zeus, Mother!" He scowled at her. "I am not in the best of moods at the moment. I have no desire to deal with your temper tantrums! Whatever it is can wait!" He still felt heartbroken and miserable from Psyche's betrayal. His temper came and went, and when it went, it left him aching to see her again. How could she have not trusted him?

"Eros!" She grabbed the collar of his chiton. "Did you *dare* marry that Psyche? You swore she had been taken by a beast!"

He flicked a glance over her shoulder and saw Eris smirking at him. Fresh anger stirred anew. He would have to deal with her later. "Psyche is my other half." He met Aphrodite's eyes. "I love none as much as I love her. I *am* a beast, Mother. And she has been taken many times by me. She is my true wife."

She recoiled violently. "I forbid it!"

"It has been done." He shrugged. "I would not change it though I am quite furious with her right now. We are having our first martial spat."

"Oh?" she bit out. "Do tell what has spoiled your bliss."

"I had been keeping her in the dark to protect her from you. I came to her during the night and left her with the dawn. She did not know my name or my face. I asked her to trust me until I could make things work; I knew you would overreact as you have thus. Last night, she tried to light a candle to see me. She tried to excuse herself by saying she wished to share everything, that she wanted to worship me with her eyes, but she simply did not trust me. Love is supposed to be blind."

A part of Aphrodite almost wanted to smack him in the head. Love was to be blind, but not *that* sort of blind! *Naturally* Psyche would wish to share everything of her husband if she truly loved him. She had deserved to be given the truth. Eros was quite the one at fault for this fiasco, and Aphrodite had no doubt that he would shortly realize it himself and rush to beg forgiveness.

Over her dead body! If it had been any other female—mortal or no—she would have boxed his ears, given him a ripe lecture, and sent him to grovel. She would *never* condone his union with that comely upstart who dared compare herself with the Goddess of Beauty. She would sooner see Psyche dead than continued to be worshipped for her looks! "You are an idiot," she told him curtly. "You are the one who is blind, my son." She made a sharp gesture and a golden cage formed around him. "I will not let you go back to her when your temper cools!"

He banged on the bars but they held firm. "What are you doing?" he demanded.

"Ensuring you will not do something stupid!" She broke off and her eyes widened slightly as she heard someone praying to her. The voice was surprisingly familiar, and she looked into the distance where she could see through the eyes of her statue in the temple. A familiar redhead knelt in prayer. Nearly malicious glee filled Aphrodite. She would have a chance to get rid of her rival!

Eros cursed as she hurried off. "Mother!" he shouted. He shot a dangerous look at Eris as she ambled closer. "Your dead heart can as yet be inflamed, Discord. Do not think I will ignore your deeds."

She clicked her tongue at him mockingly. "See me shake in my sandals, Eros. By the time you get out of there, you will realize what an idiot you really are." She flew up into the air. "Maybe you should think about things, young God of Love. Who is truly to blame for your fight with your wife? I think someone else around here had a problem with trust!" She disappeared into the air.

Sobered and suddenly a bit afraid, he slowly sank down to sit on the ground. Was it his fault? His temper tried to tell him it was not, but he could not dismiss Eris' words—or his mother's. Heart pounding, he forced himself to start thinking about everything that had happened. Had he not seen something?

The wolf had taken Psyche all the way to Aphrodite's temple, and its disarray disappointed her as deeply as it upset her. It had been abandoned by the people wishing to worship her, and she was not a goddess. She did not *want* to be worshipped by any except her husband. Unable to stand the sight, she got to work cleaning everything up. She replaced the dead flowers and got the candles burning anew. She cleared debris and dusted statues. Only when everything was as it should be did she go to the altar and kneel in prayer.

She was not sure if her words were being heard until a strident feminine voice sniped behind her, "At least you are not entirely helpless! I would thank you for cleaning up, but it was your fault in the first place."

She slowly got to her feet and turned around to discover a woman too beautiful to be mortal behind her. Objectively, she was reluctantly forced to admit that, actually, she really was more beautiful than the Goddess of Beauty. She still did not feel as if she deserved worship for such a thing. "How do I address you?" she asked only. "You are my mother-in-law, and you are a goddess."

"Hmph. 'Aphrodite' will suffice." She sauntered closer. "I do not think you are that beautiful at all. You cannot hold a candle to me."

Psyche said only, "You are the Goddess of Beauty."

"I am." Her eyes narrowed as she looked down at her daughter-in-law. The mortal was a few inches shorter and overall more delicate. Even Aphrodite was reluctantly forced to admit her appeal. She could not question her son's taste; she simply did not like it. "Tell me. Do you love my son?"

Ripe agony filled Psyche's black eyes. "No one loves him more," she whispered. "Forgive me for saying so, but I believe I love him more than you do."

Aphrodite wanted to be offended, she really did, but she could feel Psyche's honesty. It would make things much simpler. She would do anything in order to get her husband back. "I shall make a deal with you. You wish to prove your worth as the bride of Eros himself? I have three tasks to set before you. Accomplish them and I will accept you as his wife, and I will personally mediate this little spat. Fail at even one, and I will see you banished for all time from his side."

Psyche took a long breath. "You have my word. What tasks do you have to place before me?"

"Come with me." She grabbed Psyche's arm and swung her around sharply.

A combination of the sharp nails digging into her arms and the disorienting transportation had Psyche's head spinning and her stomach churning. She shook off the feelings to the best of her ability and looked around quickly. She barely kept her jaw from dropping in disbelief.

They seemed to be standing inside a storehouse of some kind, and it was covered in stacks upon stacks of rice and grains that had been thoroughly mixed together. Aphrodite released her and gave her a shove forward. "Here is your task, *daughter*." She smirked. "Before you is the storeroom of the gods. We keep grains in here for our festivals. They have become quite disarrayed. There are more than a million pieces in here, and you are to sort them into individual types before sunset." She turned on her heel with a toss of her golden hair. "Have fun!" Her laughter lingered in the air long after she had disappeared.

Psyche squared her shoulders and lifted her chin. It seemed an impossible task but she would not give up. Too much was riding on her succeeding at these tasks. She knew that Aphrodite did not expect her to succeed—that she was, in fact, deliberately trying to make her fail—but it only firmed her determination.

The first thing was to make herself some room. Everything

was mixed up already, so she simply started shoving and pushing it all to one side of the room. Once she had an area cleared, she lifted her skirt and filled it with the first batch of grain to begin sorting. They were all different colors, blessedly.

It still took her two hours to get the first small stacks started, and it didn't even look as if she had made a dent. She needed help. Hoping that Demeter had not led her wrong, she closed her eyes and sent up a prayer to any god who may heed her call and give her aid. That unusual knowledge she was still only just becoming accustomed to having seemed to stir, and she found herself calling out to Hestia, the Goddess of the Hearth.

There was no sound, yet she became aware that she was no longer alone. She opened her eyes quickly and discovered what looked like thousands and thousands of ants marching across the floor toward her. She did not move for fear of accidentally stepping on some. Very carefully, she knelt down. "Are . . . are you . . .?"

Across her mind, she heard a feminine voice say, *They are there to aid you, lovely Psyche. You called, and I have answered. They will tend to this impossible task. I feel it is a chance to give back to Eros for his kindness. I am grateful for the way he has honored my wish to remain untouched and has never pierced my heart with an arrow.*

"Thank you," Psyche whispered. It was humbling to hear the direct opinions of the other gods after she had indirectly been told by Eros of his difficulties with them. It seemed much as if they respected his power and did, in fact, love him a great deal, despite the problems he might cause them. Personally, she did not feel he caused any problems that were not justified.

The ants were hardworking and efficient little creatures. She moved out of their way and sat down safely to watch. With each carrying one or two grains at a time, it took only a few hours in order to get everything sorted. The individual stacks were completed and the ants had left the scene long before the sun set.

Aphrodite returned just after sunset and she was singing

merrily as she entered the storage room. She broke off sharply and stopped in stunned shock as she beheld the sight of Psyche sitting calmly in front of very obviously sorted grains. She had even found the time to start storing them in barrels with labels! "How did you do this?" Aphrodite demanded harshly.

Sensing a rhetorical question, Psyche kept her mouth shut.

It was just as well. Aphrodite swung away and paced in a short circuit as she drummed her fingers on her arm. Perhaps this had been too easy. She needed to increase the danger as well as the difficulty if she was to be rid of her rival. "Well then!" She swung around and smiled though it did not reach her eyes. "Congratulations on a job well done, Psyche. I see I shall have to test you further." She made a vague gesture and a plate of scraps clattered onto the floor beside the girl. "Eat, sleep, and in the morning I shall return."

Psyche watched her sweep out with the grandeur of a queen and then gingerly poked at the scraps. They barely looked edible. It was also quite chilly in the storage room, and it was getting dark as well. She found where she had placed her lamp and lit it so that she could at least see. When she returned to the plate, she was surprised to discover it had somehow been replaced by a different one entirely. The new plate had a fresh loaf of bread and large clump of grapes on it. A glass of wine sat beside it.

Eat, a male voice said in her mind. *Eat and rest, my niece. I, Hermes, shall watch over you this night. I am the God of Good Fortune, am I not? You seem in need of a bit of fortune.*

She found herself smiling for the first time in a long while. "Thank you," she said softly. More than grateful for the food for she was very hungry, she ate both bread and grapes before gingerly sipping the wine. The warm spiciness lulled her toward sleep, and she curled up around her lamp for warmth. It would seem she had won over all of the gods except the two that counted most. Perhaps it was just the irony of her life.

She woke when the morning light came in the high windows,

and she discovered a blanket had been placed over her during the night. It bore the symbol of the Queen of the Gods herself. She wrapped it further around her shoulders as she waited for Aphrodite to arrive and tell her what to do next.

Her mother-in-law arrived barely an hour later and breezed in as dramatically as she had left before. "Get up," the goddess ordered. "I am taking you to the far side of Olympus. There is a stream that flows in a place where we cannot reach easily. I wish a chalice of this water before sunset." She tossed a gold chalice to Psyche. "You will have to climb to it. I hope you are nimble."

Psyche was smart enough to close her eyes when she saw Aphrodite reaching for her arm. A quick rush of power swept over her and she opened her eyes to see that she was standing alone on an outcropping of stone. The cliffs overhead looked ragged, sharp, and near impossible to climb with two hands let alone only one. She looked around quickly and spied a sharp rock on the ground. A few minutes of work shortened her peplos to a length normally reserved for men but would better aid her efforts. She used the cloth she had removed to tie the chalice in a way where she could carry it across her body.

Her hands got gouged and torn as she climbed, and her feet fared little better. She spared some cloth to wrap all of them, but the strips were shortly bloodied. She just ignored the pain and kept moving. She had to prove she was worthy of the faith of the gods, Aphrodite's approval, and, most importantly, her husband's love.

It took a bit before she heard the waterfall that created the stream, and it gave her renewed strength. She hoisted herself up onto a ledge and discovered that she had a whole new problem. The water poured over the cliffs from just out of her reach by leaning, and the stone beside her was too flat and straight to climb. She did not have the time or energy to climb back down the way she had come in order to take a new route up to the outcropping that sat closer to the fall. It was far too wide for any mortal to jump.

She closed her eyes in order to send up a prayer but was

startled out of it by the strange feeling of static along her skin. She looked up sharply and found a glorious stag standing on an outcropping over her head. He glowed softly in the light, and lightning arced between his antlers. She stopped breathing as she realized who he must surely be: Zeus, the very King of the Gods himself.

Breathe, an amused male voice said in her mind. *It would do you no good to swoon here. I admit I do not mind when a beautiful woman falls at my feet, but you belong to one of the few I would never dare challenge.*

She found a trembling smile. "I would think he was the one you would most wish to get vengeance on."

I have cursed that boy many times for the way he delights in making me want what I cannot have, so I consider it quite fair that he be enraptured by a woman himself. I would be pleased to see you keep him distracted for a long time to come, and perhaps I might find peace of my own. The stag leapt down to her level. *Onto my back, girl. I shall carry you across the divide.*

She climbed onto his back and held on tight as he ran at the divide and gracefully leapt over. She slid down to the ground again and ignored the protests her feet made when she landed. The waterfall fell close enough to spray on her face, and she filled the chalice with water. When she turned around, the stag had left her alone. She slowly sank down onto the ground to catch her breath and strength. She knew Aphrodite would locate her wherever she was with the hopes of finding her a failure.

The cawing of a crow made her look up swiftly and she found the black winged avian delicately landing near her feet. It tugged and pulled at the cloth around her damaged feet until they were revealed. Sensing yet another god's power, she said nothing. The crow brushed a wing over the wounds and yellow power flowed. The marks disappeared entirely. It looked at her expectantly and she held out her hands. They, too, were healed back to new. Duty done, the crow flew off into the sun, and she knew it had been sent by Apollo.

The sun had only just begun to sink when Aphrodite appeared on the cliff. A blend of fury and loathing turned her normally beautiful face into a displeasing mask. "So." The word was bitten off through teeth. "It would seem you are resourceful and courageous alike. I think I shall give you a task that no god let alone no mortal would ever dare accomplish."

Psyche got to her feet and braced her shoulders. She knew her mother-in-law was seeking her death rather than her worthiness, and she did not care. She would succeed, and she would win back her husband. Every event lately just felt more and more as if it was weighted in stone. It just seemed that, somehow, she could change the path the stone took if she only *knew* something. "I am ready."

"I doubt that." Aphrodite tossed her hair. "You shall find the route down into the Underworld, charm your way past Cerberus, and find Persephone herself to speak with. She and Hades have been guarding a relic of great importance that should be brought to Olympus where more gods can watch over it. I will not lie: you are very likely to die if you try this." She spread her hands wide. "You can risk your life for your love, or you can die alone and miserable. It is your choice."

Psyche drew herself up to her full height and looked Aphrodite dead in the eye. "I begin to think I know more about love than the very goddess of it. I would not try to destroy true love. I would do everything within my power to protect, cherish, and nurture it." She dropped the chalice at Aphrodite's feet where the water splashed onto the stone. Without waiting for permission, she climbed up to the next level of stone where she could safely and easily find a place to call to Zephyr and ask for journey to the River Styx that led to the Underworld.

A very shaken Aphrodite slowly knelt and picked up the chalice. She wanted to be outraged by the girl's audacity, but the words had sounded far too much like prophecy.

"Well, you just made a mess of things!"

She slowly looked up as a red light appeared and her favored lover strode out of it. He wore his normal armor as if preparing for battle but he was not armed. He never came to her armed; in fact, she was the only one he ever let down his guard for. "Ares." She closed her eyes. "I cannot shake her words."

"And rightfully so!" Temper lit his eyes warningly as he grabbed her arms and gave her a shake. "How dare you do this to our son?! You have sent Psyche to her death, and we both know it! For what? Jealousy over something she did not ask for, did not encourage, and could not change even if she wanted? You are trying to stop true love!" He gave her another shake. "You have doomed that girl, and you have doomed Eros with her! He *bound* himself to her with one of his agreements!"

She looked up in horror. Eros' agreements were powerful, profound pieces of magic that drew on the very force of love. Completing such an agreement ensured a future of happiness and joy. Failing to complete the agreement, voiding it entirely, would doom the signers to an eternity of pain, loneliness, and despair. Not even Aphrodite had the power to create such documents; they were proof that even she, the Goddess of Love, bowed to her son's gifts. "Why would he do such a thing?" she wailed.

"Is there wax in your ears?" He released her on a disgusted oath. "He *loves* her! I saw the way he looked at her when he found her. *She is his destined other half!*"

The color fled from her face as she faced what she had been confronted with: the one person who should protect love was the one who had tried to destroy it. If Dike and Aletheia, the Goddesses of Justice and Truth, had still been alive, they would have had her soundly punished for her actions. "Oh no." It was barely whispered. "We have to stop her!"

He grabbed her arm. "She is a resourceful girl, and our fellow gods and goddesses have been aiding her. We must move quickly to catch her. She may already have found Persephone!"

Aphrodite could only send up a desperate prayer of her own to the forces that lay beyond the control of the pantheon in the hopes that she had not doomed her son and his worthy lover to an early death, or worse. An eternity of suffering borne from a voided contract. She felt sick at the very idea.

CHAPTER FIVE

Aphrodite was not the only one who had been deeply cowed and forced to confront what she had done. Eros himself was in a near state of frenzy as he struggled to free himself from the cage that held him. His anger had entirely fled and left behind nothing but agony and despair. Psyche was not the one who had not held enough trust. Love was blind? The only thing blind around there was *him*. He had been blinded by his own sense of competence. He had been blinded to the very reality of love.

His wife had deserved to know all along who he was and why he could not be with her. If he put himself into her sandals, he could see himself acting the same and demanding the same. *He*, of all people, had forgotten that love demanded the giving and receiving of whole selves. True love, more than any other, was a selfish emotion that would not settle for less than everything.

The God of Love had not been willing to stand up and fight for the woman he loved. He should have claimed Psyche, told his mother off, and petitioned Zeus for approval. The Thunder God would have easily given it in exchange for a few promises to make some of his conquests easier to catch.

"Eros!" The voice barely preceded the glow that heralded Hephaestus, the blacksmith of the gods. Though he was married to Aphrodite and should have rightfully disliked her illegitimate child with Ares, he was in fact quite fond of Eros. "By Zeus, boy, what a mess you are in! Stand back from there!"

Eros backed up hastily as his stepfather hefted a mighty

mallet and gave the cage a sound smack. The ceiling popped off and the bars fell onto the ground with a clatter. "Thank you," he said quickly. "Please forgive me for not staying, but I must find my wife!"

Hephaestus grabbed his arm quickly. "That is why I came to free you!" he protested urgently. "Aphrodite has sent Psyche to retrieve Pandora's Box and bring it to Olympus! She has sent your wife to her death!"

White climbed Eros' face. "What?" he barely managed to whisper. His stomach churned violently. "What has been happening?" he demanded sharply.

"Psyche offered herself to Aphrodite to prove her worth, and Aphrodite sought to either force her out of your life, or to kill her entirely! Your Psyche . . . she is *powerful*, Eros! She has a power that has reached the other gods, and even Zeus himself was willing to give her aid! But this . . ." He shook his head sharply. "This is murder! If she were a goddess, or if she were in command of whatever power she holds, she may be fine. She will charm Persephone as she has done the rest. We must hurry!"

Panic gripped Eros as he whirled and rushed from Mount Olympus. Prove her worth?! He called himself every type of fool he could as he desperately headed for the Underworld before it was too late. Another folly upon his shoulders; he had not intended to awaken her into her powers in such a way! She did not know what they were, nor did she know how to control them. He could *not* lose her!

Zephyr had dropped Psyche at the edge of the River Styx. The place was far more beautiful than she had ever imagined it might be. The river was made of a thick silver liquid that flowed between two very high cliffs. The tops of them were covered in a series of steppes and plateaus decorated in wildflowers of every type. It seemed like such an odd place to be found around the river that took the dead to the Underworld, but then again, the Styx was death, life and rebirth. She doubted even the Elysian Fields would be as beautiful as this place.

A small boat stopped beside the shore where she stood, and the creature steering it stared at her from empty eye sockets. Though a cloak covered him from head to toe, his skeletal hands and face could be seen still. Charon, the one who ferried the dead to the Underworld.

She reached for her knowledge and it came to her shortly. She reached out to touch his hands without fear, and she smiled at him. No one had ever smiled at him. The dead were in limbo until the Underworld, and living beings ran from him. The gods and goddesses barely spared him a look. "My name is Psyche. Please. I must ask for a ride to the Underworld to speak with Persephone herself."

It almost seemed as the ferryman's boney face shifted into something of a smile. It certainly softened somehow. He graciously offered a hand and helped her into the boat. When he saw her shiver as she sat down, he produced a himation from nowhere in order to wrap around her. The thick linen drape would keep her warm, and it reached her toes to maintain her modesty where her torn peplos no longer could.

He ferried her all the way to the entrance of the Underworld and just as graciously helped her from the boat again. She impulsively dropped a kiss on the top of his head in gratitude, and she unknowingly earned his eternal devotion. Nerves returned as she turned to look at the massive cavern entrance that marked the beginning of the Underworld. She did not think it was her imagination that the ceiling had stalagmites deliberately formed to resemble sharp teeth.

More sharp teeth waited further in. She had only gotten so far into the cave before a mighty snarl shook the very ground. A massive three-headed beast lunged out of the darkness and landed directly in front of her. Cerberus' heads snarled and snapped at her so close that his heated breath seared her, and yet she managed to hold her ground. She held out a trembling hand as she would to any large dog. "I am friendly. See?"

He paused before slowly lowering his heads to let each sniff at her hand in turn. Whatever he found, he liked. He laid down with a whine and let her gently scratch him behind all of his ears. She looked past him to deeper within the Underworld, and he leapt to his feet. Gently, he began to nudge her down the path. She could not help but be a bit bemused as he danced along behind her like a puppy following a favored person.

The Queen of the Underworld was sitting on her throne looking over a list of some kind when Psyche walked in. Persephone looked up, and for a moment, she could only stare. Somehow this slip of a girl had won over Charon, enchanted Cerberus, and earned the affection of nearly every god in the pantheon—and then some! "Well!" She got to her feet. "Greetings, mortal. I am Persephone."

Psyche respectfully knelt. Close. She was so close to success that she did not dare make a single mistake. "Greetings, bright one." She kept her gaze lowered. "I have been sent by Aphrodite to retrieve a relic of great power that needs to be brought to Olympus for safety."

Persephone began to frown as she realized what may be occurring. "Psyche," she kept her voice gentle, "this relic is exceptionally dangerous. We gods and goddesses can barely stand touching it. I am not certain you can handle transporting it."

"Please!" The words burst from her lips on a wave of pain. "Please let me do this! I want to prove myself worthy of being the bride of Eros! I want him to love and trust me again, the way he did before I ruined things!" She shook her head so hard that her matted red hair stung her cheeks. "Do you know how you feel to be apart from Hades for six months of every year? I have endured that every minute of the last few days!"

Persephone very badly wanted to wrap her arms around this

child and promise everything would be better. The simple fact was that she could not make such a promise. Sensing there was nothing she could do, she left briefly to fetch the relic. She could not shake the feeling that something terrible was going to happen whether she did or did not hand over the relic.

She returned with the relic and brought it to Psyche. It was a small gold box of beauty and mystery sure to entice any into opening it to see what lay within. "This is it," she sighed. "You must *not* open it. Carry it swiftly from here and call to Zephyr as soon as you are beyond the entrance of the Underworld. It must arrive in Olympus quickly in order to be kept safe."

Psyche nodded fiercely. "I will not even look at it. *Nothing* would sway me." She gingerly reached out to take the box and winced hard when the metal seemed to sear into her flesh. A strange and disgusting bitter scent clung to it. Rather than risk her hands, she wrapped the box within a length of her himation. "Thank you," she told Persephone. She hesitated briefly and then rose up to kiss the goddess' cheek.

Persephone watched her hurry out and finally realized what the gods and goddesses before her had. She was truly Eros' other half. She loved just as deeply, gave just as generously, as he did. They would do truly amazing things together.

Cerberus escorted Psyche partway back toward the entrance. He left her to go the rest of the way, and she tried to hurry faster. Having gotten so used to the peplos being short, she misjudged a step and tripped over the edge of her himation. She gave a startled cry as she hit the ground with a thud, and the box tumbled away. It bounced off a rock and cracked all the way down the center.

The broken pieces clattered onto the ground and, slowly, a softly sinister laugh rolled through the air. A disgusting smell rose from the box all the stronger as an ugly black cloud began to lift into the air. A misshapen face formed within the center and bared broken, ragged teeth. On a screech of triumph, it lunged for Psyche, who could only throw her arms over her head desperately.

Eros shot in front of her at the last moment. The cloud consumed him over her terrified scream and tried desperately to devour him whole. It could not succeed. He was a god, and he was immortal. An immortal could not die. The cloud recoiled back several feet in disgust, and Eros collapsed to the ground.

Psyche scrambled to his side on a broken sound and cried out anew as she saw the condition he was in. He had been torn and ravaged by thousands of bites and cuts. He did not bleed—his immortality had halted the blood loss to save him—but he barely breathed either. His heartbeat was terrifyingly slow and halting. There seemed to be almost no life left inside his body. The cloud had devoured all but the tiny bit that could not be taken because he could not die.

She felt the cloud gathering and looked up quietly as it moved in. So be it. She would atone and she would repent in her next life for what she had caused here. She had released evil, and it had taken her husband from her. Had he forgiven her? She simply did not know. Had he saved her, or would he have protected anyone? She just . . . did not know. That sense of knowing in the back of her mind had silenced entirely.

When Ares and Aphrodite rushed into the scene, all they saw was the cloud of evil hovering over the prone forms of Eros and Psyche. A battle cry ripped from Ares' lips as his sword appeared in hand. "Athena!" he bellowed. "Artemis! To my side!"

The two goddesses appeared in their armor and with their weapons, and while Athena rushed in with Ares, Artemis stayed back to fire her arrows. She was shortly joined by Apollo, and the twins' lethal accuracy drove the evil away from the fallen lovers. The God and Goddess of War did their very best to destroy the evil, yet they knew it was futile. They had never before been able to destroy it. All they had been able to do was seal it within the box it had come from.

Zeus landed on the scene and began firing lightning bolts. The evil, perhaps sensing the fight was doomed to last forever, merely fled from the area entirely. It had been badly wounded, and it had been sealed for ages. It would take many millennia before it came into its power and sought to destroy the thing it hated most: the very power of love that brought forth life and happiness.

Weapons were lowered as eerie silence fell. A sobbing Aphrodite gathered her son in her arms and rocked him back and forth. "Does she live?" she demanded brokenly of Apollo. "Does my daughter-in-law live?"

Apollo slowly shook his head. "The evil devoured all of her life. There is nothing left. Her spirit has already fled to the Elysian Fields not far beyond here. She is gone." He waved a hand softly over Psyche's body, and it dissolved into little ribbons of silver color. It had been rendered as nothing but a shell by her death.

"We must take Eros back to Mount Olympus," Zeus ordered. "He will not be able to recover anywhere else. Ares, carry your son."

Ares knelt to take Eros from Aphrodite, and he hefted his child with little trouble despite their similar heights. Something fell out of Eros' chiton and clattered onto the floor, and all eyes lowered to see it was a scroll. Only Artemis had the courage to kneel and open it. Red color flickered in the middle of the text and abruptly formed the word VOID. The agreement had been voided. She looked up and her lips trembled. "There will be no happy ending."

They brought Eros back to Mount Olympus and moved deep within the domain to the center where the power was most concentrated. Hephaestus built a coffin of crystal for the younger god to rest within, and Apollo made a thorough examination of his wounds. When he finally gestured for the lid to be sealed, he looked old and tired. "I do not see him recovering for at least two millennia. A mortal would have died a thousand times from what he endured."

Aphrodite collapsed to her knees on a broken sob and buried her face in her hands. Athena watched her coolly for a moment before kneeling beside her. It was time for some cold, hard facts. "This is your fault, Aphrodite," she warned in a low voice. "This entire thing could have been avoided if you had merely made Psyche a goddess!"

Shocked looks were exchanged. "How could it be that simple?" Hera demanded.

Athena got to her feet on a disgusted sound. "Making Psyche a goddess means that she would be a goddess *of* something! The people would cease to worship her for her beauty and instead worship her for whatever she was in charge of doing! They would admire her no more or less than I and Artemis, and Aphrodite would be worshipped as the Goddess of Beauty once more. You shame your own power, Love Goddess, by your petty jealousy and unreasonable hate of a mortal girl!"

Ares crossed his arms. "I think it is time to point out that Psyche was *far* from mortal." He shrugged as everyone now stared at him. "Did not anyone notice how quickly we leapt to her aid? How we treated her as one of our own? It was not merely because Eros chose her. She has a gift the likes of which none of us can comprehend. We claim Eros as being more powerful than we are. Well, so is she. Given the time to mature, to grow into her power, she would be his perfect equal."

Zeus immediately turned and walked from the room. In moments, he was striding into the throne room of the Underworld where his brother and sister-in-law ruled. It did not at all surprise him to see Persephone crying in Hades' arms. She would always feel the guilt for the role she had played. "Brother, walk with me. I have a question."

Hades smoothed Persephone's hair back and tenderly kissed her before gaining his feet and crossing over to join his brother. They fell into step together as they moved toward the Elysian Fields. "This is about Psyche."

"What else?" He sighed deeply. "Has she earned a rebirth?"

"It is hard to say. She was very young, brother. Young by mortal years let alone immortal. There was a great deal of good packed inside her, but she did not do enough deeds to truly earn a rebirth." Hades stopped at the edge of the Fields and gestured within.

Zeus' heart ached as he looked and saw the spirit curled into a ball under a tree. Her misery could be felt at a distance. She would suffer eternally from her voided agreement. "What if we . . . perhaps amended the rules?"

"How so?"

"What if we were to have her reborn and *then* do the deeds needed to earn it? A debt, we shall say. I do not see it as being hard for her to do. She is the other half of the God of Love, and that means she can use the force of love energy as well. Not in the same way, perhaps, but in a way no less important or profound."

Hades thought about it critically. "I think it is very possible that we can make this happen. Should she have longevity? I do not think I am wrong in thinking you hope to buy time for Eros to recover."

"You are not wrong, and yes she should."

"Where shall we send her? Here in Greece may be too painful for her."

"I think we should let her decide the where and the when, as most spirits to be reborn do. Her gift to see the future, if that is indeed what I think it is, will dictate to her where she is needed and where she can do the most good." He lifted his hands and the voided scroll appeared on one palm even as the broken box appeared on the other. "She will remember. Hermes will see to it. It will pain her, but it would pain her more to never understand her own existence."

"She will endure, Zeus. She has a strong heart."

A wry smile tugged at his lips. "Of course she does. Things would have been so much simpler if she did not." He released the scroll and box to the ether to wait until they could be claimed by Psyche in her new life. Both he and Hades turned away from the Fields, but they knew they would not soon forget that ugly red VOID in the middle of Eros and Psyche's agreement.

One hundred years later, along the East Coast of America, before it was America, the magic boiling under the surface from the River Styx began to produce children with exceptional gifts. One of them was a girl with red hair, black eyes, and a strange ability to make things happen as she wished.

They named her Rhianna.

Status: File Voided
Analysis: Pending

Folder Two
RHIANNA
Rhianna Taber

CHAPTER SIX

(Present day)

New York City was home to many things. Large buildings, big companies, millions of people, and a small den of magic. The magic was housed within the small 3rd District within the greater city, and it was overseen by one of the—arguably—biggest companies in the country. The Enforcers had been around as long as its District had, and that meant it predated the very government. Some people suspected it had been around for far, far longer than that, and that perhaps the co-owners had as well.

Rhianna Taber had never bothered to confirm or deny the rumors just as she had never bothered to confirm or deny any of the other tall tales of her District. She had watched the world change greatly over two millennia and she had seen beliefs in magic come and go. It was in a coming phase, and most people accepted 3rd District at face value as a historical landmark that might just be home to gifted humans and people who were not human at all.

Truthfully, it was more the former than the latter. Any child born in the District would be gifted. Children born to District people who lived elsewhere would be gifted. Faeries and werewolves walked alongside elves of half and whole blood. Rhianna and her partner, Eric Mason, knew every inhabitant by name. Knew every gift. Knew, in fact, where every member was even if they were beyond the limits of the District. They protected all of them.

That protection could cover everything from offering medical insurance to helping find jobs to arranging scholarships. And sometimes . . . a little bit extra was needed. Some happy endings required a bit more . . . punch. It was a punch that could only be provided when someone was placed under contract with the Enforcers. It gave liberty to Rhianna and Eric, and their associates, to do whatever was needed to ensure things ended well.

Rhianna's black eyes were warm as she studied the young woman with blue hair sitting in her guest chair. She had been expecting this visit for many years. "How goes the training, Marina?"

"It goes well. I'm almost ready to start training for the Olympics." The long-distance swimmer's hands clenched together before she blurted, "I want to try out track running!"

A delicate red brow lifted. "The water elf wants to find her land legs?" A smile tugged at her lips. "Do tell why. You were swimming before you were walking. It's often a surprise you even leave the water at all."

"I just feel like a change."

Rhianna shook her head in fond amusement. Her people knew she knew everything and yet they tried to keep secrets. "His name is Markus, correct?" She smiled when she received a wide-eyed look. "He is quite handsome. And quite the nice guy from what I hear. A track runner and trainer, right?"

"Uhm." Pink climbed Marina's pointed ears. They barely peeked out around the headband that she wore to disguise them. Her hair could be excused as being dyed, but her ears would give her away each time. "Yes." Her shoulders slumped. "He can't swim. I fished him out of the pool but he doesn't know it was me. I just can't get far from water, and he can't swim because he's *terrified* of water! It's not fair, Ms. Taber. Is there anything you can do to help me?"

"Hmm." Rhianna opened a folder on her desk as if she hadn't had the documentation sitting by for ages. "I think it's time you came under contract, Marina. This is a bit more complex than merely arranging for your training to be put on hold." She slid the document across the desk. "I will arrange for your training to be paused for two weeks, and I will also give you something to allow you to get away from the water for extended periods. At the end of the two weeks, you will have to make the choice whether to give up the water entirely or give up Markus."

"It might not be love," Marina insisted as she signed the contract. Even saying it, her stomach sank at the idea of having only one of the things she wanted so badly. "I just want to get to know him better." Her lower lip quivered. "Maybe I'll love to run as much as I love to swim." She scooped up the contract and tucked it into her backpack before she could change her mind. Her braid trailed behind her as she hurried out of the office.

Idly, from the doorway that connected Rhianna's office to his, Eric Mason asked, "Gee, I wonder whatever might happen if Markus could get over his fear and learn to swim. It's much easier for a human to adapt to the District's needs than the other way around."

Rhianna looked at him innocently. "I have no idea what you are inferring, Riku."

He snorted rudely at that and went back into his office. She just grinned. He had accused her of manipulating people since before they could walk. No one knew her better than her surrogate twin brother, but she still liked to keep him on his toes. Content, she stretched and leaned back in her chair. She loved her job. Ensuring the happiness of her people was her greatest pride and honor.

The rest of the day was a relatively normal one. She had meetings in the morning with a few associates—Enforcers had alliances with nearly every corporation in America—and she then had a lunch meeting with Eric and another Enforcer, Taylor Vincent. Taylor was a part-timer, and though not District born, he had extremely powerful gifts of his own. His wife, Gwyn, was Eric's sister-in-law, and she was the Goddess of Justice. Gwyn's almost-twin sister, Rayna, was the Goddess of Truth. Five years separated their ages but it was impossible to tell by either appearance or action.

It was for that reason that Rhianna approached the lunch table and grinned to see what Taylor was idly sketching. The depiction showed the twins racing in cloud cars as they tried to catch up to the other vehicles in front of them. Taylor's most potent gift was his art, and it was the cornerstone of the game company he owned. Rhianna dropped down into the open chair at the table and asked, "Are we branching into racing games, Taylor?"

"It's a mini-game," he answered absently. "I'm working on a sequel to *My Fair Faerie*, and I decided to bring in Rayna. She's married to the intimidating warlock that gives out quests. Can't imagine where I got that idea."

Eric smirked at him. "You're just sour that I beat you at poker."

"*You* cheated."

Rhianna sighed fondly. "Now, boys, let's play nice. Let's talk about something else. How are the other things going?"

"Just fine," Eric assured her. He dug into his peach cobbler contentedly. Both Rayna and Gwyn were exceptional cooks and kept him and Taylor happily fed. "I checked on two active works, and things are going as expected. I'd give it a few more months before it comes to fruition. On a different subject entirely, I have D.J. arranging to have the entire building baby-proofed. Glory is starting to walk."

Rhianna winced with good nature. "Uh-oh." Glory was a half-Faeriekin, half-warlock who literally charmed anyone she met. Even Rhianna had dreaded the day her niece found her feet. "We need to distract her. Teach her to garden."

"I'm working on it. She likes computers more." He grinned. "She's her mother's child."

Rayna, in addition to being Truth, was also the company hacker. She couldn't be kept out of any system, and even the government had given up trying to stop her. With a sort of 'if you can't beat them, join them' attitude, they now often hired her as a consultant. It kept Rhianna happy, too; she always made sure that Enforcers honored and respected its long-standing alliance with the feds. It had been useful more than once to call in a few favors. She kept an even closer association with the state level. Enforcers needed the authority to be able to tell police and doctors when to step back and let the District handle its own affairs.

Thinking of similar things, Taylor asked, "Is the new birthing ward at our hospital done now?"

"It is!" Rhianna bit into her *souvlaki*. She had been feeling an unusual craving for Greek food lately. There was probably something stirring somewhere from the past. It happened sometimes. Maybe the River Styx under the District was in high flow season. "Freshly painted, freshly remodeled, and they've finished hanging up all of Rayna's landscape paintings." She grinned. "Are you still trying to coax her into drawing backgrounds for your games?"

"I tried offering cookies. It didn't work. I'm hoping that, you know, I might have a trump card soon." He flipped pages and went to another drawing. He spun it around with a grin. "I'll finish it once we need it."

Half-finished on paper was a beautiful baby crib. Eric laughed and clapped Taylor on the back. "Rhi and I noticed a while ago. Congratulations, Taylor. Let us hope for the sake of everyone's sanity, your child is like you and not Gwyn."

Taylor snorted. "Heul told me the horror stories. Trust me, I agree."

Rhianna hid a smile by sipping her wine. Heul Trahern was Gwyn's eldest big brother and had raised her from the age of nine. He would certainly be the expert on her frustratingly innocent trust in the inherent good of mankind. "Speaking of Heul and birthing wards."

"Remy's recovering just nicely," Eric assured her. He smiled. "Heul is waiting on her hand and foot, despite her protests. Nicole is *very* happy with her new baby brother and is already insisting on learning to change him and clothe him."

"Naturally." Rhianna dug in her purse for money. "Her future revolves around children. She has a gift our District needs very badly; Audra can't do all of the tutoring. Having our own kindergarten will do nicely. It will prepare our young ones for the outside world." She tossed bills on the table to cover the cost of her lunch. "No food fights after I'm gone."

Eric and Taylor watched her head out of the restaurant and noted the many wistful eyes that followed her. It was neither uncommon nor unexpected. Rhianna was almost unnaturally beautiful in a way that seemed to transcend gender and perhaps beauty itself. Her thick red hair hung to just past her shoulders in a blend of curls and waves. She was fairly small at a five-two height, and she seemed deceptively slender and delicate. Her vibrant black eyes could almost literally mesmerize people.

Over the entire two thousand plus years that Eric had known her, he had only *very* occasionally seen her date anyone, and those dates had been casual to the point of almost not being dates at all. "She's waiting," he murmured.

"Yeah." Taylor sighed it as he sat back. "Do you know who she is waiting for? Neither Gwyn nor Rayna can determine it."

He hesitated visibly. "I don't know his exact identity," he said slowly, "but something terrible happened. I think this is her second life, and it happened in the first. After everything that happened to the Lucinos, I cornered her. She's been slipping away from me, and it's breaking my heart. She wouldn't tell me anything except that the 'end' is coming and she will face her final redemption or punishment. The one she's waiting for . . . his spirit is growing stronger. She doesn't know if he'll come to her again, though."

"Why not?"

His hands clenched together. "She gave me a very old contract. I can't read it because it's in Ancient Greek. But it—it is voided."

Taylor's heart stopped for a moment. No contract in

Enforcers' history had ever been voided. Some had gotten painfully close though, particularly recently as Rhianna's grasp on events lessened. A voided contract meant no protection for the signee. No happy ending. Nothing but an existence of loneliness and pain or, sometimes, even death. The one person who created happy endings for others could not have her own. "I wonder what went wrong," he murmured.

"I suppose we'll find out when 'he' returns." Eric stared out the windows with eyes that could see most anything but not the futures that his sister created for everyone. Even he did not know the extent of her true power. Perhaps that, too, would finally come to light. "Just who were you?" he asked softly. "Just what story are you living?"

(Mount Olympus)

The 3rd District was not the only place of concentrated magic on the Earth. It was the only physical, reachable, place, but it was not alone. A second place was the River Styx. It ran around the world like a band, invisible beneath the surface and only accessible from the basement of the Enforcers' Headquarters. Only District members knew how to get there, and only a select few had actual access.

The third and final location was not underground but instead in the skies. Hidden beyond an invisible film of clouds that could not be seen, sensed, or touched unless you were a god was the legendary place of the Grecian Gods, Olympus itself. The closest point where it touched the Earth was the peak of Mount Olympus. Another point dipped close to the District since the Styx acted as a magnet of sorts that drew in other magical places. Most infamously, the Styx had latched onto another world entirely. The world of Mirage could only be seen on Earth as vague impressions on hot days, but it could be *clearly* seen from the land around the Styx . . . or the sky of Olympus.

It was the first thing that Eros saw when he opened his eyes for the first time in more than two thousand years. Through the cloudy glass of the casket that he rested within, he could see the obvious presence of the faerie tale world. It was not an unfamiliar world. His body had been incapacitated, but his spirit had grown enough in strength over the last few centuries that he had been able to reach out to that beautifully magical place.

He reached out and pushed aside the casket lid. It clattered onto the granite floor and sent off an eerie echoing noise. He gingerly sat up and found that there were no physical aches and pains left from his ordeal. Emotionally was another story. A living, breathing agony churned inside his heart and soul. His blue eyes were ripe with pain as he accepted how much time had passed. "Psyche." He could still smell the scent of her skin and see her mane of red hair. His beautiful wife.

He carefully got to his feet and grimaced as he realized he was still wearing the same chiton he had been wearing in the past. His bare feet made no sound as he walked slowly through the empty halls. The gods and goddesses were gone. Had *been* gone for centuries. Nothing but dust, echoes, and the lingering bitter scent of evil remained. He ignored the last for the time being. It could not touch him.

He found the old scrying pool and it still held water. A wave of his hand cleared the surface to let him look down onto the Earth. He had been somewhat prepared for it by his brief excursions outside his body, but his jaw still dropped when he saw the metropolis that his beloved Greece had become. That would take getting used to seeing!

He scoured every inch of the country with the pool, and he did not find his Psyche. He knew she lived. He had felt her more than once. He had even seen her on Mirage recently. She was out there somewhere, waiting for him. She needed him as terribly as he needed her. They could finally be together.

He sat down on the side of the pool and set about the arduous task of examining every large city. The further he moved from Greece, the stronger her power felt and the more foreign the language and land felt. He landed in a relatively new country that had veritably exploded over the last two centuries, and he found a city of sparkling lights and glass buildings. Her power permeated every mile.

The Styx itself aided him. He recognized its presence and followed it until it bubbled just under the surface of a small district that stood as a reminder of the history that had passed. The buildings looked quite old and historical though there was a single skyscraper that had been modernized. The streets *oozed* magic into the very air, and it had been saturated by his lover's beautiful power. She was far, far stronger than he remembered. She had finally settled into her gifts and almost embraced them wholly.

His breath wedged painfully in his chest as the pool suddenly revealed her to him. His eyes devoured her greedily. Her thick red mane. Her velvety black eyes. Her lithe and supple body. Had she gotten more beautiful, or had he simply forgotten how she made him feel? He knew it was not his imagination or his personal opinion that she was the most beautiful in the world. It was that very thing that had caused all of the trouble in the first place.

His impulsive nature demanded he jump out of the clouds and grab her up immediately. *That* was not a good idea at all. It, too, had caused many problems in the past. He needed to put himself into her world. He would descend, learn to live among humans, and he would put out the signals only she could read that would finally bring them together. At the least, integrating into society would not be hard. Being a god had its merits.

He strode swiftly toward the exit. Every step made a chilling darkness close behind him to cut off his return. It was no darkness that brought the restful night. It was the darkness that brought fear; it was evil itself. The acrid scent seared his sensitive nose as he continued to walk. He did not look back. Olympus was his home no longer.

The moment he broke through the invisible clouds and hovered unseen in the sky of Earth, he felt the palace seal entirely. He pressed against the entry, just out of curiosity, and it held firm. If he ever wanted to return, he would need to find another way to pierce the clouds. So be it. His future lay on the land below.

He did not go right to the district where his love waited. The way her power had saturated the land meant that she quite literally saw everything. He instead landed out of sight beyond the district and took care to mimic the average wear of the male passerby. When he became visible and stepped out of the alley, no one saw anything but a surprisingly and shockingly handsome man in blue jeans and a t-shirt. If they noticed he was barefoot, they didn't say anything. Eros only noticed it himself when he stepped on a discarded cigarette. He winced wryly and made himself some sandals while no one was watching.

The culture shock was a bit horrific. He could make himself understand the language but that did not mean he *understood* the language. These people had words that simply did not translate over for him. Everyone had interesting little devices attached to their ears that they talked into. Others were using their fingers to poke at the screen. Tiny little things were stuck in ears and attached by wires to those devices and others. Strange, giant, glowing signs seemed to be trying to sell things. Why did a partially-eaten apple need a sign that big?

It was noisy, it was smelly, and it was insane. Eros tried to duck around a corner to get out of the way of an oncoming crush, and he smacked right into a young woman. He grabbed her arm quickly to hold her on her feet. Melancholy brown eyes looked up at him. "Sorry," she sighed. "I wasn't watching."

"Neither was I."

She looked at him for a moment before cocking her head slightly. "You have an interesting accent. Sounds kind of Greek."

"Well, that is because I am." He gave her a courtly bow and quick grin. No grin greeted him in return. The God of Love was no slouch for emotions. He ducked his head and peered into her dark eyes. She stood a handful of inches shorter than his five-ten height—something he had quickly noticed was now a norm rather than a sign of being a god. "Do we have a problem, my lady?"

"I lost my sense of humor."

"Literally?"

"Seems so. Weirdly, it happened after I banged my funny bone."

He arched a pale brow. "Funny bone?"

She held out her arm and pointed to the spot in question. "Got me as to why it's called that as it isn't funny to hit. It hurts a lot. I used to laugh a lot but now nothing is funny." She offered her hand. "Priya." He studied her hand and she shook her head. "You *are* from far away. Handshake? Sign of greeting?"

"Ah." He took her hand and felt bemused by the entire thing. "Tell me, Priya. Are you gifted?"

Her eyes widened and she looked around hastily. "Uhm, maybe," she whispered. "I can sometimes feel others' emotions."

"Then I can help you." He caught her elbow and escorted her further down the sidewalk. "My name is Eros," he told her. "I am the God of Love."

New York had its crazies, to be sure, but Priya found herself unable to doubt him. He definitely looked like what she would expect from the tales of Eros: hot, sexy, and way too good for mortal women. "I need my sense of humor, not a lover."

"I did not offer to find you a lover." Though he intended to do so, given how lonely her heart felt to him. "I am a god, Priya. I can make things happen." He snapped his fingers and a scroll appeared in his hand. "If you do exactly as I tell you, then you will be happy and humorous again. Will you sign yourself into my care?"

She frowned at the scroll. "You won't own my soul, right?"

"Do not be silly. I have no need for your soul. This contract

will simply allow me to do everything needed to ensure you are happy again. You may read it as slowly as you wish. It is in your language."

It was indeed. "Do you really fly and have wings and shoot people with arrows?"

The corner of his mouth kicked up into a wicked grin. "Frequently."

She huffed out a breath and signed the scroll without letting herself think about it. "You're still going to set me up, aren't you? I can feel it inside you."

He cuffed her chin. "You will have to trust my instincts to know what you need. It is my job."

"You're a matchmaker?"

"I believe I am." He looked around at the bustling streets and could see the diminished force of love. The world had become quite cynical. "In fact, I believe that is exactly what I am and should be. I suppose it is time I put my powers to good use. This world certainly needs them!" He smiled at Priya. "I could use a friend and an assistant. I cannot yet pay you, but it will not take long."

"I guess working for a god would be better than working for McDonalds." She couldn't find the ability to smile, so she hugged him instead. "I can teach you how to handle our world. I think it's probably really different for you."

She had no idea, he reflected ruefully. She proved to be a valuable ally, however, and he was as pleased personally as he was professionally to watch her 'coincidentally' meet a young doctor while having her elbow X-rayed. He obtained a small building just on the outside of Psyche's district—the 3rd District, it was called—and he opened up his new 'marriage consulting and matchmaking' business.

By the end of the first month, he was no longer feeling the culture shock as badly. He could even read a newspaper without asking Priya for a translation. They were sharing a bag of donuts before their doors opened for the day when he flipped to the business section of the paper and felt his heart stop.

The look on his face had Priya peering over to see what he was looking at. A beautiful color photo of Rhianna Taber greeted her eyes. She looked again at Eros and saw the blend of longing and suffering in his eyes. "You know Ms. Taber?"

"I did," he admitted. "A long time ago." He trailed a finger over her familiar features. He knew what she had been doing and how hard she had been working. He shoved to his feet and walked over to look out the front windows. Only a single street separated him from the one he loved. The 3rd District began right across the road. "I am so sorry I left you alone for so long, my love," he murmured achingly. "We will be together again soon."

CHAPTER SEVEN

(Two months later)

Rhianna was never not busy. There was always something to do, a meeting to attend, or simply people to watch over. At least every other day, she would see something in her dreams that meant there was someone who needed her. She would arrange the situation and get things moving; sometimes a contract was involved from the beginning, and others it came along later. It varied.

Perhaps that was why she was so puzzled one day to discover she had reached an impasse. All currently issued contracts were in a phase where she wasn't required. Others were not due to come around for another year or two. She could still feel the flow of love energy in the world and knew it was running just fine—perhaps even stronger than usual—and yet there were no new clients coming in from the outside. Even people who did not stay in the District would find their way there if they needed a happy ending. In fact, most people knew that crossing paths with the District could make dreams come true.

So what the hell was happening? She swiveled on her chair and grabbed her phone. She punched a button and waited until it picked up. "Rayna? Are you busy?"

"Define busy."

"Are you currently engaged in anything that you can't put down for five minutes to come help out your doting sister-in-law?"

"Nuh-uh. Be right up."

The delicate Faeriekin did not arrive alone. Eric was tagging along at her heels. "Rhi," he said as he walked in without looking up from a printout, "Rayna and I have almost finished reorganizing Failsafe. She has to keep getting into their system for org charts, though, as they won't provide them willingly."

Rhianna just shook her head. "Color me not surprised. They were not very happy when I called to tell them that you were on the verge of visiting. They either abide by the policies of Enforcers or they get a reboot."

Eric's presence was a bigger threat than Rhianna's for the simple fact that he only went to a company when someone royally screwed up. He typically handled the behind-the-scenes details of their various companies, and she took care of everything on the front. The contrast of their personalities—her more inviting, friendly air versus his colder, more intimidating one—made them best suited for the role they filled.

The *only* person that Eric had never been able to intimidate (other than Rhianna) was his wife, Rayna. She barely reached his shoulder in height, was even more ridiculously delicate than Rhianna, and she faced the world with the same innocent sweetness of her sister. Rhianna had known from the very beginning that Eric would need someone special, and she had been very happy to find that someone for him. "You're being followed, Rayna."

Rayna's violet eyes lit with humor as she smiled. "I can't get rid of him," she said solemnly. She giggled and dodged when he made a mock swipe for her. Her fingers skimmed down his arm tenderly for a moment before she headed over to where Rhianna's desk sat. "What do you need help with, Rhi?"

Rhianna vacated her chair. "Have a seat. I need you to hit the web and see if you can track down what the hell is going on. The flow of energy that I always sense is still moving and yet I haven't seen any signs that someone needs help."

"Huh." Eric leaned on the edge of the desk to watch as Rayna started typing. "That is a bit out of the ordinary, to be sure."

"What am I looking for?" Rayna asked.

"Anything relating to happiness, love, etcetera. The stuff that we normally take care of handling with contracts." Rhianna crossed her arms and watched over Rayna's head as she zipped through the internet like an international speed-reader. No one would ever think she hadn't learned to read until she was twenty-one. Then again, one of her gifts was her exceptional intelligence. It blended quite well with her ability to hear, see, and reveal the Truth in all living creatures.

Rhianna adored Rayna, obviously, but she always had to be *extra* careful around the tiny goddess. Rayna's ability to hear someone's heart speak the truth at the same time their voice issued a lie meant that Rhianna had to work hard to keep her associates from knowing things that she simply did not want them to know yet—if ever.

"Ah ha!" Rayna sat back happily. "I think I found our energy diverter. Look at this." She pointed at the screen. "Cupid's Grove. It's a relatively new matchmaking agency and marriage counseling services place. The marriage counselor who runs it just 'always seems to know who is right for you.' They claim a one hundred percent accuracy."

Eric whistled softly. "That's a hell of a claim. Where are they located?"

"Wow. Right outside the District. The website is just a placeholder, basically. It has the info, the reviews and references, and a downloadable questionnaire that you fill out and submit in order to book a meeting. Says he only deals with people face-to-face because he can only help people he knows."

Rhianna began to scowl. "He is messing with energies best not messed with."

Sympathetic, Rayna put a hand on her arm. "He's no different from other counselors, Rhi."

"The hell he isn't!" Little sparks filled Rhianna's eyes that Eric had always called her 'temper sparks.' "If he was like the rest, I wouldn't be feeling the flow of love energy moving stronger without at least one person knocking on my door! Mortals should *not* be interfering with this sort of thing!"

"Ah ha!" Eric shot to his feet and there was a similar temper on his face. "Damn it, Rhianna! I *knew* you were manipulating people all these years!" His hands hit the desk with a thump. "You've been setting up people like a damned matchmaker for two thousand years—including me!"

Her hands hit the desk too as she went nose-to-nose with him. "If you dare say you're mad at me for making people happy, I'm calling you a liar, and your wife will confirm it!"

Rayna was a smart cookie; she knew better than to get between Eric and Rhianna when they were going at it. The office door cautiously opened, and Taylor and Gwyn looked around the edge. Gwyn was almost perfectly identical to Rayna except for hair that was pure white and eyes that looked as much gray as violet. "Uhm." She cleared her throat. "You guys are kinda scaring the natives. Heard you downstairs."

Both heads turned. "She's finally admitted to the fact that she's the reason there are no coincidences in our district!" he snapped.

"He's just pissy because he hates when I'm right and he's not!" she snapped equally.

Rayna got to her feet and put a hand on each of their shoulders. "Okay. Fists down. Play nice."

Striving for humor to diffuse the tension—fists had indeed been known to fly in the past—Gwyn joked, "I guess that means Rhianna is the bride of Eros!"

Eric snorted. Rhianna couldn't. Something obviously shocked moved through her eyes and was noticed by all of her friends. Rayna was still touching her, and she felt the truth of the statement blasting down her nerves. Her jaw dropped. "Ohmygod she is!" she blurted.

Taylor and Eric's jaws dropped as well. "B-but!" Gwyn could

barely wrap her brain around it. "But we don't remember you!" she protested. She shook her head hard. "I remember Eros! He was our favorite god 'cause he wasn't stuck-up like the others could be. Where were you, Rhi? We should remember you! It's not fair that we don't!"

"You died before I came into the picture!" Rhianna snapped. "All of you get out of my office right now!"

"Rhi, please!" Rayna tugged on her sleeve. "Let us help you!"

"*Get out!*"

Not even Eric was willing to take her on when she got that note in her voice. He and Taylor hastily escaped into his office. The twins scrambled out the front entry. Both doors slammed tight behind them. Under his breath, Taylor muttered, "I think things might finally be starting to make sense."

Eric muttered back, "We can sic the girls on her later when she hits the point of feeling guilty for yelling at them. She hates yelling at the people she loves."

"Then why do you provoke her?"

"*Someone* has to."

Rhianna scowled at both doors and tossed herself down into her chair. She was going to have to apologize to all four of them, but she just did *not* feel like it. Events of the past were still too raw and too painful for her to bear remembering. Worse still, the memories had a tendency to overwhelm her abilities and leave her psychically burnt out.

Rather than do nothing, she downloaded the questionnaire and opened it. She would fill it out, send it in, and see what happened. If the company was just a normal one with an unusually gifted owner, she would let it slide. If they were deliberately messing with the energy, she would take action. They could cause far too much trouble if they were left unchecked.

The questionnaire was surprisingly lengthy. She very nearly started just randomly answering, but something made her change her mind. What the hell. Being honest would prove whether or not they knew what they were doing.

The questions ranged from standard likes and dislikes to political and religious beliefs, and she was bemused to find that her Hellenism was listed among the Christianity, Judaism, and other sundry items. Few people believed in the Greek gods anymore; they had become nothing more than a series of myths and legends.

The next question surprised her: *Be honest. What is your ideal in a physical lover? Hair color, eyes, ethnicity, etc. Don't be ashamed if you like a type.*

She paused for a moment before marking the blond hair, blue eyes, and golden/tanned skin boxes. Her husband's image had been imprinted on her mind though she had only twice gotten to see him in the light. Her body knew his touch. Her ears knew his voice, and her lips knew his taste. She knew how he felt and how his skin always carried the scent of peaches. Only her eyes had been deprived of the chance to love him, and when she had tried to claim that chance, she had ruined it all.

A headache threatened behind her eyes and she shoved out the memories. A bit defiantly, she used the 'Other' box to write *He should look like a Greek god.* Good luck to them matching *that* one. Nothing and no one was as beautiful as a god or goddess.

She sent the questionnaire off to the email address provided and went to get herself some coffee; she badly needed caffeine. Much to her surprise, she had a response waiting for her when she returned only a few minutes later.

Greetings, Ms. Taber!

I am happy to say that I think we have the perfect match for you! To ensure that we truly do know you as well as we think, we would love for you to come in tomorrow for a personal meeting with the counselor. We have an opening at 9:00am; the rest of his day is booked. If you cannot make it tomorrow, please let me know and I can easily find you another time.

We look forward to meeting you at Cupid's Grove!

Priya Martinell
Administrative Assistant

Rhianna drummed her fingers on her desk for a few moments, then shrugged. She responded to say she would be there at nine and made sure to put the meeting on her calendar. They obviously did not know what they were doing, and that made her feel a bit better. She would go in, clarify her instincts, and then wash her hands of it. Maybe there was something else messing with the energy. She was going to have to apologize to Rayna and ask her to look again.

The rest of the day went normal enough for Enforcers, and her dreams that night were strangely empty. She had known she was losing her grip on events because she was too close to them, but had she passed the point where she would have even a hint of the goings-on? Perhaps the end was closer than she thought even though she had not seen evil moving for several months.

She contemplated her closet in the morning before the meeting. She really wasn't inclined to go out in her normal suits and business wear. The Grove was all but across the street from her District, and she had effectively taken the day off anyway. She grabbed the lovely yellow sundress that Brian Matthews had made her as a thank you gift and paired it with white leggings. Most yellows did not work with her coloring but not this one. Its buttery hue perfectly flattered her red hair.

She walked the blocks over to Cupid's Grove and felt the familiar tingle that meant she had left her District behind. Much to her bemusement and reluctant admiration, she rather liked the look of Cupid's Grove. It was done with a heavily Grecian architectural style, and she recognized the familiar work of Seven Wishes Design. Lexie and Joseff must have had a ball with the nearly invisible windows that made it seem as if the pillars were entirely open between them.

Her second surprise came as soon as she walked in the front door. She felt . . . strangely comfortable there. The décor likely helped, but it went deeper than that. She just felt welcome and secure in a way she normally only felt in her District.

The lovely young Indian woman behind the desk looked up curiously and began to smile. "Good morning, Ms. Taber! I'm Priya. Welcome to Cupid's Grove. Have a seat and I'll buzz Aaron that you're here."

"Thank you." Bemused because she wasn't used to people acting so blasé about her presence, she instead wandered along the lobby and admired the paintings. Most were depictions of the gods and goddesses, of course. She almost felt as if she had gone back in time. It was more nostalgic than bitter.

"Ms. Taber?" Priya called. "Aaron will see you. He's just down the hall. His office is on the left. His name is on the door."

Rhianna linked her hands behind her back as she started down the hall. It was a short one, and there were only two doors anyway. The one on the right went into what looked like a break room of sorts. The left indeed had a name placard: Aaron Konstantinos. Of course it would be Greek. She glanced at the end of the hall and found a statue of a bow and arrow carved from olive wood.

Her ire stirred anew. She opened the door and walked in saying, "I hate to call bullshit, but I'm afraid I must. My perfect match isn't even on this plane." She broke off and stopped sharply as she reached the center of the office and realized it was empty. Were they yanking her chain?

The door shut behind her. Before she could turn, a powerful male arm slid around her waist and a hand covered her eyes. The scent of peaches crept into her lungs and dug in with velvet claws. Familiar, achingly familiar, lips tenderly skimmed over her ear. "I think that for once in your long life," an equally familiar, husky, voice murmured in Ancient Greek, "you might be wrong about something, my beloved."

Memories ambushed her on a wave of powerful emotions and dormant desires. A headache tore through her head behind her eyes, and she felt him murmur something soft and soothing. The pain evaporated, and her body lost its strength. She couldn't keep up with her own heart and mind. She barely noticed him lifting her into his arms before everything blessedly shut down and she didn't have to think or feel at all.

Her escape was only disturbed when she felt another presence invade her mind. It was not Eric despite the bond they shared. She could barely feel him at all anymore; she had thoroughly burned her telepathy out. The presence slipping past her defenses was the one person who held as much power as she did. *Come back to me, beloved,* his voice murmured soothingly. *I am here now.*

Cognizance returned in the form of feeling arms around her. A heart beat, strong and sure, under her ear, and the sound brought back memories anew. Heated summer nights where they had slept with the covers thrown off and she had used him for her pillow. The autumn chill where they had snuggled under blankets. Tender fingertips caressed her face. "Beloved. Look at me."

She forced herself to open her eyes. The face that looked down at her was the one burned into her memory. Thick blond hair that fell in loose curls around a face too handsome to belong to any mortal. Intense blue eyes that glimmered with a hint of iridescence. A mouth made for kissing. She tried to smile but it trembled. "Eros."

His fingers skimmed over her lips. "My name is Aaron now," he told her huskily. "I have placed myself within your world the way you once tried to place yourself within mine. My Rhianna." He said her name slowly, savoring it like wine. "I want to hear myself calling your name. Hear you finally calling mine." His mouth skimmed across her features and steadily lower. "Come lie with me."

Any protest died as his lips claimed hers in a kiss that seared her to her soul. Two thousand years had not gone by; he kissed her as he always had before. Hard, urgent, hungry. Her fingers fisted into his thick hair as she twisted up to meet his passion halfway. Sleeping nerves awoke with a vengeance and rushed into overdrive as pleasure flooded her body and erased loneliness. "Aaron," she whispered thickly when he lifted his head slightly.

A light shudder moved through his body. He shot to his feet with her cradled in his arms and strode swiftly down the hall. "I have need for my wife, and you have need for me." His eyes burned with bright sparks as he looked down at her. It was his desire for her that fueled his power. "Our marriage contract may be voided, but it is neither broken nor dissolved. You are still mine. I am still yours."

"I've been waiting for you." She nipped at his lower lip. It looked wonderfully bitable. "Let go of my legs." He did so, and her grip on his shoulders meant that she did not fall. She lithely boosted herself up and hooked her knees on either side of his hips. "I am stronger than I look, my husband."

He swung her with a suitably romantic flair into the bedroom, and she found a laugh welling up. She spared the room enough of a look to see that it was the same style as his office and she noticed the night sky beyond the tall windows. "It's night?"

"You had need for rest." He slowly lowered her to the bed. "I have dreamed of this. Even when I could not feel, could not reach out, I dreamed of you." He dragged her up for another of his drugging kisses. "I need to feel your body."

A moan answered him as he raked his hands down her figure and savored every supple curve even through her clothes. It was beautiful music. The act of love, of desire, always seemed more beautiful with her. "Mine."

He had never been a quiet lover. He demanded, he coaxed, and he gave. He gave so generously. There was nothing like being loved by the God of Love. Perhaps she should have known all along just who she had married. Perhaps there could have been no two thousand years of pain. No evil in the distance. She grabbed onto him with all her strength and poured herself into a kiss that made the sparks flare in his eyes.

A rough curse left his lips as he shot to his feet. He could not wait. He crossed quickly to throw the curtains closed. The room was plunged into darkness that entirely shielded him from her sight. The same was not true of him; he could see in the dark and saw her clearly.

His action rocked her to her soul. Her emotions tumbled over themselves as she tried find him in the dark. Why would he insist on darkness still? She knew his identity. The gods were gone. There was no need to hide. It couldn't be that he did not want to see her; she knew his sight was literally godlike. It had to be that he did not want her to see him. But *why*? He had absolutely no modesty or self-consciousness. What didn't he want her to see?

A memory rushed past her eyes. Her first glimpse of him when he had snuffed the candle she had lit. His bare arm had reached past her, and he had been glowing. A god only glowed when they were in their 'true' form. He was the God of Love and Desire. His true form would be his naked one. Even socks would dilute the effect. If he was wholly bared, he would reveal his true self. *He did not want her to see his true self.*

Mortals were not typically capable of beholding a god's true self because they did not have the capacity to feel deep enough emotion. If she did not feel a deep enough love or desire for her husband, she would be torn apart by her body and heart struggling to comprehend his beauty. He did not believe that her emotions went deep enough to endure. He still did not believe in her love!

His hands suddenly closed around her waist as his hot mouth caressed her neck. She began to push at his shoulders and try to twist away. "Stop!" she ordered as firmly as she could, but the rasp to her voice gave away her desire.

"Do not be afraid. I know it has been a while but—" He broke off in absolute shock as a pillow smacked him right in the nose. He released her immediately and sat up to turn on the bedside lamp. Light spilled into the room and revealed the tableau. He had stripped down to his pants, and she had gotten off the bed to back away several feet. She looked rumpled, flushed, and too damn beautiful for his sanity. He could *feel* her frustration even at range, and it was only the sparks of temper in her eyes that kept him in place. "What is wrong with you?" he demanded.

"I will not give myself to a man who won't give me all of himself in return!" she retorted hotly. "You won't give me your true self, Aaron!"

"What are you talking about?" He shot to his feet. "I have been naked with you a hundred times. You know every inch of my body. I have felt your fingers and lips everywhere. How can you say I have not given you my true self?"

A blend of humor and sadness moved through her temper as she realized that he genuinely had no idea that it was *only* her fingers and lips that knew him. She could excuse the past—he had been trying to keep his identity a secret. He had given himself away by insisting on darkness now that there was no need to hide. "You are hiding from me," she said only. "Protest all you like, I know it for fact. I will *not* accept the half-relationship that I was given before!"

He tried to grasp her shoulders and her power rose to slap him back a step. Frustration burned out of his blue eyes for long moments as he stared at her. She was not the Psyche he remembered. She was stronger, more powerful, and far more stubborn!

A flash went through his mind of the questionnaire that she had filled out. It had matched his perfectly. A one hundred percent compatibility from the part where she had admitted liking having her own way (so did he) to the part where she had confessed that she disliked yelling at loved ones but would do it anyway if they pissed her off (and so did he). Delight began to rise inside him. "You are perfect."

Red brows began to slowly lift. "Beg pardon?"

"You are perfect for me! We *matched*, Rhianna. Were you honest on your questionnaire?"

"Well . . . yes, actually." She shrugged wryly. "I figured it would reveal you as a fraud." She scowled. "I did *not* expect the God of Love to be the one messing with the energy, but I think I should have! No one else would dare."

"It is my job, my love." He grabbed her shoulders. "We matched. We matched one hundred percent. The person you are now is perfect for me. I am finally perfect for you. Give me access to your building so I may see you tomorrow."

She shook her head slightly. The way he could change gears put Taylor's cloud racing cars to shame. "Aaron, I'm sorry, but I am emotionally and mentally fried harder than an overdone *baklava*. You lost me. Again."

"Give me access to your building," he repeated patiently. "I wish to see you more."

A ladylike snort answered him. "You're a god. You can do whatever you want."

"I *want* to prove that I am hiding nothing. I want to meet you halfway. We will have an equal relationship, Rhianna. I do not want what we had before either. I will proudly claim you as mine alone. Let me see you at work. Share your world with me."

He could not possibly learn the depth of her love if he was not with her. She wasn't even sure if he ever *could* trust that she loved him as deeply as she did. What would she do if he never did? She didn't know, but she *did* know that they had a chance for the happy ending they had been deprived of before. He had forgiven her and he had come back to her. She had to take the chance that they could have it all. "Alright," she conceded. She made a slight gesture and a plastic card appeared in his hand. "You will not need to sign in nor need an escort upstairs. I'm on the top floor."

"I will be there." He dropped the card on the bed and reached out to thread his fingers into her thick red hair. "Let me kiss you one more time and then I will send you home. It will be just a kiss. You have stated your feelings and I will try to abide by them." He teasingly nibbled at her lips. "I will not promise to not kiss you."

She slowly spread her hands across his chest. Her fingertips tingled deliciously at the feel of his skin and the power that burned beneath. She rose up on her toes and took his mouth before he

could take hers. It slowly deepened and unraveled with a sweetness that did not keep it from being as hungry as the rest. There was nothing quite like a man who loved to kiss, and he certainly did. She eased back a breath and said huskily, "I had forgotten how well you scattered my thoughts."

It took a great deal of willpower to resist the urge to seduce her right there. His cranky and frustrated body was only a minor problem. It was *her* hunger beating at him that drove him mad. Only he could bring her the pleasure she craved, and he knew it. Love made everything else pale in comparison. They had ruined each other for the rest of eternity from that very first night some two millennia before. "Go home," he muttered against her lips.

She blinked and was inexplicably back in her house. Her purse was even on the couch. She looked around slowly and then sank down to sit on a chair. Her lover had come back to her as she had always prayed, but he didn't even see the wall he had placed between them. She couldn't even tell him the problem! Losing her ability to see the future in no way kept her from having premonitions of the present. To tell him what was wrong would be to make worse happen.

Omniscience could be nothing but a pain in the ass sometimes. She shoved to her feet and stalked into the kitchen to find her favorite wine. She was going to have a glass, take a hot bath, and try to pretend that she would be able to get any sleep before work the following day. Thinking it, she winced as she took the first drink. She still owed Gwyn, Taylor, and Rayna an apology. (Eric deserved what he got, the fink.) She would buy some flowers and donuts on the way in. Maybe if she bribed them with sugar, they wouldn't ask any awkward questions.

Yeah. And pigs could fly.

CHAPTER EIGHT

Rhianna arrived at work the following morning to discover that the receptionist, D.J., was busily hanging new paintings that Taylor had completed. The lobby was decorated with his original art, though perhaps 'original' was not the word for them. Each fancifully depicted Rhianna and Eric's favorite jobs. They showed the Shaughnessys, the Carmichaels, and the Deases. Now being added were the paintings to represent the Lucinos.

The first showed two identical young women, one a princess and one a commoner, sitting back to back. Each looked up at a different man who was smiling at her. The second painting was split in two. The first half showed a gosling being rejected by ducks. The second half showed the now grown swan being drawn into the arms of another. The third in the series depicted a tall tower with a braid of hair spilling from the window. Shadows on the walls inside implied the owner was in a lover's arms.

The other side of the lobby had paintings of the events on Mirage. There was a new one there too; an image of a dark-skinned faerie holding an upside-down spell book while a prince holding an arrow peered over her shoulder.

Rhianna's mood lifted at the reminder of the good that had been done. She handed off one of the flowers in her hand to D.J. "Since you don't eat donuts."

"Carbs and I are not friends," he agreed with a grin. "Oh," he added as she headed for the elevator, "wolf's on grounds."

Rhianna stifled a groan. She normally loved getting a visit

from her 'wolf', but she really didn't feel up to dealing with her at the moment. She was tired, frustrated, and cranky. Lucky for her, she ran into Rayna and Gwyn first on the top floor where she and Eric had their offices. "Peace offering?" She held out the flowers and box of pastry. "I'm sorry for yelling at you. I'm just touchy on the whole thing."

They both looked at her with solemn eyes and then hugged her tight. "S'okay," Gwyn told her. "We love you so we don't mind if you get mad." She pulled back and grinned impishly. "You wouldn't get mad at us if you didn't love us, so I guess we can know it's a sign that we're important to you."

"Two of my favorite people." Rhianna sighed. "Share with Taylor, please. I owe him the apology as well."

A matching impish grin lit Rayna's eyes. "But not Riku?"

"Your husband deserves what he gets, and you know it! Pleh. Anyone make coffee yet?"

"Rayna did," Taylor said from the doorway to the conference room right across the hall. "I'll grab you a cup. You look a bit peaked, Rhi. Didn't sleep well?" He grinned. "Let me guess, you spent yesterday yelling at the marriage counselor for things beyond his control."

She winced. "Yeah, I guess you could say that."

Rayna frowned thoughtfully. She was still hugging Rhianna so she could feel that what she had said was the truth, and yet . . . something felt *off* somehow. She just didn't know what. Movement in the corner of her eye had her turning her head with a smile. "Look what we found, Audra!"

Audra Shaughnessy leaned a shoulder against the door to Rhianna's office and slowly lifted a black brow. She had never seen her oldest friend in quite such a condition. Her sensitive werewolf nose scented the air, and an odd look crossed her face. "Rhi?"

Rhianna stifled a sigh. "Yes, dear?"

"What—or rather *who*—have you been doing lately that would change your scent this much? You have the scent of a male all over you! Sure as *hell* it wouldn't be there unless you'd been doing an impersonation of a clinging vine on him!"

She groaned and shoved past her friend into her office. "Damn it, Audra! Why can't you ever have any tact?" She scowled as she saw Eric watching her cautiously from the entry into his office. "Now what?" she demanded.

"Er, pardon my asking, but just what happened at Cupid's Grove yesterday? I got a headache from the backwash of your brain going into overdrive, and now I can't even reach you at all. You're completely burned out, Rhi." He frowned. "I'm worried about you."

"I'm fine, okay?"

"No, she's not." Rayna scowled. "She's cranky and frustrated!"

"Damn it, Rayna!"

Audra grinned a bit. "This gets better by the minute."

Rhianna's temper had never exactly been a tame one to begin with, and despite two millennia of learning self-control, events lately had pushed her to the edge and kept her there. The combination of physical frustration and lack of sleep on top of her burnout had her snapping, "At the risk of repeating myself, get out of my office! All of you!"

Audra straightened and leaned down until they were eye level; she stood eight inches taller than the older woman. "Quit taking out your problems on us! It's not our fault that you're getting a dose of your own medicine!"

"You have no idea what you're talking about!" she retorted hotly.

"Yeah, because someone around here never tells anyone if there's something wrong!"

"Excuse me for not wanting to concern you with things you can't help!"

"Excuse me for calling that a load of bullshit! You know damned well that you can't get a happy ending alone!"

Someone knocked very loudly on the door, and all eyes turned. Aaron struggled as hard as he could to keep from laughing out right at what he had heard and seen. He had been wondering just who would receive the sharp edge of his wife's inevitable temper. "I suppose I am interrupting, but Rhianna said that I could come by anytime." He smiled. "I am Aaron Konstantinos. I am Rhianna's husband."

Heads swung toward Rayna, but the way her jaw hung open said that he was, in fact, telling the truth. He was also a far safer target for Rhianna's temper for she knew he could give as good as he got, and she didn't risk damaging him. She snatched up the book on her desk and chucked it at his head. "You can't call yourself that!" she snapped. "I was *reborn*!"

He gracefully dodged the projectile. "I beg to differ, my love. Your heart and soul are the same as it always was, and therefore you are still my wife. It was those things that I bound myself to. I am a god." A little smirk touched his lips. "You will never escape me, Psyche."

"I am not the Psyche you knew!"

He had known that, of course, but that did not stop him from standing by his beliefs. Their contract still bound them. It would bind them until the day they ceased to exist entirely. If he ever faced a future where she left him for good, he would sacrifice every drop of his power to follow her. "No," he finally agreed softly, "but I love you no less."

Taylor and Eric exchanged a wide-eyed look as they finally realized just what story encompassed Rhianna's life. Gwyn and Rayna looked at Aaron hopefully, as if worried he did not recognize them, and he smiled. "My favorite little goddesses," he teased gently. "I am glad to see you again, Dike, Aletheia."

They gave happy cries and rushed forward to hug him tight. The moment Gwyn touched him, his brows shot up. He looked at Taylor, and Taylor just smiled. "I would assume the God of Love and Desire might sense such a thing. Yes, she's pregnant. Rayna—er, Aletheia—and Eric have a daughter already."

"I will wish to meet her and give her a blessing."

Rhianna could feel another headache brewing and pressed her fingers to her eyes. Eric studied her, studied Aaron, and then her again. "Rhi?" he asked as gently as he could. He knew she was pushing the edges of her control and he feared that she might exhaust her temper. He would not be able to handle it if temper became tears. "Did you really take the God of Love as your husband?" It was *her* truth he sought. He stood by what *she* wanted, not Aaron.

She sighed. "Kind of."

At the same time, Aaron promptly said, "She did not take me nearly often enough."

Audra barely turned a laugh into a snort. Seeing the hot look Rhianna shot at Aaron, Gwyn and Rayna grabbed their own husbands and beat a hasty retreat. None of them wanted to stick around for the fireworks. Audra feared next to nothing, and she would be damned if Rhianna suffered any longer. She strode over to Aaron and looked him dead in the eye. "I'm Audra Shaughnessy. Rhianna saved my life."

"I can see the threads in your soul from the imprint of your contract," he concurred. "I am aware of your story, she-wolf. I am pleased to see you are happy." He held out a hand with a smile. "As you like."

She sniffed at his hand intently and was not at all surprised to, at last, find the illusive tang that matched perfectly to Rhianna. She turned, looked at her friend sharply, and then left the office entirely. She had troops to rally just in case they were needed.

Rhianna had not needed the confirmation that Aaron was her perfect mate. Everything else about them fused like two halves of a whole; why shouldn't their scents do it as well? Everything she was and stood for welled inside her painfully as she fought the urge to throw herself into his arms and never let go. He could not yet give her what she needed. As long as he withheld his true self, there would never be the absolute fusion they so desperately needed in order to be happy for eternity.

She began to sway on her feet as too many years of grief and loneliness dragged her down. She would have fallen to her knees if he hadn't materialized in front of her and caught her in his arms. He was solid, safe, and secure. Her promise of a life filled with the things she had lost forever.

Tears began to well without stop. They slid down her face as she stared up at him almost blindly, and she did not know that they ran dark from the gouges on her soul. Panic briefly stopped his heart. She was far more fragile than he had believed. Those who felt the most were the ones who hurt the most. He knew it intimately. He just had not realized that she did as well.

He wrapped her fiercely in his embrace and transported them away. She needed sanctuary. She needed a place where she felt safe to break apart so that he could put her together again. "When did you last cry?" he asked her roughly as he walked through his house toward the gardens out back.

"I don't remember," she whispered. She buried her face against his shoulder. "It seemed like such a useless exercise. Tears can't change what has already been done."

"Some can. Tears hold magic, my beloved. Tears shed in grief can bring healing. Tears shed in love can create miracles." He stepped out into the lush backyard and moved toward the immense bath surrounded by peach trees. A padded bench waited, and he sat down with Rhianna still held tenderly in his arms. "Heal," he murmured into her hair. "Let go and begin to heal."

The fragrant scent of the flowers, the sweet scent of peaches, and the steamy mist of the water reminded her anew of the beautiful, happy, days before everything had fallen apart. She buried her face against his shirt and let the tears come freely. She wanted to heal. She was so tired of being unable to escape the past. The curse of her ability to love as deeply as her immortal husband.

He rocked her back and forth and sang softly in Ancient Greek. He hurt for the pain she endured, but he refused to stop the tears even though he could. They were long overdue. If she had only cried back in Greece! But, no, his leaving her had been the thing to awaken her gifts, and she had immediately set out to prove her worth. His blind stupidity had caused far, far too many problems that he now had to unravel.

The tears were eventually spent and she rested in his arms. She felt exhausted from her soul out but strangely more peaceful. She could have the strength to endure. She could find the will to continue to wait until he believed. It would come. It had to come. Whether or not it came before she faced her final judgment was the only question.

His eyes narrowed as he felt the odd sense of guilt inside her. He pulled her back and caught her face in his hands. "What are you thinking? You have nothing to be guilty over."

"Aaron." She turned her face into one of his hands. "You know what I did. I have been paying off my sin for two thousand years."

"*No.*" He shook his head hard. "Curse it to the Underworld, you are *not* paying off a sin! You have no sin! A debt, yes, you had and you have repaid." He brushed his lips over her still damp lashes as she frowned. "My beloved, you were reborn early. You had not yet earned a rebirth by dying as young as you did. Zeus and Hades bent the rules a bit to have you be reborn and *then* earn it."

"Why did they choose the time they did?" she whispered. "It was a scant hundred years later. Did they feel I needed this long to pay off my debt?"

His lips curved. "You chose the time and place. A soul that is to be reborn *chooses* its new destination. I believe that you knew that this was the place you were needed, that the 3rd District had to be made, and that only here could you truly grow into your gifts and powers."

She was not at all surprised that he knew she could see the future. She even had the feeling that he knew *why* she could, but she didn't expect him to tell her even if she asked. She had always wondered about it though she had come to accept it and use it. As always, she put it aside until it was worth thinking about. "I still have a sin, Aaron." She shook her head. "You know that the evil is growing stronger and preparing for the final siege. It's my fault it got free in the first place!"

"*It is not!*" He scowled and gave her a little shake. "If anyone is to blame, it is my mother for giving a mortal the duty of carrying that vile thing to Olympus for safety! She sent you to your death and nearly doomed the world as well for her petty jealousy!" His fingers combed back into her thick hair and held on. "I will fight by your side," he vowed fiercely. "I will fight for you as I should have from the moment I knew I was yours."

She pulled away from his grip with a decidedly rude snort. "You only became mine because you're a klutz!" As if quoting from memory, she intoned, "The god Eros looked upon the sleeping Psyche and accidentally stabbed himself with his own arrow. Upon beholding the beauty before him, lo did the arrow's power inflame his love and he sought to possess her for his own."

He just smiled. He had been expecting the accusation for a while. "I have looked upon these tales told by mortals, and many are either wrong, exaggerated, or perhaps only telling half of the truth." He tipped her chin up. "I did stab myself upon my own arrow, but it was not an arrow that induces love. It was one of my instigators, my beloved. The arrows I use to remove inhibitions on existing emotion." He tenderly caressed her lips with his. "I saw you lying there and I could see the beauty inside your heart that had caused the beauty in your face and body. I had intended to leave you be for you were too good for me—too good for even a god, my love—but I misjudged and got myself with the instigator." His lips teased hers again. "I could not let you be without claiming the kiss I craved."

She frowned. "You loved me on your own?"

"Mmm." He traced the lovely line of her cheekbone. "When I escaped you, I did not go far. I watched you." He trailed his fingers along the outside of her eyes. "Your eyes. I saw your eyes and I knew I had found my other half. It had been told to me many centuries before that my other half would have 'eyes as black as the velvet night that embraces lovers.' I knew then that I must have you no matter what else. If only I had been wise enough to understand that 'else' included my mother. Such a bitter and ironic lesson for the God of Love to learn."

She hesitated and then asked softly, "Did you ever shoot me, Aaron? The legends . . . but I don't remember it . . ."

"No." A hint of a wry and yet self-mocking smile touched his lips. "Your love was your own just as my love was my own. We are made to be together. It is our love together that gives me power. Your desire for me, my desire for you, gives me power. We belong." He rested his forehead against hers. "Tell me. Tell me what I am not giving you. I feel as if I have given you everything, Rhianna. You cannot possibly own more than you do. My very soul rests in your small hands."

She sighed and framed his beautiful face with the aforementioned hands. "Aaron. My Eros. I can't tell you what you need to give me for to tell you will make worse happen. There is a fear inside you to give me the thing you hold back. That is all I can say."

He nodded firmly. "Very well. I believe you." He smiled when her brows lifted. "I have never and will never doubt your gifts, my love. If you say I fear something, then I surely do. I will try to understand what I fear so that I may move past it. It is connected to my true self somehow?" She nodded and he kissed her nose. "I do not understand how, but perhaps the fear is inside my subconscious. I will seek it and remove it. All I ask in return is that you let me be in your life. If you cannot yet let me be your lover, then let me be your husband. Let me be your confidant and your friend. The person you turn to when you need something."

She could not deny him that when it was something she wanted just as terribly. She needed *him*. Her physical need for him, and his for her, was merely a small part of the complicated ways that they were bound. Alone. She had been so alone for so long.

The curse of their voided contract. Could the void be erased and the contract made active again? She had to try. "Alright." She rested her head on his shoulder where it had always belonged. "I do love you, Aaron. Never doubt that."

"If you did not, I would seek to correct it. I would not even need arrows for it. How could you not love the God of Love?"

The arrogance was more deliberate than deeply felt, and it made her smile as he had intended. "I suppose that is true." She reluctantly straightened up. "I have work, Aaron. No doubt you do, too." She sighed. "I owe my friends *another* apology."

"I would think they rather wish an explanation."

"They can have it when I am ready. I'm too busy today."

"Are you busy tomorrow?"

"No more than normal." She tilted her head. "Why?"

"I wish to see your District." He smiled. "I have not entered it for fear you would know I was there before you were ready. I wanted you to come to me of your own will. I would like to see this beautiful place that you have given your heart to protecting."

"I could show you around," she agreed. "You will like it there, I think." She smiled as well. "We always say that those who belong in the District will eventually find their way home. People who belong nowhere else will always belong in the 3rd District. Eric and I made it to be a sanctuary."

"You will have to tell me the story tomorrow." He slowly and reluctantly released her to let her get to her feet. "Will you spend the night with me?"

"Only to sleep?"

"You know I wish more, but I trust your sight. We will be lovers when I find what it is I have not given you." He stood as well and bent to teasingly nibble at her ear. "I could shoot myself with a dulling arrow. It minimizes desire."

She shook her head. "I love the way you want me. I trust you, Aaron. Of all the gods, you never took what was not freely offered."

He shrugged. "That is not true desire, and it is certainly not love." An arrogant brow lifted. "I do not deny *influencing* someone to offer something freely, but there is nothing wrong with a dalliance purely for pleasure. My consorts were never unhappy—physically or emotionally. I did not break hearts." Under his breath, he groused, "It was my fellow gods that had that problem. People think I caused all of the mayhem, but it was all I could do to keep it to a dull roar!"

She hid a smile and patted his cheek. "There, there."

"Only you would dare placate me." He covered her hand on his cheek and leaned down to kiss her with an edge of hunger that made their hearts mutually race. She was the only one he had ever wanted enough to consider seducing against her wishes, but she was also the one that he most wanted to have willing. "I am not used to learning self-control," he muttered against her lips. He took another hard kiss. "It is a good lesson for me." His hands curved around her bottom to hold her against his aching body. "I burn for you, my beloved. Never doubt that."

Burn? She was in danger of self-combustion. She craved the feel of his hands on her body and the taste of his skin in her mouth. Her head fell to the side weakly as his knowing mouth sensitized secret nerves behind her ear. "You know that saying?" she asked huskily.

"Which?" He took a tiny nip at her earlobe. She wore clip-ons rather than piercings, and he tugged one off for better access.

"Absence makes the heart grow fonder. Beginning to think it might be abstinence."

His low laugh was as sultry as the feel of his fingers dancing down the inside of her arm. "It is an addiction with no program to cure it. We will simply have to accept that we will always crave our ecstasy. The gift for feeling true love is to feel true desire. Flames that will never extinguish." He dragged her up onto her toes and kissed her wildly for a moment before releasing her entirely and stepping back. "I will pick you up tonight to come home with me," he managed to rasp. "Off with you, temptress."

She quickly closed her eyes. Air conditioning rather than steam touched her skin a moment later and she carefully opened her eyes again to see that she was in her office. She reached up to her ear and discovered her earring was still missing. "Damn it, Aaron," she muttered.

A little 'clink' noise made her look at her desk and she saw her earring sitting on her keyboard. It was, appropriately, on the X key. The letter that in shorthand meant a kiss. The symbol had come up well after his time, but he had probably started researching modern symbolism in order to resume his duties.

"Rhianna?"

She sighed and turned to where Eric stood in the doorway to his office. "Not a single word out of you. I know I owe you an explanation, but I just can't do it yet. I'm so sorry, Riku." She broke off as he crossed the room and pulled her into his arms. All she could do was hold on in turn. Truthfully, the only person she loved more than her surrogate brother was her husband. "I think I needed that."

He let her go and skimmed a hand down her hair. "Glad to help. Now let's get your mind off things by getting some work done. You can take out your frustration on Failsafe. You get to call them and tell them that I'm coming in with new org charts and a pair of pruning shears."

She had to smile. "That sounds like a plan."

Putting her life back into its normal operations did wonders for her overall sanity and brought her temper back down to its regular level. She was able to get a great deal of work done and free up the following day to show Aaron around.

As the end of the day approached, a part of her wondered if he would just wait for her downstairs and a bit brazenly take her home. She still hadn't yet come up with an excuse for the inevitable rumor and gossip sure to fly the moment she was seen with him more than once. Only an idiot would think there was only business between them. She was hardly ashamed of her relationship, but she didn't really know what kind of relationship they *had*. They were married but not yet lovers. It made things sketchy.

He appeared out of nowhere in the middle of her office while she was shutting down her computer for the day. At her lifted brow, he told her solemnly, "I can be discrete, my beloved. I would think you ought to know that by now."

"You have a point." She went around the desk and did not protest when he tugged her into his arms. He was incapable of being near her and not touching her in some fashion. "Your place or mine?"

"Mine for now." He kissed her warmly, lingering over her flavor. "You always taste so good," he murmured thickly against her lips. "I love how you taste." He drew out another kiss until a soft purring noise emerged from her throat. "And that." His lips continued to tease hers. "I love the sounds you make." With obvious reluctance, he released her. "Welcome home."

She shook her head hard and looked around in bemusement. He had so thoroughly distracted her that she hadn't noticed the transport. Now conscious and cognizant, she was able to actually admire the décor and the way he had built his home. It held the Grecian flair, yes, but it had all of the modern amenities. She trailed fingers across the widescreen television in the living room. "A prop or do you like it?"

"I enjoy it to some extent. It is a good way to learn things. I am still learning this new world. Shall I make dinner?"

She shook her head. "Let me. I suspect I'd be eating old school if I let you be in charge. Let me offer some other cuisine as well." She shrugged out of her jacket and tossed it over the back of the couch. "I should have brought an overnight bag from home," she noted ruefully. "I am not used to spending nights elsewhere."

He paused at that. It seemed a surprising statement for a woman over two millennia old. He looked at her very seriously. "Rhianna."

She smiled as she met his eyes. "I am faithful to the man I

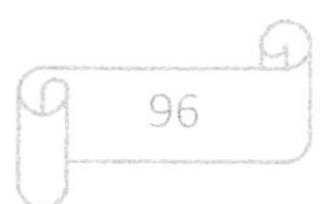

married. Who would ever compare to my God of Love?" She heeled off her shoes and gratefully tugged off her stockings. "I'm not a virgin, though. I technically never have been. I suppose my body remembers you as thoroughly as the rest of me does. I should have clarified before that I am *emotionally* not the Psyche you remember. Everything else seems to have carried over."

"It does not bother you?" he murmured.

"Not at all. Our story never ended, Eros. We are merely in a new chapter. My rebirth was a layover of sorts. I know that now. We will take it a page at a time until you can find and eliminate what you fear." Her black eyes seemed to burn as she looked at him. "Do I want to pretend that it could be enough to have only part of you, just for a few moments of pleasure? I'd be lying to say I didn't want that. It would just never be enough for my heart and soul."

A blend of awe and pride filled him. She carried herself as regally as a queen and with the same calm confidence of any goddess. His beautiful, perfect, mate. Still, he would have to do something about her frustration soon. He could not handle knowing she suffered. "I could give you something to wear," he offered, "if you would like to not wear your suit." A bit wistfully, he added, "I miss the *peplos* you used to wear, but I think I like your suits as well. I am fond of those pants you wear."

She hid a smile. "They show off my legs?"

"They are beautiful legs. I anticipate having them wrapped around me again." He ambled down the hall and returned briefly with a t-shirt. "It will be big."

"And that works for me." Because modesty was truly ridiculous, she tugged off her blouse and pants without bothering to tell him to turn. She tugged the shirt on over her head and found the neck dipped over one of her shoulders while the ends went to her knees. He was watching her hotly, sparks in his eyes, and she could not resist yanking his chain. Without removing the shirt, she unfastened her bra, pulled down the straps, and tugged it out through a sleeve. As it dangled from her fingers, she grinned at the astonished look on his face. "Bras are a bit different from an *apodesmos*."

"So I see!" He was still not entirely sure she hadn't used some sort of magic, but he let it slide. He studied her intently in his t-shirt and finally decided, "I think I am growing fond of modern things."

"They grow on you." She wandered into the kitchen and began to poke around in the pantry and fridge. She hummed softly under her breath as she got out ground beef and the other items needed to make cheeseburgers. She would have to introduce him to sushi eventually. He had always loved fish.

The burgers were happily sizzling in a pan when she heard the sound of a familiar talk show's theme. She quirked a brow as she carried a glass of wine into the living room. She leaned over the couch to hand it to him, and she eyed the large screen. A smile started tugging at her lips. "Do I *dare* ask why you are watching Jerry Springer?"

"It reminds me of the pantheon."

She thought about that. "Hmm. I think that does sound about right. Zeus was certainly the biggest baby daddy on the block."

He choked on his wine and began laughing. "Off with you, woman!" He swatted at her halfheartedly. "You are distracting me."

She bit back a laugh as she went back into the kitchen. She would have to introduce him to a few of her favorite shows as well. The idea of snuggling on a couch to watch them together was deeply appealing. This domestic situation felt wonderful to her. What a strange feeling it was to share her life in such a way with him. They had not had this in Greece.

Arms slid around her waist. "You are sad."

"Melancholy," she corrected. She let his arms stay as she added cheese to the burgers. When he rested his chin on her shoulder, she hooked an arm around his neck. "I'm fine, Aaron. I promise. I was actually just thinking of how much I like where we are."

"I am fond of it as well," he admitted. He sniffed at the burgers as she put them onto buns. "What have you made?"

"Food." She handed him a plate with a smile. "You'll like it."

In fact, he *loved* his cheeseburger. He happily polished off his share and munched through a handful of the zucchini fries she had made as well. "I will cook tomorrow night," he told her firmly as they were cleaning up the kitchen much later. "I will ask Priya to find me some recipes tomorrow."

"She's your Eric?"

He contemplated that. "I suppose she is. I do love her a great deal. You will like her and her husband, Pablo. They are gifted as well. I believe they would have found your District if I had not found them first." He smiled as he saw her pat away a yawn. "It is getting late and it was an eventful day."

"That's one word for it. I'm using your toothbrush since I don't have one."

"I do not mind." The smile he shot at her was decidedly sensual. "Our mouths have shared space often enough."

Much to her bemusement, she had a shorter bathroom routine than he did. She only had to wash off her makeup, and he liked perfumes and lotions. Not that *she* was complaining about such a thing; she would get to sleep snuggled against that soft skinned and fragrant body. She was the first to go to bed, and she slipped under the silk covers with a contented sigh.

The lamp clicked off behind her, and she watched as he crossed to the windows to shut the heavy drapes. The room was plunged into darkness where she could not even make out his outline. Perhaps a bit ironically, he warned her, "I will not wear pajamas for your 'delicate sensibilities.' I do not own any."

She was not surprised by his actions, but she was a bit disappointed. Of course one day would not be enough. She knew that for fact though she did not know how much time it *would* take. Rather than reveal her sadness, she just snorted softly at him.

He slipped into bed beside her and snuggled up along her

back. "Side, back, or stomach?" he asked her softly.

"I'm still a side sleeper."

"I still sleep on my back. Turn over."

She did so and cuddled against his side as he lifted his arm for her. He dropped it around her waist and her head found its spot on his shoulder as if no time had passed at all. She let out an unconsciously contented sigh and closed her eyes. He was a terrible distraction to her poor body, and she barely resisted an urge to start petting the peach-scented skin so deliciously close at hand.

Sensing it, he smiled. He brushed his lips over the top of her head and murmured something inaudible in Ancient Greek. He briefly encountered her instinctive resistance to his power—which in and of itself was a sign that she was his other half—and then she gave in and let him calm her nerves. She slipped asleep within the next breath.

He stared at the ceiling overhead and thought about his possible plans of action. Finally deciding he might as well do what he did best, he snuggled her closer and slept as well. Just having her in his arms where she belonged was enough for the moment.

CHAPTER NINE

Rhianna awoke alone in bed to the feel of the sunrise spilling across her face. She could still feel the warmth from where her husband had slept, and the déjà vu was briefly disorienting. Loneliness rose and threatened to close her throat. Just once . . . just once, she wanted to wake in his arms. To know he had not let go all night. But, no, that was denied to her for as long as he slept naked and the light would give away his true self.

"My beloved." His husky voice teased her ear. "Wake up, beloved. Let me see your eyes."

She opened her eyes and looked up to see him leaning over her. He was naked except for a towel knotted around his hips. She eyed it for a moment, deeply tempted to get rid of it. Why should she be denied the beauty of his body? It was not fair. "Are you taking a shower and didn't want to wake me?" she asked on a delicate yawn.

He tugged her up to a sitting position and smiled as her tousled red hair fell in her eyes. He brushed it back for her. "I was thinking we should enjoy the bath instead. You will like how it looks in the dawn."

She drummed her fingers lightly on her leg. "Hmm. Why do I not trust you . . .?"

Blue eyes lit with humor. "My only ulterior motive is to offer you something beautiful, enjoyable, and relaxing."

Pity she didn't have Rayna's ability to hear the truth. He sounded sincere enough, though. "I will settle for a shower."

"No, you will not. I have already placed soaps and towels for you." He lifted her out of bed before she could protest. "You will come enjoy the dawn with me, and I promise you will feel better after."

She could only sigh as he carried her through the house. "Why can't I tell you 'no'?"

"You cannot argue with me when you know I truly have your best interests at heart. If you did not want what I offer, your heels would dig all the way to the Styx as they did the day we met again. What I give, I give freely. I am not asking for anything in return." He teased as they entered the garden, "I will keep my towel on to prove my intentions are honorable."

Another irony, she decided, since him removing the towel would reveal his true self in the light. Keeping it on showed his as yet subconscious lack of trust in the depth of her emotions. Still . . . it *was* a step closer. Half-naked was half more than she'd had before. Her eyes ran over him wistfully. She had asked for a Greek god. She had gotten one. Her eyes at last could know what her fingers and lips did. It only stirred the craving to have more.

He smiled to himself and gently put her on her feet beside the bath. Again, she was able to see it for the first time now that she was not emotionally distraught. It was truly beautiful with lush flowers and peach trees surrounding the marble and stone pool. Statues and pillars dotted the landscape. A fountain shaped like a dolphin sat in the middle of the bath itself. "It's beautiful," she said simply.

"I thought you would approve." He waded out into the water and toward the other side where a shelf held soaps and bottles. "Come join me."

Her eyes riveted to his powerful back. Finally bared to her eyes was the fact that he bore a mark representing his power. Etched into his skin right on each of his shoulder blades was the shape of a wing. It looked black until the light flowed over it and revealed it to be the deep red hue of desire and love. Here she had thought it was just a thought of fancy that he had wings, and it turned out that he actually did. She *ached* to memorize the curves and lines with her lips. What else did she not know?

She could only sigh and strip off the borrowed shirt. She dropped it on a bench and then shed her underwear as well. She stepped down into the pool and waded in deeper. At the lowest point near the fountain, the water came up to just under her breasts. Built in benches along the sides would allow her to sink deeper and soak.

The water was covered in rose petals and they clung to her skin as she moved to where Aaron waited. Her brows lifted as he caught her around the waist and casually lifted her onto one of the lowest steps. It brought her onto eye level with him. "What are you about?" she asked warily.

"I am washing you." Suiting action to words, he began to smooth a cake of soap slowly down her arm. His fingers trailed along the sensitive nerves near her elbow and inner arm as he did, and he seemed to ignore the way her breath caught.

She told herself he was not doing it on purpose, but she knew it was a lie even before soapy hands skimmed across the inner curve of her hips and slowly upward along the base of her ribs. She wasn't breathing at all as she waited in agony for his hands to travel higher. Fingers skimmed the outer curves of her breasts and slowly trailed in toward the sensitive skin between. His lips curved as he felt the wild race of her heart. Her fingers caught his shoulders for balance and her nails bit in.

He continued his slow and thorough journey of her body. The secret nerves at the base of her spine were teased, and the heated flesh of her upper thighs were caressed. Her legs began to tremble as he worked lower. There were dozens of hotspots to be found, and he knew all of them.

By the time he had finished with the soap, it was only her grip on his arms that kept her on her feet. "Aaron." It was whispered thickly, and it sounded like a sultry siren's call. "I shouldn't let you do this."

"What I give, I give freely," he repeated huskily. He grabbed the pitcher and began to rinse her clean. The last of the soap was floating away when he tossed the pitcher aside carelessly and began the journey of her body again, but this time with his lips. He hotly caressed her breast until the taut nipple begged for his further attention. "Do I please you?" he asked thickly as he nuzzled and tasted. A moan answered him and he greedily caught the tip of her breast in his mouth. Perhaps someday milk would come from there to feed their child. How beautiful it would be.

Her knees buckled and he lifted her off her feet. He carried her to the edge of the pool and slowly lowered her to the towels waiting there. Steam curled up from her skin and a flush rode her cheeks. Her black eyes were as consuming as the night as she watched him, and the feel of her hunger for him made the sparks leap inside his eyes. He pulled himself out of the pool and leaned over her. "I will not take you." He slowly slid down her body and tormented her navel with his tongue. "I will give you what you need."

Protesting was far from her mind by that point. He was a god, but he could not turn off the sun. Either he would love her selflessly, or he would give selflessly of himself. It was the middle ground that she resisted. A hot mouth buried between her legs and the sensation made her cry out. He had revved her body so skillfully that it took him only a few moments to drive her ruthlessly to the peak and then over. The way his name broke from her lips in ecstasy raked over his aching body and made his hands shake.

She barely managed a whimper as he lied down beside her and gathered her against his chest. After the recent highs and lows, it was a blessed relief to feel nothing except that wonderful sensation of absolute pleasure. She would have tried to hold him but he had completely melted every muscle in her body.

He studied her face contentedly. The sleepy, satiated expression made her radiantly beautiful to him. It was worth every

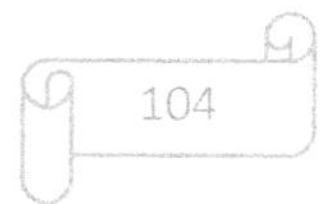

bit of his gnawing need to no longer feel her frustration beating at him. Now he could find the control to wait. "Shall I wash you again?" he asked teasingly. The little rasp to his voice gave away his need, but he did not care. Contrary to his body's annoyance, he felt incredibly full of energy and power.

She found the strength to bury her fingers in his wet hair. Drowsy black eyes opened as she smiled. "I don't think you ever had to induce anyone into wanting you, Eros. You are far too good at what you do."

"I am a firm believer in doing your best at whatever job you have. My job now is to please only one woman. I shall happily spend eternity doing so." He leaned down and kissed her slowly with a famished heat. "You are happy?"

"Depends on the context." She skimmed her fingers over his lips. "This was not fair to you, Aaron."

"I disagree. I am the one who has the problem keeping us apart. I could not handle feeling you so tangled up in your desire for me without having a way to appease it." His lips curved. "Perhaps my being so frustrated as well will drive to me to find faster what I am afraid of and remove it so I may make love to you more thoroughly. And repeatedly. And perhaps in a few ways I never taught you before. You may wish to arrange for a week of vacation."

She found herself laughing as she was reminded anew why she loved him. That wonderful, mischievous manner always lifted her spirits. Those whispers in the night two millennia before had stolen her soul. "Speaking of work, I think I am glad that I arranged to have my day free for you. I can imagine myself walking in feeling like this. I would never hear the end of it."

"I do not know why it is called 'getting laid'," he admitted wryly. "There are so many more interesting variations than merely being horizontal." He grinned when a sudden rumble from her stomach was echoed by his a moment later. "I suppose we should be less horizontal now and take care of a different sort of hunger." He rolled to his feet and winced a bit. "I would prefer a *chiton* over a towel right now," he groused as he bent and scooped her up into his arms.

She tried to hide a smile. "Chaffing?"

"Well, it certainly itches." He swung her around the corners inside the house and looked down to see her smiling. He gently placed her on her feet in the bedroom. "Have I amused you?"

Her fingers trailed up his chest and then skimmed down his jaw. "I was just thinking again that I am a lucky woman to have a man so unashamedly romantic."

A golden brow lifted arrogantly. "I invented romance."

A sudden thought of what would happen in a few months when Valentine's Day arrived made her struggle to keep back a laugh. The thought was followed by the reminder that she may not even survive to the day of lovers, and her lighthearted mood evaporated.

She was immediately drawn into his arms and rocked tenderly. "You are sad." He buried his face in her soft hair. "You were happy. What has you so unhappy, my beloved? I will be entirely yours soon enough."

Lies did not belong between them. Too many had ruined their lives already. "It's not you. It's the evil out there. It still looms, Aaron. I feel it. With every day, it grows stronger. I've had to work so quickly to ensure it cannot hurt anyone but I nearly lost someone anyway. She should never have been shot, and yet she was. I was able to use it to my advantage to help her, but it should not have happened." She dropped her head onto his shoulder. "I will carry that guilt for the rest of my life."

"Is she happy now? Healed? Healthy?"

"Of course."

"Then that is all that matters." He slowly released her and smiled because he knew she needed it. "I am going to take a shower. I will join you to make breakfast."

Entirely unsurprised, she smiled. "Alright." She watched him head into the bathroom, and she was equally unsurprised when the

door shut behind him. She was becoming a bit fascinated in a strange way; his inability to be naked almost seemed to be a form of modesty. How offended would he be when he figured it out? It would be amusing, to say the least.

She had to travel around the house a bit to retrieve her clothes. Pieces had ended up all over the place. Rather than pull on her blouse and jacket again, she rummaged in his closet. He liked the same neutrals paired with jewel tones that she did. She spotted a silk shirt in warm brown and tugged it out. Once cuffed at the wrist and tied at her waist, it fit well enough to suit her. She was only going to be in her District, and her people would actually be *glad* to see her with Aaron. Just desserts, so the saying went.

She was crisping potatoes when he walked into the kitchen. His eyes lit with hungry sparks as he spotted what she wore. "And I thought you never went out without your version of body armor," he teased.

"When I'm not on the clock, I wear whatever I like. It just happens that, usually, I use my days off to stay home or visit my grandkid." She hid a smile as she heard him choke on his coffee. "Do you know the Gentle Brook Inn? It's owned and run by Madelyne and Kienan Shaughnessy. When Madelyne lost her parents, I became her legal guardian. I and Eric raised her to adulthood. She is enough like a daughter to me—and Eric and Rayna—that her son calls us his grandparents."

"Thank you for explaining," he grumbled. "I could not imagine how it be possible you have a grandchild, let alone a child, if you had not been touched by anyone except me." He nuzzled the back of her neck through her hair before getting out some eggs and frying them up. He glanced over where she had already placed strips of bacon to drain. "I have grown fond of bacon," he confessed.

She contemplated that as they were serving themselves and taking a seat at the dining table. "How are you sustaining your immortality without nectar and ambrosia?"

"It takes but one serving to make a god. We are not required to continually consume it in order to remain as gods. We chose to do so because it placed us so much higher above the normal mortals who ate the flesh of animals." The smallest hint of sarcasm had entered his tone. "I have actually discovered that I enjoy mortal living. Oh, it has its downsides, but it is nothing that I cannot overcome or avoid by my power." He arched a brow. "As you well know. I believe someone else shamelessly uses her power to have her way in things."

She just smiled. "Why have it if you do not use it? I have limitations on what I can do, though. I'm not a goddess."

Not for the first time, he could not help but think that she *should* be a goddess. She was all but one already. Truly, only a lack of full omnipotence and immortality (which was different from longevity) kept her from his station. He would have made her one right then and there, but Olympus was sealed and he had no access to nectar and ambrosia. "Would you be one if you could?" he asked softly.

She thought about it very seriously. "If it would help me better protect the people who need me, yes. What would I be a goddess *of*, though?"

He just smiled as well. "It would be interesting to find out."

After breakfast, he obligingly transported them to her home so that she could put on makeup. He watched with deep fascination at the entire process. There were many different sorts of products and items than he remembered from Ancient Greece. More colors as well. The basic ideals—emphasizing lips, eyes, and cheekbones— were familiar, though. "Why do men not wear makeup these days?" he asked as he picked up her powder and sniffed at it.

She contemplated her words and then decided that it would be something he never understood. "Cultural shift," she finally said. "It's considered feminine to wear makeup now. Men really only wear makeup if they are actors or models, and most laymen don't even realize they are." She smiled. "I have been told a dozen times that I don't need makeup, that I'm pandering to male ideology, that I am being fooled by commercialism, and that a woman should not be expected to wear makeup in order to be considered beautiful. I *like* it. I like the feel of pampering myself and knowing I'm playing up my best features. I feel naked if I'm outside without it."

It made him smile. "A part of you is still in Greece."

"Perhaps so." She offered him some lip-gloss. "I'm a bit paler than you, but we have the same hue to our skin. You can wear most anything of mine except the powder. I'll pick you up some of your own if you like. I know the modern stuff better than you do—for now."

"I would be grateful." He sniffed at the gloss. A slow and sensual smile curved his lips. "No wonder you tasted of strawberries that first day." He deliberately put on a layer. It gave his already bitable lips an effect that made them seem as if he had just kissed her. "I will kiss you again later and we will be even."

"Deal."

As he had only ever transported her in and out of her home, and he had only transported himself, he was pleasantly surprised to discover that it was actually built as a part of Enforcers HQ itself. The house was decent enough size, and it had a garden space that rivaled his. The garden was protected by glass panels over the top that let in light but were reflective on the other side so that people could not look inside. Like his home, she had decorated with their homeland in mind. "I did not realize you lived attached to where you work," he murmured.

She smiled up at him. "Nearly everyone in the District lives in a place attached to their place of work if they own the business. Eric and Rayna are on the other side of the building. Most everyone who lives here also works here. We have a large tourism trade nowadays, and we offer handmade goods as well as historical tours. We are primarily mercantile with only a small residential area. We keep it looking a bit on the rundown side so that only the people who truly belong will wish to stay. We see beyond the surface."

He certainly could see beneath the surface himself, and what he saw was a beautiful, thriving, community where everyone knew each other and shared whatever was needed with whoever was in need. He spotted several smiling glances sent toward Rhianna and impulsively caught her hand with his. Her brows lifted and he grinned. "I am enforcing the belief that you are interested in me."

She leaned her head against his arm. "As if my wearing what is obviously a man's shirt—and then being seen with a man—was not enough of a clue." She stopped walking as they reached the front gate around a beautiful bed and breakfast set behind a lush garden. "Welcome to the Gentle Brook Inn."

"Gramma!" A boy of no older than seven came rushing down the pathway and happily threw himself into Rhianna's arms. His hair was a fascinating shade of gray with only a few hints of brown to imply it had ever been anything else. Chocolate colored eyes watched his grandmother with obvious hero worship. "We have cookies."

"Well, how can I turn that down!" She snuggled him for a moment before putting him down. She knelt beside him and gestured to Aaron. "Conner, meet Aaron." She smiled up at Aaron. "This is Conner Shaughnessy. He is Madelyne and Kienan's son."

Aaron knelt as well. He could not help smiling. He had always loved children of all kinds. "I am pleased to meet you."

"I like your voice." Conner planted a kiss on his cheek. If his grandma brought him, then he must be family. "I'll tell Mommy and Daddy you're here!" He scampered back into the inn and his shoes could be heard skidding on the floors.

Aaron stood and tugged Rhianna up and then tucked her under his arm as they followed the gray-haired tornado into the building. They were promptly greeted in the lobby by a surprisingly plain woman who happily threw her arms around Rhianna. "I'm happy for you!" Madelyne exclaimed. "I was so happy when Riku called me and told me I might have a stepfather! You need to be happy, Rhianna. Tell me you're happy."

"We're getting there." Rhianna hugged her back as well. "This is Aaron Konstantinos." She winced wryly. "At least, that is who he is now. He's actually Eros, the God of Love."

Violet eyes filled with humor. "I think only a god could keep up with you, Rhianna." She turned to Aaron and studied him intently before smiling anew. She had once been wary of beautiful men, but even if Kienan had not cured her of that, she would have still been comfortable near Aaron. He radiated such a wonderful sense of compassion and acceptance into the air that she *knew* he judged only on someone's heart—if he judged at all. "My name is Madelyne, but I am Maddie to friends and family."

"Maddie it will be." He bent to kiss her cheek. "I would not mind being your stepfather. I have never been a father, but I imagine I can figure it out."

"The one god who would have a good reason for having a hundred kids has never had any?" Madelyne asked Rhianna in amusement.

Rhianna smiled. "He is also the one god who truly respected all of his consorts." She heard a footstep and looked up to see another male approaching with Conner on his shoulders. "There you are, Kienan. I was beginning to think you were lost."

Kienan Shaughnessy just grinned. As a marked contrast to his wife, he was almost as handsome as a god himself, and it was his chocolate eyes passed to his son. His hair was a thick golden brown instead. "I was in the middle of cleaning the hot spring." He eyed Aaron speculatively. "Do I like him?"

Sensing a powerfully protective nature, Aaron gave him a graceful bow. "You have my word of honor that there is nothing I could ever do to harm Rhianna. I will spend the rest of eternity filling her life with love so that she is never alone again. *She* is why I have power." He looked at Rhianna and did not bother to hide the emotion that turned his blue eyes incandescent with sparks and power. "The God of Love and Desire has need for only one woman's love and desire."

"Wow." Madelyne looked up at Kienan with a grin. "He made her blush. He's good."

Kienan was just happy to know that Rhianna would be treated the way she deserved. He considered Rhianna to be a part of his family thanks to Madelyne, and he put his family first and foremost in everything. "I'm sure that's not all he's good at."

"Behave yourself!" Rhianna scolded him, but she was smiling. "We have other places to stop. I just wanted to introduce him for now." She kissed her daughter and son-in-law's cheeks and then her grandson's puckered lips. "I will bring him over for dinner one night."

"I'll make something Greek," Madelyne offered impishly.

Aaron chuckled at that as he followed Rhianna out of the inn. "Your daughter has impeccable taste," he noted. "Her Kienan would have been chased by many of the gods if we were still in the past. I may have joined the hunt myself."

"They needed each other," she murmured. "My favorite nightingale and swan." She caught his hand and tugged him along down the sidewalk. "We have another stop to make, and a few things to see along the way. I'll tell you how it all got started."

He listened intently as she laid out the history of the 3rd District starting from the day she and Eric had realized how very different they and their families were from the rest of the tribes along the coast. His heart wept that he had not been there for her, that he had not been strong enough until recently to even reach out in another form—and only on Mirage anyway. And yet, there was pride for her accomplishments. She had done deeds worthy of her own heroic legend.

He tugged her even closer instinctively and she absently tucked a hand into the back pocket of his jeans. She smiled as she saw what they approached. Two nearly identical young men stood with a rusty haired young woman and another young woman who had pink streaks in her hair. They were arguing avidly over the clipboard that the redhead held. "Are we having trouble?" she asked dryly.

Heads swung around and smiles replaced temper. "Ms. Taber, you surprised us!" Kenneth Dease said warmly. "No trouble here; we're just not in agreement about how we want to handle the commercial we're going to be shooting for the inn. It's going to be the District's first foray into television."

His wife smirked. "You should have heard him and Kienan going at it," Sera Dease noted dryly. She studied Aaron intently for a few moments before smiling. "Welcome home."

Cameron Dease looked solemnly at Rhianna but there was a sparkle in his eyes. "Is he a keeper?"

"I like to think so." She smiled at the redhead. "I trust you to sneak me things on the side so that I can be kept up-to-date on the process, Sarah."

Sarah Dease just grinned. "It isn't much of a sneak when you announce it. And you think Cam or Ken would tell you no?" She saluted sassily. "I'll send you an email tonight with what we have so far."

Rhianna and Aaron let them be and continued on their way. They passed by a small house undergoing construction, and the front area was packed with stunning clothworks. The weaver's wife stood bickering with several exceptionally large Vikings, and there were a handful of redheads discussing colors and patterns with the weaver himself.

Rhianna murmured, "Brian and Louise Matthews. They have a little girl of about five months. The house was splitting at the seams, so to speak. You know the Traherns, of course. You hired them to do Cupid's Grove. Seven brothers matched with seven sisters because of seven wishes on a golden locket."

Aaron slid a smile at her. "You planned that one early. You must have been holding onto the golden apple for a while."

"A century or two. I would infrequently visit Greece to seek out the hidden places of my memory in order to obtain the items needed to ensure—enforce—the happiness of my people. I borrowed thread from Hestia as well."

"We will go together next time." He brought her hand to his lips and delicately teased the tender skin between her fingers with the tip of his tongue. A delicate flush climbed her face and her eyes darkened until he could barely see her expanded pupils. "I will take you to my temple and make love to you under the stars."

She refrained from mentioning the temple was a ruin and probably always surrounded by visitors. He was a god. He could make anything work. It was an encouraging sign, though, that he wanted to have her outside, even if it was in the night. "Will you disguise yourself and pretend you are seducing a poor, hapless mortal girl with your wiles?" she teased.

The sparks returned to his eyes. "I shall become a stag and chase you down, and then I will turn back and ravish you most thoroughly. Will that suit you?"

Her breath hitched as she tugged her hand free. "We have a date."

He insisted on holding her hand anyway as they continued along their way. She pointed out two couples that were window-shopping for baby furniture, and he smiled as he noticed both women were pregnant. One had hair too long to belong to a normal human, and the other was as lovely as a swan. The husband of the one with long hair looked quite hard at the edges, but Aaron could see the gentleness inside his heart. The other man had an oddly familiar shape to his face that took Aaron a moment to place. "Ah! Italian?"

"Indeed." Rhianna sighed happily at the scene. "Theresa and Van D'Angelo, and Rafael and Tori Lucino. Rafael is an associate of mine. He took over the family company a month ago. Van works as a consultant for Enforcers. He has skills of . . . particular use. Theresa is District-born. Tori is not, but she is special in her own way." Her gaze lowered. "She is the one who was wrongfully wounded."

Aaron smoothed his hand down her arm. "She is alive and she

is happy. That is what is important, my beloved. And she seems to be thriving. Four months?"

"Thereabout. Theresa is at six. She is a gifted healer. I look forward to their daughter's gifts as well." She stopped outside a glittering club and lightly gestured. "Welcome to the Faerie Club. Kienan's younger sister is the owner and manager of the place. This is *the* place to be in NYC. It is so safe that parents can drop off their children without fear of harm happening to them. Aenya runs a clean ship."

He was charmed even before they went inside and found that the middle of the day made it no less lively. There were few children around since it was during school hours, but there were teens of various ages about the place along with young adults. A beautiful blonde that bore a resemblance to Kienan was on the dance floor and currently teaching a class how to do the waltz.

Rhianna looked around and was reminded again of the good that had been done. She saw Isabelle LaGuardia and Brie Viani sitting with their husbands, Alex and Roberto, and the rest of the Shaughnessy family was present as well. Taegan was teaching some of the few kids present how to do math. His wife, Kalliope, was fussing over a teenager's hair and putting it up into a fancy do. Audra was talking with her husband, Mel, and they were keeping an eye on their two children as well as the kids belonging to their siblings. Aenya's husband, Hiro, was playing at a waiter and serving tables.

The fact that all of them had day jobs, particularly Mel and Kalliope, yet they had found the time to be there when she needed them did not surprise her at all. All had completed contracts. They would instinctively respond to her call. She had wanted Aaron to see the best of her world, and it was all there in front of them.

"Rhi!" Aenya waved happily. "You saved me an email! Come look at what Heul and Remy came up with for our remodel. Van's paying," she added impishly. "He still owed me one from when he was helping Theresa."

Aaron watched Rhianna head down for a quick conversation, and he saw her stop along the way to talk to anyone who spoke up. Everyone in her District loved her as much as she loved them. They all knew who she was even if they had not met her.

Understanding began to fill him. She had said she was not his Psyche emotionally anymore, but he believed now that she was wrong. The loving, giving nature that had imbued her in the past had not gone away. She had not suddenly become more stubborn or independent. She had merely grown up. She was everything she had been before, and now also more. He would never have been able to love her in the past in the way he did right there.

"You have an interesting look on your face," Taegan noted as he stopped beside Aaron. He followed the god's gaze to where Rhianna was intently studying the plans while Aenya talked animatedly. "You didn't realize how much you love her? Odd thing for you, I think."

"I suppose even the God of Love must learn about his power firsthand. It is beginning to feel a little like destiny."

"Well, it sure wouldn't be a coincidence. Not around here anyway."

Aaron and Rhianna spent the rest of the afternoon exploring the District, and he only fell more in love with the place and its main protector as time passed. He *belonged* there. Still, he was a discrete gentleman when he chose to be. He made sure that everyone saw them part at her door and took himself away where he could not be seen before he transported himself into her living room.

He made dinner for them both and let her convince him to watch one of her favored sitcoms. Things stayed lighthearted and casual to the best of their ability, but it was not easy for either of them. He was incapable of keeping his hands off her, and the taste of strawberries on his lips had done nothing for her self-control. The interlude by the bath may as well have been a year ago. As he had said, some fires were just not meant to go out.

He borrowed her toothbrush this time and noted while she was washing her face, "We will need to place items at each other's house until we decide how to compromise on where we live. You are needed here, yet I know you were happy at my house."

"I don't mind alternating until we figure it out." She dug out one of her favorite t-shirts to sleep in and tugged it on before getting into bed. "Warm your feet before you join me. They were cold last night."

He chuckled softly. "As you wish." He padded half-naked across the room to shut the curtains and tugged off his socks as he crossed back to catch the lamp. The darkness had barely settled before he slid naked into bed beside her. She promptly turned over and scooted in where she belonged and he skimmed his fingers down her arm. A delicate shiver was his response. Her frustration gnawed at his hormones until even his teeth ached with the urge to be deep inside her. "I can ease you again," he offered huskily, a note of anticipation in his voice.

"Odd as it sounds, I don't trust you to do only that," she answered wryly. "I don't trust you in the dark, my love."

He paused for a moment as that turned over inside his mind. Why would she not trust him only in the dark? Was there a connection between whatever fear he held, his true self, and the dark? He frowned as he tried to sort it out, but it still made no sense. He would have to wait, watch, and hope she said something else that might give him a clue. Their contract would continue to remain voided until they gave all of themselves to one another. Only when it was active again could they fight for their happy ending.

Something stirred in the distance. It felt cold, slimy, and malevolent. Rhianna went very still and Aaron held her even closer. He brought her hand up to rest over his heart and laced their fingers together. "When will the war come?" he asked softly. "It is inevitable now."

"I don't know." She closed her eyes. "I only know that it will happen. If needed, I will give my life for the safety of all that lives."

He froze. "You will *not*," he vowed harshly. "You will not die on me! Enforcers needs you. The District needs you. *I* need you. I will not let you go, Rhianna. You *cannot* leave me again."

"I will try not to," she soothed. She rubbed her cheek against his skin for a moment before yawning and snuggling closer. She was asleep a few moments later.

He forced away the disturbing feeling that she was being prophetic and let himself follow her into sleep. As was his way, he woke at the first light of dawn, but he was surprised to find himself waking alone. His eyes flew wide and he discovered his lover had left him. Her side was still warm and he could still feel her skin. A sense of the house told him she was not there.

A strong and bitter sensation of loneliness filled him. He loved waking with her in his arms. The way she felt and looked so perfect. The way she had of making him feel needed, wanted, and loved. How could she have left him that way? Didn't she know how much it hurt to wake without your lover in your arms?

Actually, yes, she did. He threw an arm over his eyes as he realized that he had always left her before she woke. He had done it to protect his identity in the past, but he had no excuse for the previous morning other than 'needing to prepare the bath.' He could have done it after she woke. Why hadn't he thought to wait?

He got out of bed and got dressed. He transported himself to his home to get ready and then headed to the Grove to get some work done. Priya was not there yet, but she did not get in until eight. He walked into his office and spotted the two questionnaires on his desk. One had his name. The other had Rhianna's. They had been clipped together, and Priya had put her usual heart-shaped post-it on the top where she had written '100%!' with a smiley face.

He sank down into his chair and grabbed Rhianna's

questionnaire. He slowly went down her answers to the questions about her thoughts on romance, and he grabbed a pen to circle something in particular. "Perhaps," he murmured into the quiet, "it is time I start practicing what I preach. I believe I owe my wife some long, long overdue courting."

CHAPTER TEN

Rhianna was already at work when she heard Eric enter his office. She said nothing. He walked into her space a few moments later and looked at her very intently. He slowly crossed the room and eased onto the side of her desk. "Rhi."

She looked up at him. "Yes?"

"Please tell me what's going on. Do I probably know what happened? It's likely; few don't know the tale of Psyche and Eros. What is real and what isn't, however, is what I don't know." A trace of pain lingered in his normally icy blue eyes. "You know my secrets, Rhi. You gave me my happy ending. Tell me what I need to know to help you get yours. I can't stand seeing you suffer."

She drew a long breath. "Alright." She gestured to one of the chairs. "Have a seat. This might take a few."

He tugged one closer and sat down with a wry smile. "Does it start a long, long time ago?"

Her smile was no less wry but it was also a bit sad. "Doesn't it always?"

Status: File Voided
Analysis: Pending

Folder Three
AARON

CHAPTER ELEVEN

Eric had taken the information with his characteristic ability to absorb and adapt though his face had reflected his horror for the details at times. Rhianna felt strangely peaceful now that she had gotten it off her chest. She had loathed lying to Eric and keeping him out of her life. It felt quite freeing to eliminate the last secrets between them.

Work continued on for the day with relative normalcy until roughly ten in the morning when D.J. buzzed Rhianna to tell her she had visitors that had been sent over by Cupid's Grove. She had told D.J. to consider the Grove another ally, but she had expected to see Aaron or even Priya, not referrals.

The two who showed up at her office after being escorted by a guard were a set of young women in their mid-twenties or so. Rhianna knew on one look that they were the type who would struggle to make their own happy ending. "Welcome," she said warmly as she got to her feet. "I'm Rhianna Taber. I understand you were sent over by the Grove? Have a seat and tell me what is going on."

They both sat down, and their knees bumped intimately. "Our parents are pressuring us to get married," the brunette explained. "We thought that going to the Grove might help us find true love; Mr. Konstantinos' gift to match people is almost godlike!"

Rhianna hid a smile. "So I had heard. I presume you two met that way? He matched you together?" She could certainly see where their souls would lock and fuse.

"He did but . . ." The blonde lowered her gaze. "We didn't expect to match to our own gender." She made a helpless gesture. "I'm bi, but I've been careful to date only men because I know my family would disapprove."

"I didn't even know I *was* attracted to other women," her partner admitted. "Or maybe it's just Cassie. She just . . . from the moment I met her, I've been so happy. But . . ."

"But you fear for rejection from your families," Rhianna surmised. Not for the first time, it made her blood boil. She still remembered the days when love was all that mattered, not the equipment used in the act of it. "Let me see." She tapped a finger on her chin as she let her sixth sense process. Events adjusted and she could see what needed to be done. She would have a bit of tinkering to do. "Alright then." She opened a file and began typing up a fresh contract. "I am putting you under contract with Enforcers."

The lovers exchanged a wide-eyed look. Just as people knew that dreams came true in the District, they also knew that being under contract with Enforcers, well, *enforced* that outcome. "What do we have to do?" Cassie asked.

"It will all be here within the contract. You will have to place quite a bit of trust in me." She printed out the contract and slid it across the desk. "I can see why the Grove sent you to me. Sometimes a little external force is needed." More specifically, a little external force that could change and control the future—something Aaron himself could not do. He could not change events previously set in stone, but she could. She still didn't know why.

The two young women signed without hesitation, and the blonde took possession of it. There was already a renewed spring to their step as they walked out reading over what needed to be done. As soon as the door closed behind them, Rhianna picked up her phone and made a few calls to adjust what she needed. She then emailed a copy of the contract to Rayna for her to keep an eye on.

"Got a referral, huh?" Eric leaned against the doorway. He

arched a brow. "Interesting that a god can't do some things."

"If the gods could have done everything, there wouldn't have been so many of them." She tapped a finger on her lips and then picked up the phone. "I think I need to give my husband a call." She ignored Eric smirking at her. She knew he considered it his revenge that she had the same problems with Aaron that he did with Rayna. When the other side answered, she smiled. "It's Rhianna. Is Aaron busy?"

"Nope, he's between meetings. Hang on and I'll transfer you."

A click and a moment later, Aaron answered the phone smoothly, "How may I serve your desires, beloved?"

Oh, the *possibilities*. "Referrals?" she asked only.

"Ah. Naturally." The smile was in his voice. "You and I have our own strengths and gifts. Where there is some natural overlap, we still do things the other cannot. It is why we are two halves of a whole, why we are stronger together than apart. I saw that there was something I could not do and I sent them to you. I would hope you may do the same."

She could not resist teasing, "Should I be having Gwyn write up legal documents to make our alliance formal? Enforcers prides itself on having good working relationships with its allies in other fields."

He laughed softly and the sound was sultry. "You and I do many things beautifully together, and working is merely one of them. I look forward to again demonstrating my best skills for you someday soon." He gently hung up the phone.

She blew out a breath and tried to ignore the way her entire body had heated at the silky promise in his voice. She needed to re-acclimate herself to the way he turned her on with merely his words let alone if he touched her.

It stayed nicely peaceful for the rest of the morning. She had a luncheon with a few former associates that she still enjoyed speaking with, and she was bemused that they had insisted on a casual dining spot rather than the fancy places most businesspeople of her experience preferred. She liked the casual ones as well.

She got there first and was quite pleased that the staff gave her a quieter table. There was never any guilt inside her for taking advantage of her clout. It balanced for the fact that she always used her power to help others. She had taken her seat and was perusing the menu when she heard steps. She looked up and smiled. "Sullivan. Jiles. What a delight." She got to her feet to greet them properly.

Sullivan Shaughnessy was indirectly related to her thanks to Kienan and Madelyne, and there was in fact a contract in his past. Actually, his entire family for a hundred fifty years had been issued contracts. Jiles Tavoularis was Kalliope's father, and therefore he was kind of related as well. Both men were in their sixties but as fit and handsome as men two decades younger. "Rhianna." Jiles gave her cheek an affectionate kiss. "What is your secret? You simply never change."

"Good genes," she demurred modestly. Truthfully, she had never needed to worry about the fact that neither she nor Eric aged because of their longevity—and neither would Gwyn, Rayna, or Taylor. By the time people had noticed she and her partner ought to look older, the first murmurs of their power had already begun. It had never been questioned since.

They all sat down and kept the conversation light as they ordered their meals. The two men were still enjoying their retirement and being grandparents, and they had quite a few humorous tales to be told. Rhianna told them about some of Enforcers' latest business ventures and amused them both when she mentioned shamelessly intimidating competition.

They were having tea with their desserts when they were surprised by a young man in a delivery uniform walking up to the table with a bouquet of red and orange roses and forget-me-nots. He stopped beside Rhianna with a bright smile. "Hi! Rhianna Taber?"

A buzz began to rise in the entire restaurant. Sullivan and

Jiles' brows seemed to lift at the same time. Very warily, Rhianna said, "Yes, I am." She eyed the flowers. "Those are not for me."

"In fact, they are." He handed them over into her arms and cleared his throat as he straightened. "I have been instructed to inform you that your loving husband sends them with his warmest regards."

As an excited clatter broke out, she closed her eyes and contemplated finding a way to kill her 'loving husband.' "Thank you," she muttered. She looked at the flowers in resignation as the boy hustled away. Red roses meant love, orange roses meant fervent passion, and forget-me-nots meant exactly what they sounded like they meant. Damn him.

Sullivan cleared his throat delicately. "Rhianna?"

She put the flowers down on the table and sought for a way to explain. "I was married a long while ago," she said carefully, "and something happened that caused us to separate. We had not seen each other in ages, and we are trying to see if we can reconcile. There are complications, unfortunately. We had trust issues."

Jiles propped his chin on his hand as he grinned. "Someone seems quite determined to overcome those issues. Will you hit me if I say that I think it's wonderful? I doubt I am the first to mention that it has always been painful to see you be alone. Some people are happy that way, but you never struck me as one of them."

"I'm not," she admitted. "I was always hoping he might forgive me and return. Unfortunately, he seems to have a few subliminal issues that he is trying to find and remove. He surprised me now, I admit, and I don't surprise easily." She winced wryly as she heard the continuing buzz in the room. "So much for him saying he would be discrete."

Sullivan grinned. "After all these years, and all of your meddling, you still thought that love could be discrete at all?"

"Touché. To be fair, he is actually quite adept at it. The fact that he came back into my life a few days ago and no one noticed is proof of it. Whatever he is up to, he is up to deliberately. He could have merely made it seem as if he was courting me, but he—" She broke off as understanding dawned. "Ah." Her smile turned wry. "He *is* courting me, but he is eliminating competition at the same time. Him courting me and my accepting would make me fair game to other interested parties."

Jiles chuckled. "As ever, you know everything. You do sound surprised though. Was there no courtship when you first met?"

"Hmm, no. Things happened quite fast. I guess he is trying to make up for lost time." She looked at the flowers with an unconscious longing. It felt kind of nice to be made to feel as if she was the only thing he wanted. She *knew* it already, yet the demonstration was wonderful. "I didn't actually intend to keep our relationship a secret forever. It's just a very complicated situation."

"You will keep us posted, yes?" Sullivan asked hopefully.

She had to laugh. "Oh, I'm sure Maddie will be quite happy to tattle on me! I'm surprised neither she nor Kienan mentioned it sooner. They met my husband just yesterday." She got to her feet and put some money on the table for her share of lunch. "I have to be heading back. It was wonderful to see you both." She scooped up her flowers and headed out past the whispers with the proud manner of a goddess.

The two friends exchanged a look before Sullivan pulled out his cell phone. They would call Kienan and Madelyne immediately and get the full scoop. If there was *anything* they could do to help, they would damned well do it!

Rhianna immediately went back to her office and ignored the giggles and grins from her employees. She put the flowers into a vase where she could admire them and turned to go to her desk. Much to her surprise, there was a gaily wrapped package sitting on the top. It was wrapped in gold paper with a white ribbon. She really didn't even need to see the signature on the card to know it was from Aaron.

She sighed and untied the ribbon. Removing the paper revealed another layer in red. Then a third in purple. She couldn't help but be impressed despite herself. A box was at last under the purple paper, and she lifted the lid to discover an assortment of custom chocolates. All of them were dark chocolate, which happened to be her favorite. She couldn't resist scooping up one and biting in, and her eyes went wide as she found herself with a mouthful of gooey cinnamon filling. A sniff of a few others revealed pomegranate and honey fillings.

The giggle that passed her lips surprised even her, and she felt glad that Eric wasn't in the office to hear her. Her impish, romantic, and sexy significant other had sent her a box of all-natural aphrodisiacs. No chocolate covered strawberries for *him*. He went right to the good stuff. As if they needed the help! Still, her non-traditional side was tickled.

The moment she realized it, she sighed and shook her head. The questionnaire she had filled out. One of the questions had been on her opinion of traditional gifts like flowers and chocolates, and she had answered that she liked them when they were adapted to the person receiving them. He had deliberately picked out things sure to stir her romantic side as well as her sense of humor. He was also deliberately playing to her senses by engaging them with aromatic scents and tastes. Odds are that she would soon be serenaded by a lyre; she had never been the saxophone type.

She couldn't resist grabbing another chocolate as she sat down and logged back onto her computer. She then promptly choked on the candy as her speakers quite merrily began to play a soft, sexy ballad rendered in a lyre and an oboe. The high notes seemed to flutter her heart, and the low notes fluttered something much lower. She grabbed her phone and punched a button. "Damn it, Rayna!"

All she got in response was an explosion of helpless giggles, and she slammed down the phone again. There was no other way the music could have gotten onto her computer. Aaron had enlisted his minions—and they had been her minions first! She sat back in her chair and drummed her fingers on her arm. Finally, with a sigh, she gave in to what he was so obviously trying to do. She rescheduled her one afternoon meeting and took the rest of the day off.

When she arrived at Cupid's Grove, Priya looked up with a smile that she hastily bit back from becoming a laugh. Rhianna merely sighed at her. "Alright. Where is he? We both know he was deliberately trying to entice me into coming to him."

Priya struggled to the best of her ability to hide her giggles. "Actually, he's not here. He had no appointments so he decided to go home. He said he was, uhm, going to get in some archery practice."

Rhianna rolled her eyes at that. She drummed her fingers on her arm for a moment as she thought about things. Perhaps it was time that Cupid got himself some competition. "Thanks, Priya." She swung around and headed out of the building. Her transportation skills were highly limited because she was not a god, but she could take herself to places that she had previously visited physically. She went home to change into casual clothes and packed herself an overnight bag. A flick of her fingers transported her to Aaron's beautiful home in the mountains and she dropped the bag inside before heading around to the gardens beyond the bath.

A large open space greeted her once she passed the line of peach trees. Several targets had been set up for practice, and her lover was calmly and expertly placing arrow after arrow into the dead center of the bulls-eye. Another bow and quiver sat nearby and she scooped it up. From ten feet behind him, she notched an arrow and let it fly. It neatly nipped over his shoulder close enough to clip a few strands of hair, flew right across the field, and smacked into the end of his last arrow with enough force to knock it out of place.

Aaron looked back over his shoulder with a slow and wicked grin. "What is that phrase mortals have? Something about 'this being war'?"

"'This means war'," she confirmed. She sauntered closer. "I

think I can keep up with you, Eros. I've picked up a few skills in my life."

He tilted up her chin with his free hand and leaned down to kiss her with his familiar intensity. "And some things," he murmured huskily, "you are simply a natural at." Sparks moved across his iridescent eyes. "You taste like chocolate." He lingered over another softer kiss. "Mm. I like it. Maybe I should get some of that edible paint for us to play with."

A bit breathlessly, she asked, "Who turned you loose on the erotica sites?"

"Priya. She claimed I might as well have all of the tools of the trade, particularly since it would seem they created the word *erotic* from my name." His laugh rippled over her skin. "I think I like that."

She had always felt it was an appropriate derivation herself. "Don't think you'll distract me into losing." She pushed him back and moved up to stand beside him. "Let's see what you've got. You might be rusty after two millennia."

A little thrill rippled through him anew at the signs of her inner strength and confidence. He did not want someone he could always boss around; he wanted a partner. An equal. He lifted his bow and fired at the target, and he knocked her arrow free. The target was beginning to be a bit ragged, and he shifted to shoot the next. Her subsequent arrow knocked his out moments later.

They traded back and forth with their shots, but eventually they both just gave up and started laughing. They were simply too evenly matched. Aaron took the bows and quivers to place them aside, and then he tugged Rhianna into his arms. "I would like to declare a tie." He rubbed their noses together affectionately. "You are quite the archer, my beloved."

"It amused me to learn," she admitted. She looped her arms around his waist and smiled. "I will take it as a compliment that I can keep you on your toes. And admit that my friends are glad that I don't have arrows like you do. I'd shamelessly use them."

"You shamelessly use other things." He tucked her under his

arm and escorted her back into the rest of the garden. "Come sit with me."

She took one look at the little table set with tea and cake and knew that he had indeed been deliberately luring her into coming over. She did not mind. He filled in the places in her life that her job and friends never could. "What is this?"

"I believe it is called a date." He helped her into her chair before scooting his closer so that they sat side-by-side. He brought her hand to his lips and lightly teased the skin between her fingers. "I am courting you, Rhianna. You once said you had hoped I would suit you. I realized I have been lax in that department. A married woman deserves to be courted no less than an unmarried. A married man, too," he added hopefully.

"I could be convinced to court you in return." She shook her head at him. "If, perhaps, you could ever get around to *asking* me about things. You never asked me to marry you. You never asked to court me. You didn't even ask me onto this 'date.' Sometimes a question is important even when the answer will be yes. It evens the field."

He tugged her hand to his heart and looked very seriously in her eyes. "Will you let me court you, Rhianna?" he asked softly. "Let me shower you with the love and devotion you so richly deserve. Let me ensure that there is no doubt in your mind how much I love you. I wish to tell the entire world."

She cupped his cheek with her free hand and tugged him down for a tender kiss. "Yes, you may court me," she whispered against his lips. Humor filled her eyes. "I think you already started on the 'telling the world' bit. Sending me flowers at my luncheon and declaring yourself as my husband!"

He smiled unrepentantly. "I have no desire to entertain rivals, and we both know that you starting to accept attention from any man would label you as 'single and looking' as far as the rest of the male populace was concerned. I suppose some things have not entirely changed after all this time."

"Except that I get to *choose*. It is entirely my decision. I think that I would be offended if my father was alive and you asked him for my hand."

"I would ask your entire family," he disagreed, "for I would be taking you away from them. I would not ask that they give you to me, but that they accept your decision to be taken away."

"Ooh, tactful." She reached for a slice of cake; it was chocolate, of course. "Tell me about your day, and I will tell you what I have done for your referral."

They lingered long enough in the garden that the sun was beginning to set before they realized the passage of time. It had always been that way for them, even from the beginning. They could always find something to talk about, and there was nothing sacred between them. And yet, they could be perfectly fine to be together and quiet. Both could envision wonderful times reading by a fire together, if they could get to that point where they truly lived together.

She made dinner since it was her turn, and they snuggled on the couch after to watch one of their programs. He then sat down with some questionnaires to evaluate while she read up on the business proposal that Mel had floated her direction. Once work was done for the night, they shut down everything and retired to the bedroom.

"Do you want a shower?" he asked.

"I'll catch one in the morning. I don't like showers right before bed. Makes it hard to sleep."

"I could make you tired." He teasingly nipped at her shoulder where it was bared by her nightshirt.

"You certainly could, but I will decline." She finished washing off her makeup and removed her earrings. "I once considered pierced ears, but back when I was first introduced to them, it was a bit on the barbaric side. Turned me off to the entire procedure. Rayna has tried to tell me it's very safe and relatively painless these days, but I just get the creeps."

He grinned. "So there is something that alarms the ever calm, never flustered Rhianna Taber."

She smiled at him. "I am only human."

"You are only a living being," he corrected softly. "Even gods feel fear. Perhaps we even feel all emotions more acutely."

Which was the entire reasons mortals could not behold a god or goddess in their true form. She brushed it aside; it seemed as if each day moved him closer to understanding. She could continue to be patient no matter how painful it was sometimes. "I'll wait for you in bed."

He frowned as she walked into the bedroom. "Why do you continue to sleep in that shirt? I know you do not like it, my beloved. Do you not trust me? I can abide by what you wish. I am not that much a beast."

She got under the covers. "If you can't trust me in the light, then I can't trust you in the dark." The curtains were already drawn, and she clicked off the lamp to plunge the room into darkness. "Don't forget your feet. I'd swear you had ice cubes attached to your legs."

It was just as well that it was dark for it meant she could not see his frown had deepened. He undressed for the night and slipped into bed beside her. She immediately snuggled up against his side where she belonged, and it did not take very long before her breathing evened out into the beautiful sound of sleep.

He stared at the ceiling overhead and tried to make sense of her words. She had said it before that she did not trust him in the dark. Because he had only ever made love to her in the dark? Of course he had. He had been hiding his identity from her. Yet now she inferred that he did not trust her in the light? That seemed ridiculous when he had spent the last few days with her quite vagrantly in the daylight.

But had he ever made love to her in the light?

His fingers stilled their absent stroking over her arm. No. No, he had not. Even now, past the time of deceit and lies, he had brought in the darkness that first night. He had made love to her by the pool in the light, though.

To her, not *with* her. She trusted him to not do more than ease her if they were in the light, and she did not trust him to hold back when they were in the dark. Because he had only ever made love with her in the dark, she rightfully was wary of it. No, it couldn't be that she was wary. She had said *he* was afraid of something, that he was afraid to give her something. Something that was connected to his true self.

You won't give me your true self.

Her words echoed and doubled in his head. It simply did not make sense when he had been naked with her quite frequently. He was naked right then and there. She had seen his true form plenty of—

The thoughts stumbled off and came to a halt. Horror began to slowly rise as understanding started to break through. She had *not* seen his true form. She had never *seen* him naked. Not even now that the truth was out had he ever been naked with her *in the light.* The towel by the bath. Turning off the lights and closing drapes before getting into bed. Leaving her before the dawn. Closing the door while he showered. No wonder she didn't trust him; he had painted nothing but a sign that he did not trust *her.*

But what didn't he trust? Why would he not want her to see him naked when he very much liked the way she looked at him? He had been savoring the love and desire in her eyes when she gazed at him. She was finally able to give him the same worship he had always given her . . . except while they made love. But *why?* She was all but a goddess, so—

For the second time, his thoughts stumbled off as understanding collided with hindsight. She was a mortal. He had thought of her as being almost a goddess and yet he had treated her like a mortal. *He had instinctively thought she could not handle his true self.* It was absolute bullshit, and he felt like the biggest fool in the entire universe for the second time in his life. She was his *equal.* Whether mortal or immortal, her emotions ran as deep, true, and powerfully as his did.

Agony welled anew. How he must have been hurting her! She must have been thinking all this time that he did not trust in her love. After the way they had parted in the past, he could not blame her for it at all. He had *never* questioned his decision to keep her in the dark, and he had never realized just what had really been driving it.

He had already accepted that he should have fought for her from the beginning, but now he had a much more bitter pill to swallow: he would have still screwed things up even if there had been honesty. Things had merely happened faster thanks to his deception. Even if they had seen each other during the day, even if she had known he was Eros, eventually she would have been driven to want to see him while they made love. Nothing could have stopped them from reaching the point where they were now— nothing except *her,* and she had not fully come into her power until this life.

His arm tightened around her fiercely for a moment and she mumbled something in her sleep as she cuddled even closer. One lovely leg hooked over his as if to keep him from escaping. Determination began to pound inside his heart. It was time to make them the full equals they deserved to be, and to give her the final thing that he had never given before.

He stayed up a little while longer in order to decide his course of action and finally managed to fall asleep close to midnight. The waiting would finally end tomorrow, and they could make that grab for their happy ending. It was time to change that VOID into an In Progress. They had come too far to lose now.

CHAPTER TWELVE

Rhianna awoke in the morning to the feel of fingers dancing down her arm. They skimmed up into her hair and caressed the nape of her neck. Lips teased hers. "Wake up, my beloved," Aaron's husky voice murmured. "You do not want to oversleep."

She opened her eyes to find him kneeling beside the bed. He was already dressed, and she glanced at the clock. It was indeed getting late. She freed herself from his grip and sat up with a yawn. "I don't normally oversleep. I'm still psychically burned out so some of my side gifts are muted."

He tugged her out of bed and kissed her warmly. "Go take your shower. I will make breakfast."

"Alright." She rose up on her toes to kiss him in turn before heading for the bathroom. There seemed to be something . . . different inside him. A strange sense of peace and determination that she could not put her finger on. She was really starting to dislike her burnout. She needed every advantage she could get, and she missed being able to feel Eric even at a distance.

He had baked cinnamon rolls for breakfast, and they both devoured their share happily. After they ate, he transported her back to her home where she could finish getting ready to go to work. He then transported himself to the Grove. He knew he could take the effort to learn to drive and perhaps get a vehicle, but why should he bother? If at any point he needed to go somewhere that he needed to arrive via vehicle, he could merely bribe his wife to take him. He was still tickled that she owned a motorcycle. He liked an unconventional streak in anyone.

Priya had dropped off on his desk the latest questionnaires he needed to review, and she had updated his calendar on his computer. The learning curve for the electronic beast had been interesting, to be sure. He was quite proud of himself for finally getting the hang of it. Rayna had promised him lessons later if he needed it, but so far so good.

His first meeting was at nine. He settled in with a cup of his new favorite Starbucks coffee and started going through the questionnaires for the markers he had placed. People truly did not realize just how much they gave away with a few simple questions. They left an energy fingerprint that read like neon to him. He compared those as much as he compared the answers themselves; he had matched up perfect opposites because their energies blended, and that was the important part. Likes and dislikes could be changed and expanded. It was how people grew.

He found two potential matches and clipped them together with his notes for Priya to make appointments to bring them in for more in-depth analysis. He was on his second cup of coffee by the time his client arrived, and he smiled when he saw her. She was an older woman in her mid-fifties who had been divorced for ten years. He quite looked forward to finding her love. It was beautiful at any age.

They were partway through expanding on her answers when he felt a familiar chill ripple down his skin. His head came up sharply as power moved across his eyes. Evil. It stirred. It must have surely sensed that he and Rhianna were on the cusp of becoming one. It hated nothing more than what they represented together; they alone could create the happy endings that evil sought only to destroy.

"Mr. Konstantinos?" His client frowned. "Is something wrong?" A sudden strong scent touched her nose and she pulled a face. "Ugh, that smells like rotten eggs." She gagged as the scent got stronger. "What *is* that?"

"Aaron!" Priya burst into the doorway. "Can you smell it?" He shook his head, and her heart briefly froze. Of course he wouldn't. *Humans* were sensitive to the scent added to gas, but that didn't mean gods were, too! "There's natural gas filling the building! We need to get out of here."

A chill ran down his back. "Grab the drive with our information," he ordered her as he got to his feet. Danger began to beat along his nerves as he helped his client to her feet and urged her toward the door. Natural gas. He could not smell it, but he knew it was highly flammable. Truthfully, the very fact that he could not smell it was a sign that it was directed at him. If Priya had not been there, he would have been a sitting duck.

They hustled outside and crossed the street quickly to be just inside the District. Priya was already on the phone calling 9-1-1. Their two neighboring buildings had begun to evacuate as well thanks to the smell leaking over. They went down the street rather than cross over. Oddly, that did not surprise Aaron at all.

With a roar of fire and a window-shattering explosion that also shook the ground, his building went up in a mushroom cloud of smoke and flames. Alarms started going off all over the street. People came out of other buildings to see what was going on. Sudden sirens in the distance meant that firemen had noticed and were on their way.

Aaron narrowed his eyes on the burning building as he still felt as if there was something wrong. A faint heartbeat touched his ears, and he realized that there was someone inside. It was possible. He left the back door unlocked so that the nearby homeless people had a warm spot to sleep at night.

Priya bit back a yelp as he went running for the building. "Aaron!" she wailed. "You'll get hurt!"

"Hurt?" the old woman blurted. "He'll get himself killed!"

Well, no, he wouldn't, but he would sure as hell get badly wounded. Priya barely hesitated before grabbing her cell phone. She turned and looked toward the Enforcers' tall building. She would bet that Rhianna already knew, but it was always better to be safe than sorry.

Aaron was reminded of his lack of true invulnerability when the first flaming piece of wood struck his arm. Burns and bloody wounds of other assorted shapes formed as he moved through the mess of the lobby toward the break room and the door inside that led to their storage space and back door. His slim consolation was that he might cough from the smoke but it could not do permanent damage.

He scalded his hands as he wrenched the knob to the storage area open. A plume of smoke hit him in the face and he was briefly blinded. He managed to wave it out of his face and ducked down to get inside. "Is someone here?"

A whimper responded and it did not sound human. His eyes covered the ground sharply and he found a wiggling lump under a blanket. Yanking the blanket aside revealed a bedraggled and soot-covered puppy. It was probably quite fluffy when clean, if the matted fur was any clue. He stared for a moment in sheer surprise and then scooped up the small animal into his arms. "It will be all right," he soothed. "How did you get in here?"

The acrid scent of evil touched his nose again. Understanding flashed. A trap. He had been deliberately lured back inside. He tried to kick down the back door but it seemed as if something heavy had been braced on the other side. Keeping the puppy wrapped in his jacket, he rushed back the other way as quickly as he could.

A beam crashed down from the ceiling and cut off his escape. Something moved in the corners, and even the bright glow of the fire could not banish the ugly black cloud creeping in. He held his ground without fear and wrapped the puppy tighter inside his jacket. The cloud rushed over him to consume him, and his power rose hotly. White light ripped from him and tore through the cloud. It evaporated with a scream that made chills run down even his skin.

His now torn and bloody skin. He grimaced as the pain

ambushed him. A quick look down told him that he looked like a royal mess. He used another blast of raw power to break apart the beam and rushed out into the safety of the street once more. There was a large crowd of onlookers standing around, and the firemen were beginning to hook up hoses to the fire hydrants.

Priya came scrambling over to his side. Fear made her dark eyes wide. "Aaron! Oh, god. You look *horrible!* You must be in agony!" Her eyes widened more as he opened his jacket to reveal the puppy. "What the . . . how did she get in there?" She gingerly took the small creature and tried to brush at the soot. It looked like a collie of some kind and barely older than a few weeks in age.

"Aaron!" Rhianna shoved through the crowd and rushed toward him. Her black eyes had consumed her pupils in her distress, and her skin was pale. She threw herself into his arms heedless of the onlookers and clung onto him with all of her strength.

A few jaws dropped in the crowd. It was a shocking thing to see the always-collected Rhianna Taber that rattled. Rumor had already spread quickly about the fact that she was married, and now understanding began to dawn. The new marriage counselor in town, conveniently right outside her district, was her estranged husband. "Talk about a coincidence," one woman murmured.

"Rhi." Aaron held her as tightly as he could and ignored the protest of his wounds. "I am sorry, my beloved."

"Were you caught in there?" she asked against his chest.

"No." Priya scowled. "He went back inside!"

He scowled at her equally as Rhianna pulled back sharply. "You *what?!*" She narrowed her eyes as the familiar sparks of her temper appeared. "You went back into a burning building? Why?"

He shrugged. "There was a heartbeat inside. I could not let it be harmed. I am a god, my love. I cannot be killed. Perhaps I can be a bit singed, but not killed." He took the puppy and plopped it down into her arms. "You need a pet. She will suit you well." He sighed as she continued to stare at him. "I wish I could placate you by saying I would have not gone in if I had known it was merely a puppy, but I am afraid I would have done it anyway. I cherish life. I am a protector."

"Get it from your father," she muttered.

A soot-covered golden brow lifted. "I had to have something from him, did I not? It is better that it be a desire to protect than not." His lips slowly curved. "Better to make love than war, no? Still, I am amused by the way people cannot be sure of my origins. It would seem many still think I predated the gods and was adopted by Aphrodite."

"Most didn't get to see your sheer *bullheaded* stubbornness!" She plopped the dog back into Priya's arms and swung around on her heel. "Captain." She walked calmly over to where the man in charge of the firemen was standing. "Enforcers stands by to give assistance as this is close enough to our District to command our attention; the Grove is considered an ally. Was anyone injured?"

"A few passersby," he admitted. He gestured. "They are being prepared to go to the hospital."

"They will go to Enforcers' hospital and we will front the costs." She accepted his handshake and moved on to speak with the police who had arrived on the scene as well. With the same calm authority, she took charge and issued orders.

Aaron stayed back a step and watched with a smile tugging at his lips. He had been doing quite a bit of research to learn about what he had missed over two thousand years, and he had found himself fascinated by how his beautiful wife had managed to be in charge of, and stay in charge of, a multi-billion dollar company through periods of time where it had *assuredly* not been allowed for women to even contemplate working outside of a home. He thought he might finally have an answer as to how she had done it. Quite simply, who would dare tell her she couldn't?

She was natural born leader. She took charge in any situation with calm control and a sort of self-confidence that never felt arrogant. She made others feel as if they were valued equals without letting it be mistaken that her word was final. Even Eric would defer to her in the event of a tie. Her friends were perfectly fine to let her lead because she was just so damn good at it. Thinking about the events of the past, Aaron had to smile. If everything had ended happily back then, she would have taken over Olympus within the first month, and not even Zeus or Hera would have stopped her.

She strode back over to his side and ordered briskly, "You're coming home with me where I can tend to your wounds. You are not to ever visit any hospital except the one owned by Enforcers. They specifically cater to the needs of our gifted people in the District."

"Yes, beloved," he answered meekly.

She stared at him before snorting softly. "Don't try to pull that subservient attitude with me, Aaron. I know you too well." Her eyes widened as he reached for her. "Don't you *dare*." The words turned into a little gasp as he yanked her into his arms and kissed her with greedy hunger. She vaguely noted the sound of cheering in the background but found she didn't care. No level of public affection could bother her reputation. In fact, it would probably *help*.

He released her and she blew out a breath as she desperately tried to ignore her rampaging hormones. The little smirk tugging at his lips implied he could feel her frustration still, but she couldn't begrudge him his smugness. It was deserved. She shoved him back a step. "Stop that or I'll lose the ability to think." She turned to where Priya was standing with the puppy. "Priya, until Aaron can get his company up and running again, you may present yourself at Enforcers' HQ and we will find work for you to do so that you don't lack a paycheck."

"Thank you, Ms. Taber," Priya said sincerely.

"Rhianna," she corrected. She sighed and took the puppy as it was offered. She had often been intrigued by having a pet, but she had never bothered to look for one. Naturally, Aaron would have unintentionally found her a way to get her one. "Alright. I'm taking my pet and my husband home and getting them both cleaned up."

Aaron amiably walked along beside her as she strode swiftly into the District. He found himself holding the puppy again as she got out her cell phone and called Eric to tell him what had been going on. Even with good dampening on the phone, Aaron's sensitive ears could hear that Eric was not a happy warlock over events. It made him feel better. He truly wished to be friends with Eric for he knew that the other man was deeply beloved to Rhianna, and vice-versa. Naturally, he expected there to be some bickering as was with Eric and Taylor, but that was what happened when strong and dominant personalities tried to be friends. As long as it was not done in animosity, it was perfectly fine—and often entertaining to all those around.

He followed Rhianna into her house and offered the puppy. "If you will tend her, I would like a shower."

She arched a brow. "What will you do for clothes?"

"I am a god." He flicked a finger at her nose and ambled down the hall.

She just shook her head. She held the puppy up at eye level and smiled as she studied the canine face. Border collie, and what was probably a red point coat under all the soot. No more than a month old. "Alright, you. Let's see just how well you clean up."

The kitchen sink was plenty big enough for washing a small pet, and Rhianna was prepared for a fight if hers didn't like the washing. Luckily for her, the puppy seemed to enjoy the pampering as much as Rhianna enjoyed hers. Once thoroughly washed clean, the puppy was revealed to indeed have a coppery red color. She even stayed obediently in the sink while Rhianna fetched a towel to dry her.

Aaron strolled shirtless into the living room while Rhianna was using a comb to smooth out the puppy's matted fur. He dropped the shirt in his hand over the arm of the couch. "What will you name her?"

"I'm thinking Juno."

"You would name her for Hera's alternate name?"

"Do admit she was one of the nicer goddesses. Most of her bad actions were sparked by Zeus being unfaithful. Besides. She was your grandmother."

"Indeed." He grimaced as he gingerly sat down on the couch beside her. The bruises were already fading, and the wounds were showing signs of healing, but they still hurt like the fires of punishment. "I should be whole by tonight."

"Well, I am still going to bind you up." She put Juno on the floor to scamper off and explore. She briefly left to retrieve bandages and then sat down again to start wrapping up the wounds. No need for antiseptic; he couldn't catch anything. There were many benefits to being immortal. The wrapping was mostly to maintain the illusion. There had been plenty of people to see the state he was in.

As she was binding one wound, she asked softly, "Will you go home for the rest of the day since working is out? Or do you want to start taking care of calling your clients? Enforcers has a few empty office spots if you wished to use one."

"I intend to ask Priya to make the calls to tell people we are briefly closed. As for permanent space, I would like to find space in the District, yes." He smiled a bit wryly. "I love the District, Rhianna. I feel as if I *belong*. I have never felt such a sense of belonging, not even within my domain so long ago. It is true what they say. If you are drawn here, there is something you can only find here." He skimmed his free hand down her cheek. "For me, there is you. But there is more. There is . . . home."

"That's how it was for Eric and me," she admitted. "I never felt as if I belonged anywhere until we settled here and built our District. I had to accept long ago that perhaps things had happened for a reason."

He smiled. "I had also realized much the same recently. The past just would never have worked out for the simple fact that you did not know your own power, and it was this life that has allowed you to so beautifully bloom into it."

She frowned at him. "Why would my power have anything to do with it?"

"You do not understand the full scope of what you do?"

"No."

"Or see your own future?"

"No."

"Have you not ever wondered why?"

"Well, of course." She scowled. "What are you getting at, Aaron?"

His fingers tenderly caressed her cheek again. "Perhaps you should think about what complements the power of Love best, and about the things that Eric has accused you of for centuries. The gift you have . . . there is no one else with it. There will be no other. There is a very simple reason for why the gods so quickly acquiesced to you, beloved."

It made her think for a moment. Only one thing seemed to make sense, but it felt more than a bit daunting to believe *she* might have that sort of power. Very softly, she asked, "If I were to truly understand my power, would there be more I could do in order to help others?"

His heart melted. Such a typically Rhianna thing to say. While contemplating having the power to command destiny itself, she merely asked if she could do more for others. Truly, she was his other half. "Yes. There will be nothing we cannot do together."

She drew a deep breath. "It's a bit unnerving, even for me, to begin to understand. Let me process it for a while. I've learned to be patient. I will know when it is right for me to accept and take full command of my . . . gift."

"You are entitled." He kissed her softly for a moment before releasing her and testing the bandages. "They will do. After today, I will wear long sleeves until a reasonable time has passed for me to heal." He gingerly tugged on his shirt. "I will be glad for them to go. They are painful."

She smirked. "Baby." She got to her feet with a sigh. "I have to get back to work. I have a meeting this afternoon I can't put off. Juno!" she called. She knelt with a smile as the puppy bounded up to her. "Already know your name, don't you? I think you are gifted as well. Once you grow into those feet, you can be our courier. I've missed having one ever since Audra retired." She laughed as Juno happily licked her face in response. "You're welcome, I think!"

"I would like to go with you to work," Aaron offered.

"You can't sit in my meeting," she reminded him reasonably.

A brow arched arrogantly. "How little faith you have in your husband." A swirl of gold light surrounded him and he suddenly changed into a much smaller, almost cherubic, version of himself. He stood barely a foot big, and actual tiny wings had sprouted from the birthmarks on his back. He laughed richly when she gaped at him. "Where do you suppose they came up with my cherub form, beloved?" Other than a slightly stronger power, his voice sounded the same, and the masculine tones seemed quite amusing coming from someone who looked like a Disney version of a Greek statue. "Normally, only gods and goddesses can see me, but I have chosen to let you see me as well."

She felt a laugh bubbling up, and it broke out as she saw Juno watching him wide-eyed. "And puppies!"

"Ah, well, animals see clearer than most humans anyway." He landed on her shoulder. "Shall we?"

What the hell; why not? At least she wouldn't bored through her meeting, that was for certain.

CHAPTER THIRTEEN

When Rhianna walked onto the top floor with Aaron trailing along at her shoulder—leaving behind gold sparkles, the smartass—Gwyn and Rayna took one look and collapsed into a fit of the giggles. Poor Taylor and Eric could only watch them in sheer confusion; the two Faeriekin had easily tickled senses of humor, but usually it was fairly obvious what they found amusing. "Do we dare ask?" Taylor groused at Rhianna.

"Not really." She opened her office door. "By the way, the puppy is named Juno. She'll be our new courier."

"Ee!" The girlish squeal came from both sisters alike as they dropped down to scoop up Juno and smother her with cuddles and kisses. Juno's tail wagged so fast it was a blur as she happily soaked up the affection.

"I'll make a note to install a doggie door in the lobby," Eric offered dryly as he disappeared into his office.

"She needs a collar!" Rayna hopped to her feet. "C'mon, Gwyn! Let's go get one! I bet Brian'll have something." She dashed off down the hall with Gwyn and Juno close behind. "We'll bring her back later!"

Taylor just sighed and went back into Eric's office as well where they had been discussing a contract they were both overseeing. Rhianna dropped into her chair behind her desk and unlocked her computer. She was actually a bit surprised she had remembered to even lock it at all. She had been in a *bit* of a hurry the moment she had sensed Aaron in their District and gotten

Priya's phone call as to why. It bothered her deeply that she had not seen it coming. Evil was truly stirring. She needed to heal from her burnout but just didn't know how.

"Beloved." Aaron ached to turn back and hold her in his arms. He very nearly decided to do so when someone knocked on the door.

"Enter," Rhianna called. She stood as a man walked into the office, and though friendly enough, there was a sort of coolness in her smile. "Assemblyman Harkin, how kind of you to join me. It's nice to meet you. I'm Rhianna Taber."

Aaron did not like Harkin on sight. He was appealing enough in the face with a pleasantly plump body, but something seemed to come through to the surface. Some sort of greasiness and lack of an ability to feel love. He didn't think he would be the only one able to see it.

Harkin gave Rhianna one of those polished political smiles that never seemed to be sincere. She had offered a hand, and he obligingly shook it. He also happened to slowly look her over in a way more than a bit derogatory, particularly as his eyes lingered on her breasts and hips. "What a delight, Ms. Taber. I am quite grateful to you for being willing to meet with me like this. I know how busy you women can be."

She freed her hand. "I do keep busy, but I make time when it is needed." She gestured to a seat and sat down herself. Under her desk, she surreptitiously rubbed her hand on her pants as if to rid herself of his touch. Aaron smirked, but she ignored him. "What can I help you with, Assemblyman?"

"I will be looking to run for re-election and I would like to receive Enforcers' support for such a thing." He gave her a placating smile. "I had explained everything in my voice mail to Eric Mason when I requested a meeting with him. I assumed he made the decisions."

She arched a brow. "Eric and I are full partners. We make mutual decisions though we will defer to each other's good judgment as needed. In the event that we are deadlocked, I am the one with the final say."

Harkin was visibly taken aback for a moment but he recovered quickly enough. "My apologies, Ms. Taber, if I offended. Women in power are still rare these days."

Bits of steam began to come out Aaron's ears. Maybe if men like this were not so quick to believe women were incapable, there might be more out there. Even in Ancient Greece, women had been respected for their skills. It was hard to not respect women as a whole when there were plenty of goddesses ready to smite anyone who dared imply they were the inferior gender. Where was Artemis when he needed her? Someone needed that smiting.

Rhianna's nails tapped lightly on the top of her desk. "I have been in power for a very long time." Her voice sounded almost gentle. "I have never had anyone question it."

Harkin loosened his collar. "Naturally not! Well, allow me to tell you where I would like to see my next term take me when it comes to the well-being of our beautiful New York."

She made notes as she listened, and she asked obligatory questions. It was purely for form. She and Eric had already compiled their list of who they would and would not support for the next round of elections—and Harkin was not on it. Rayna had been doing the research for a few months and already knew everything that might possibly be illuminated about new and old candidates.

"You certainly do have some interesting plans," she finally said when he paused. "I will pass my notes along to Eric." And enjoy watching him set them on fire. "How has your wife been lately, Assemblyman? I last saw her at Rafael and Victoria Lucino's engagement party."

A hint of pink climbed his neck. "She is well enough. She is expecting now, and rests quite a bit."

"It is probably not even his," Aaron muttered. "He has the look of a cuckold about him. And who can blame his wife? Few have Hera's patience."

Rhianna bit back a smile. "How delightful for you, Assemblyman. Congratulations to you both."

"I hear congratulations are in order for you as well, Ms. Taber. Everyone is talking about how your estranged husband has come back. Such a shame for the rest of the men of the world that such a singularly beautiful woman would not be available anymore." His eyes ran over her again. "Truly a pity. Will you retire in order to keep a home for your husband? I suppose that might be quite boring to a woman like you, though. I do hope you might consider some interesting alternatives if he can't keep you entertained."

Aaron's considerable temper blew. The sheer offensiveness of this creature in Rhianna's office could not be defined. On both the principle of it as well as a personal level, Aaron refused to condone this sort of brash attitude. There was a vast difference between genuine admiration, natural reactionary desire, and this disgusting harassment.

Before Rhianna realized what he was about to do, a familiar bow appeared in his hands. He drew out a blue tipped arrow and quite calmly fired it directly at Harkin. The other man did not feel nor sense it piercing his chest and into his heart, but he did blink rapidly a bit as if dizzy. "I feel a bit odd."

"You are a bit pale, Assemblyman." Rhianna hit a button on her intercom. "Hoang? Could you come pick up Assemblyman Harkin and escort him out to a taxi? He is not feeling well."

The guard showed up a few moments later and graciously helped a clearly disoriented Harkin out of the office. As soon as the door shut behind them, a swirl of golden light returned Aaron to normal. He leaned against Rhianna's desk and crossed his arms. "He deserved what he got."

She lifted a brow. "Do tell what it is that he got. I don't know your arrows on sight."

"Do you recall I mentioned my dulling arrows? They briefly diminish desire without erasing it. Think of a more effective variation on a cold shower." A tiny hint of menace entered his smile.

"I shot that vile thing with a neutralizer instead. It permanently erases all capacity for desire so that only an inducer may return it—and it leaves behind the longing to feel desire anew." He shrugged unrepentantly. "When you are born with the capacity for lust and desire, and you abuse it, you should not be allowed to have it. It is the other side to my personal rules."

"Other side?"

"If you are born without the capacity for lust and desire, I do not induce it unless you can never be happy without it. I seek to create happiness and joy, my beloved, and that definition changes from one human to another. That creature within your office knows only greed and cruelty and personal pleasure. He deserves to live without the thing he covets most."

"You certainly won't hear me complaining about your actions. I have never actually liked him. And the women of the world will be glad to be spared his sly looks and casual grabbiness, as well. Pity you don't have something to erase his sexist attitude."

He pursed his lips. "I wonder what might happen were I to shoot him with an inducer and make him fall madly in love with his wife. Would it help?"

"Probably not. Some people can't be helped, Eros." She began to shut down her computer. "After that *delightful* meeting, I have a need to scrub myself from head to toe. Cerberus' breath smelled less than Harkin's." She smiled up at him. "Can I go home with you tonight?"

"Always." He caught her in his arms for a fierce hug before hoisting her off her feet and kissing her with a slow, famished heat guaranteed to scatter her thoughts. As they eased back, he murmured huskily, "Welcome home."

Sure enough, they were in the living room. "So glad I've gotten used to that style of travel," she sighed as she released him. Somehow her hands had ended up in his hair again. She suspected magnets existed under her skin that were drawn to his curls. "I think it's my turn to make dinner."

"Ah, but you want a bath." He flicked her nose lightly. "You can just make dinner two nights in a row later. I will get things started if you would like to go to the pool and soak. It is quite beautiful in the evening."

She asked politely, "Will you fetch me clothes from my house in order to wear?"

"You can wear my shirt tonight." He stole a kiss. "Tomorrow we shall stop at your home in the morning for you to change for work." He turned her and gave her a gentle nudge. "Go," he urged. "Relax, my beloved. I think you will find everything to be better soon enough."

She eyed him as she sensed again that he had secrets but finally sighed and grabbed some fluffy towels before heading out to the gardens. It truly did look spectacular in the evening light. Everything was illuminated in golds and reds, and she lit some lamps around the edge of the pool in order to stave off the coming night.

The water felt wonderful on her skin. Even better was scrubbing away the lingering grubby sensation of being near something icky. Much more relaxed, she sat down on one of the ledges and sank in to her neck. Jets suddenly began to pulse, and she smiled without opening her eyes. "The benefits to marrying a god."

"There are many," her husband concurred huskily.

She opened her eyes and found him wading into the pool. A towel was knotted around his hips. He watched her eyes flicker to it and briefly fill with pain before it disappeared. She said nothing, and he moved to sit on another ledge nearby. "Well, beloved." His voice was quiet and calm. "I believe it is time to talk about the past and determine our future."

She straightened up. "I see." Her fingers curled together under the water. "I guess I should start by apologizing for breaking your trust."

"No." He shook his head sharply. "The fault lies with me. I am

far more at fault for what occurred than you are. I hid my identity from you and did not trust that you could keep our love a secret. I, of all people, should have understood your need for more than mere whispers in the night." His breath came out softly. "*I* am sorry. I am sorry I did not fight for you from the beginning. And I am more sorry for having made you feel rejected over and over again lately."

Her gaze lowered slightly. "Only a bit rejected."

"Now you are lying to me, love. You do not think I can see your emotions? Truly, it is a wonder that I ever had this issue at all. I am a fool, I suppose. I see you as all but a goddess and yet I instinctively treated you as a mortal. What rubbish." He got to his feet and waded closer to her. "I trust nothing more in existence than I trust the depth of your love. You feel as deeply as I do. You burn as hotly. Cry as hard. We are equals, and it is time to make us so."

Her breath hitched as he deliberately untied the towel and tossed it aside. It mattered not that the water technically covered him from the waist down—he was not *wearing* the water. No clothing barred his naked body, and it took only a moment until he began to produce that incredible glow she had only once before glimpsed. It was truly metaphysical—it hid in the darkness—but eyes would register it as nearly a halo.

She stared at him for a long moment and then inexplicably began to laugh. His brows came together with more bemusement than annoyance. "It is not very kind of you to laugh at a man who stands before you naked. What has you amused?"

The laughter only came out harder. "All this time! All this time you fretted I could not handle your true self, and *I can't want or love you any more than I do!*" She shook her head hard and tried to bite back more laughter but it felt too good to stop. "You know what it is? It's your makeup! It does nothing except emphasize what I already love and desire!"

Her laughter turned into a startled gasp as he buried his hands in her hair and jerked her up for a wild kiss. When they had to part for air, he explored the skin behind her ear until she shivered. "Mine!" he breathed huskily. "Let me love you, my Rhianna. Let me be yours again. Here, in the light."

She wound her arms around his neck and turned her head to find his lips with hers again. A blinding well of joy seemed to be rising inside her soul to erase the pain and loneliness. The gouges were beginning to heal at last. She boosted herself up and hooked her knees around his hips as he waded to the edge of the pool without releasing her from the kiss. She felt as if she was *starving* for his taste and his touch. That wonderful intimacy of being one.

He released her only to grab the towels and toss them down to protect them from the stone. He then lifted her out onto them before hauling himself out as well. His hand curled around the back of her neck and he dragged her into another consuming kiss. He could not get enough of her flavor. He felt her hands pushing at his shoulders and gave a husky laugh as he obligingly fell over on his back. His arms spread wide. "I am all yours, beloved."

For a moment, she merely stared at him and let her eyes finally learn and cherish what only her other senses had known. The blend of love, awe, and arousal in her eyes made the sparks in his iridescent eyes flare brightly. Her pleasure at seeing him was matched by his pleasure in seeing her—or rather, was *finally* matched. He groaned as her fingers began to softly explore and caress so that her senses could at last share information. "I have missed your touch," he told her roughly.

"I missed touching you." Her lips trailed along behind her fingers. "I love how it feels to want you. To be wanted by you." She laughed, and it seemed a sultry sound. "There will be no shyness inside me to banish now, Eros. I know what I want, what you want, and how to get there."

His laugh was no less tempting. "There has been no shyness since the first night." The laugh turned into a moan as her questing lips and fingers found his aching arousal. His eyes all but crossed as she slowly savored his taste. "Rhi."

The rasp to his voice made her shudder. Needing his mouth instead, she shifted back up his body and caught his face in her hands as she poured herself into a kiss that had his eyes glowing bright with power. She just did not realize that similar power briefly glowed from her eyes in turn. It, too, was meant to blend.

He caught her around the waist and rolled over to be on top. His unsteady hands raked a wild course over her body to find the most sensitive places. His heated breath murmured husky promises of love against her skin as he lingered and savored until she was crying out as she had made him cry.

As terribly as he wanted to linger, to take all of the time they had lost, her hunger was throbbing inside his body along with his own desperate need. They could linger and savor later when it had not been two thousand years since they had last loved each other. He rolled again and braced her over him. His breaths stopped entirely as he stared up at her. How was it possible she could be more beautiful to him? Perhaps it was the glow of light in her eyes that revealed her love and desire for him. "Beloved." He tried to urge her closer. "Take me as I have taken you."

She did so slowly, enjoying every moment of how he felt and how his pupils seemed to be consumed in sparks. When he was as deep as he could be, when they were finally one again, tears welled in her eyes and spilled down her cheeks. They were still a bit dark as they began to finish the healing that would erase the void on their contract and make it active once more. A happy ending. There was a chance for it.

His fingers bit into her hips and urged her to move harder and faster. Nothing seemed to matter except that glorious ecstasy luring them in. That perfect fusion of two as one. It started deep and spread wide as it consumed them, and it tore a cry from her lips that was echoed by one from him. It resonated into their very power until gold color rippled over his skin as silver rippled over hers. Where the two colors met, they merged to the radiant white light that was the power of immortal love.

He caught her when she lost the strength in her arms, and he wrapped her up fiercely in his embrace. The sound of them both struggling to catch a breath was like music, and he loved the scent of their skin lingering to mix with the flowers and peaches. *Happiness.* It glowed as deeply inside him as it did inside her. "Rhianna."

The rasp to his voice delicately teased her ears. She merely snuggled closer and tightened her arms around his chest. "Don't make me move," she murmured drowsily.

"I am afraid I must." His fingers skimmed slowly over her still sensitive skin so that her breath hitched. "I wish to take you inside and make love to you in my bed. This was an . . . appetizer." He shifted to tumble her down onto the towels and disentangled their bodies. He looked down at her and stared anew. "I cannot believe you are mine," he whispered. He scooped her up into his arms and got to his feet. "We have two millennia to make up for, beloved. I would like to take my time now."

A blend of anticipation and justifiable caution filled her. "How much time?"

"You will have to see. I will feed you after." He slowly lowered her to the bed in the nearly darkened room and deliberately turned on the lamp to spill out its golden glow. "I will love you again after I have fed you. I will spend all night loving you. Every night. For eternity." He sank into her arms for a kiss that threatened to set the sheets on fire. Against her lips, he muttered, "Perhaps in a hundred years, I will have at last recovered from two millennia without you."

She suspected it would take closer to another millennia for her, but she had no objections to the idea that things would always remain more volatile between them. Age matured everything, and the good things were like wine. And if the end truly was coming and she would not get that millennia, then at least she would this time go on knowing what it meant to be whole.

It was well after dark before their stomachs demanded another hunger be appeased. Her legs weren't the only rubbery ones as she pulled on a borrowed shirt, and she found herself giggling as she saw him struggling to put on pajama pants. "Why bother?" she asked in exasperation.

"I have learned a painful lesson about cooking while naked."

The mental image brought up fresh laughter. "That's why I always wear something, too. I may not be that built, but I have enough of a bust to be wary of leaning over a stove. Especially because I'm short!" She couldn't resist jumping onto his back and holding on tight. "Mine!"

His heart melted entirely. "Beloved." He pressed his face against the slender arms encircling his neck. "I love nothing more than I love you. I will never have enough time to make up to you what I have done."

She slid off his back and pressed her lips to one of the wing marks on his back. He had removed the bandages and barely any residue of the event of the morning remained. "Just love me," she murmured. "Just love me, and I'll call us even."

He swung around and caught her up in his arms for a fierce hug and kiss. Still holding her, he began striding toward the kitchen. "Food," he said firmly, "before you are allowed to seduce me again."

She smiled. "Was I doing that?"

"Ha!" He put her down on the couch. "I promised to make dinner. I had it prepped beforehand." Ruefully, he added, "I had a feeling we may not get to it until late."

Dinner was happily consumed by both and they went through their normal evening routine by watching their shows on his DVR. She had no makeup to wash off thanks to her bath, but she did borrow some of his lotion. She was still the first to go to bed, and when he stepped out of the bathroom, she was sitting on the side of the mattress. He cocked his head as he undressed. "Rhi?"

She stood and deliberately stripped off the nightshirt. Just as deliberately, she turned off the lamp and let the room be in darkness. Strangely, she found she could actually see his outline now. As she slowly let herself take in her true power, she seemed to be evolving somehow. "I am the light," she told him huskily. "You are the dark. There are no secrets left between us."

He pounced and tumbled her flat onto the bed. "I rather like loving you in the light where I can see the way you look when you watch me." He hotly caressed her breast. "But there is something to be said for the darkness where you have to go by touch only." He closed his eyes briefly as he let his eyesight dull a bit. He opened them again and only saw her outline. "Now we are even. I will have to stay quite close to you, beloved."

She moaned softly as his lips unerringly found a sensitive place. "If you insist."

When desire was tempered again for the time, they slept tangled together like a two-piece puzzle. Neither stirred once at all for the rest of the night, and she only began to rouse when she felt sunlight spilling on her face. She turned to escape and found herself burrowing into her husband's steady warmth. Her eyes flew wide and the first thing she saw was the wonderful rise and fall of his chest. His arms had not released her at all.

As happiness and peace welled inside her, the last lingering grasp of the past finally let go. Her empathy and telepathy returned in a rush that made her wince very lightly since it was not unlike turning on a voice mail system after a vacation. She could see and sense Eric again, and his surprised delight at feeling her in return warmed her heart.

She briefly paused before reaching out for her true power. The vision came obediently and seemed to process like a series of unconnected images inside her mind. She sorted and rejected unimportant things that could carry out their course and looked for anything she could use even when her own future was grayed out. Something, an interesting flicker, came and went as an impression of someone else's future, and she knew what needed to be done. She knew what had to be done to ensure a happy ending finally came.

Aaron stirred and his arms tightened. "I can hear your mind," he murmured sleepily. "It is buzzing in my head. You have your mental gifts back?"

"I do. I'm not burned out anymore." She rubbed her cheek against his shoulder. Her eyes stared at a future she could not yet see but somehow still sensed what it might hold. "We have a busy day, Aaron. It is time to call in my reserves and prepare them for what may be coming."

"What is coming?"

"The final confrontation."

CHAPTER FOURTEEN

They lingered over a shower together and enjoyed being able to do so. He could only watch in fascination as she shaved her legs. "Why do you do that?"

"Came up in the, hmm, early 1900s? 1920s maybe." She studied her toes and decided she needed a pedicure if they survived what lay ahead. He would enjoy one too. "Skirts got shorter and razor companies leapt on a chance to say that women were uncouth if they didn't have silky smooth skin. Turned into a societal norm like makeup usage. I rather like how it feels, actually." She shot him a slightly wicked grin. "I have a thing for smooth skin."

Very little hair covered her husband's body. It never had. Few of the gods had been hairy except for the ones who chose to grow out heavy beards. They found how they liked to look and stuck with it. She rather envied that sort of power. She had nicked herself with a razor enough times to wish a way to just be done with it.

He glided a hand down her leg and smiled. "I must admit, I grow fond of how it feels as well." If anything, it also allowed him a better view of the sleek muscles in her lovely legs. He had missed having them wrapped around him, even in sleep. "We will have to go out to dinner so you may wear a short skirt and I can admire them at my leisure."

"It's a date."

They playfully toweled each other dry, though perhaps their hands wandered a bit, and he got dressed while she pulled on another borrowed shirt. Breakfast was prepared and consumed,

and he transported them to her home so she could finish getting ready. They were greeted upon their arrival by happy barks from Juno. The puppy skidded into the living room and leapt up into Rhianna's arms to enthusiastically lick her face. "Hi to you too!" she laughed. She smiled as she saw the red collar and gold tag. One side of the tag had Juno's name, and the other had the Enforcers' logo.

Aaron took charge of the puppy to take her outside while Rhianna went to change. She called D.J.'s desk while she was putting on her makeup. The receptionist was always there early because it was the only place he could get some quiet time for reading. Rhianna had made the deal with him that if he took calls from an Enforcer before the clock started, he could read as much as he liked.

"Enforcers Headquarters."

"Hello, D.J." She contemplated her eyeshadows. "I have a few calls for you to make for me. I want a meeting set up for nine am, sharp. I don't give a damn if they have previous engagements; they owe me, and they know it."

"This ought to be good. Whose arms am I twisting?"

"Mel Shaughnessy, Kenneth Dease, and Rafael Lucino. I also want Eric, Rayna, Gwyn, and Taylor to be there."

"Whoa." It was breathed softly. It was always a bit daunting when all five head Enforcers met together—it meant something big was happening—but to throw in the head members of the most famously contracted families? There was something *massive* going on this time. "I'll make the calls, Rhi," he promised. "Should I order coffee and pastries?"

"Please do. The least I can do is feed them." She disconnected the line and fastened on her earrings. They were her favorite pair; Madelyne had given them to her as a birthday gift one year. She fastened on the matching bracelet and paused to study her left hand. It was bare of rings.

Arms slid around her and strong hands slipped under hers to lace their fingers together. Aaron rested his chin on her shoulder and smiled. "I believe I owe you a ring or two, do I not? That is the custom these days. A diamond ring for engagement, and a gold ring for marriage. I do not think you are the diamond type, though." He contemplated things. "I should give you a pearl. After all, I trace origins back to the sea."

Memory made her snicker. "Technically, wasn't Zeus your grandfather *and* your cousin? Aphrodite was kind of a daughter of Uranus, so she was Zeus' aunt, right?"

"We never had much of a family tree in Olympus as much as we had a family bramble bush." He nuzzled her neck. "I shall find you a perfect pearl to be fashioned into a ring. In the meantime," he trailed his fingertips over her ring finger where power began to gather, "you shall at least have a wedding ring made from the gold that heralds my power of love."

She watched as the power solidified into a beautiful gold band with a sort of white marbling through the center. It actually glowed softly in the light. A happy thrill rippled through her soul. Such a tiny thing could make her so happy merely because of the permanence it represented. "You need one too."

He offered his other hand and opened his fingers to reveal another gold band on his palm. "Naturally, I do. I would like an engagement ring as well. Why should I not have one?"

"Why indeed!" She slipped the ring over his finger and admired it. "Would you like a pearl as well? I think it should be something associated with me instead. You claim me, I claim you."

"*Elektron.*"

"*Elektron?* Oh, you mean amber?" She turned in his arms and rested her hands on his chest. "Why amber?"

"It is formed from the beauty of nature and placed under pressure to become a stone that endures for millions of years and floats upon the waves where it comes to shore." He smiled. "Pearls are born of the sea, and amber is carried upon it. It represents our similar gifts and where they overlap while letting us still be unique to one another. Perfect equals."

She could only sigh and kiss him. He had the wonderful gift to say such romantically sappy things and make them sound only beautifully sincere. "Very well. I will hunt a bit of amber if you hunt a pearl. Then we will both be suitably claimed."

"Deal." He kissed her again and then released her reluctantly. "Let us collect Juno and head into the office. I do not imagine anyone will turn down your invitation."

"Particularly since it was not an invitation. It was an order."

D.J. was an efficient secretary. By the time Aaron and Rhianna arrived, he had already gotten the conference room on the top floor set up with coffee from Starbucks and pastries from a local District bakery. Rhianna laughed at Aaron as she saw him happily consuming his beloved Starbucks. "Addict. Remind me to introduce you to a Frappuccino."

"A what?"

"Trust me."

He smiled slowly. "Always."

A justifiably confused Eric and Rayna showed up shortly thereafter. Neither commented on the emergency meeting since they knew Rhianna would explain soon enough. Instead, they focused on what they noticed immediately upon entering the room. "Welcome back," Eric told Rhianna softly. He stopped to lean down and kiss her cheek. *Do I have to like him now?* He asked it into her mind.

She shot a grin at Aaron. *I would be grateful if you did. It would be far too awkward, and far too much of déjà vu, for my brother and my husband to not get along.*

A bit mildly, Aaron spoke to them both, *Please do be aware that I can hear both of you. Do try to keep from talking about me unless it is complimentary. I do not mind that.*

Rayna was not telepathic and could not hear the conversation, but she could make a guess based on Rhianna's smirk and Eric's glare. "Oh stop it!" she scolded Eric. She hugged his arm tightly and smiled up at him. "You like him because he makes Rhi happy."

The trouble with being married to the Goddess of Truth was that telling lies, even little ones to get someone's goat, were out of the picture. She happily tattled on him frequently. "Of course I do," he sighed. "God knows—no pun intended—that she deserves some damn happiness after all this."

Deciding a diversion was in order, Rayna asked Aaron curiously, "When will you get Rhianna pregnant? She needs to be a mom again. Madelyne doesn't need her as much now, and Rhi never did get to enjoy those first early years the way I and Eric are enjoying Glory's."

Aaron shot Rhianna a decidedly sensual smile. "I am not sure if I would *get* her pregnant as much as I would *help* her with such a thing. Anything between us is always half her fault." He sighed gustily. "I do admit I would like to be a father at last. And she will be radiant when she is carrying."

Taylor and Gwyn happened to walk in the door at that point, and the former asked hopefully, "Think I'd get her to finally pose if I bribed her with handcrafted baby stuff?"

"You could always try cookies," Gwyn noted reasonably. "It works for me and Rayna when we want something."

Rhianna looked at Aaron solemnly. "Would you believe I *like* working with these smartasses?"

"Perhaps because you are one yourself?"

Hard to disagree with that one! It was also why Aaron fit in as well as he did. The subject was thankfully shelved when she spotted new arrivals in the doorway. She smiled. "Come in, gentlemen!"

Mel walked in with rightful wariness, and Kenneth and Rafael were right behind him. They were quite dissimilar men in some ways, but quite a bit alike in others. The most notable difference lay in the fact that Kenneth and Rafael were un-gifted humans and Mel was a full-blooded werewolf. All were the respective leaders of their families though both Mel and Rafael's fathers were still alive. Kenneth tended to share with Cameron, but being the eldest, he typically had final say.

"I can't help but feel the same way I did many years ago when I got called into my father's office and told to get my grades up or else," Mel sighed as he sat down.

"Do admit that turned out well," Rhianna murmured.

"Am I complaining about being madly in love with a hot, though slightly cranky, wife and having two furball kids with more sass than sense? Not a lick."

Kenneth sat down beside him. "Did you know Cam's Sarah threatened at one point that she would sic your wife on our mother?"

Mel's grin looked almost menacing for a moment since it revealed his slightly, non-humanly, sharp canines. "Pity she didn't."

Rafael merely shook his head at them and bent to kiss Rhianna's cheek. "*Ciao, bella*. You are as a beautiful as ever. More, perhaps. Is this the reason why?" He lifted her now ringed left hand. "If you should have a renewal ceremony, *mia famiglia* would be honored to attend. We owe you much."

"If we do, you will." She patted his cheek affectionately. "Alright, everyone. Grab a chair. It's time we did some talking." She remained standing and was not surprised when Aaron opted to sit as well. He and Eric took the chairs at the head of the table with the others spreading out down the table from them. "I suppose I should begin by saying that I am," she glanced at Aaron and then back, "indirectly responsible for the evil that has been plaguing our world for many millennia."

"Huh." Kenneth tapped a finger lightly on the table. "How did that happen?"

"Have you heard of Eros and Psyche?"

"Sure. Oh." Mel eyed Aaron. "You know, I wondered about you. Maddie wouldn't spill the beans, but you don't smell human." He ignored the god's quick grin and turned back to Rhianna. "So the evil was released from the box you fetched from Persephone? The stories never clarified what it was, only that it killed you and would have killed Eros but not for his immortality." With a sigh, he added, "The great Greek romantic tragedy."

Rhianna held up her hands and the broken box appeared on her palms. "This and something else came to me a very long time ago. Eric and I had found the River Styx and were building our sanctuary. I was drawn to the river." Her gaze lowered. "Charon had been waiting for me faithfully. He had refused to let any but him guard the things meant for me. As soon as I had reclaimed them, I remembered it all."

"What was the other item?" Rafael asked softly.

"My marriage contract. It was voided."

Several faces paled at that revelation. "Is it still?" Gwyn whispered. Under the table, she desperately grabbed for Taylor's hand to draw on his ready strength.

"No," Eric spoke up. His eyes looked slightly shuttered. "She gave it to me to Enforce, so to speak. As of this morning, it is In Progress."

The held breaths were let out. Rhianna put the box down on the table. "This box is the infamous Pandora's Box that when opened released into our world all manner of illness and the ability to despair. As that despair got stronger, it began to . . . corrupt. Twist. And evil was born. The gods engaged it and managed to encase it once more inside the Box, and it was taken to the Underworld for guarding."

"And then your story came along." Kenneth blew out a hard breath. He felt a bit queasy. The tale of star-crossed lovers had always somehow struck a chord as if it had truly happened. Now, at least, while he knew it had, he also knew there was still a chance for a happy ending.

Aaron straightened up slightly. "I was there at the first fight against evil. I was young at the time. Young by mortal standards let alone immortal. It came right after me. It hates nothing more than the power of love. It hates nothing more than I and Rhianna for we alone can access the pure force of love energy and use it to create happy endings."

"That's why completed contracts protect people from evil," Rayna whispered.

"And why I called for Mel, Ken, and Rafe." Rhianna sat on the edge of the table. "It has been your families, as well as Rayna and Gwyn's, that have been directly involved in our fight. It has come out in stronger waves over the years. It was there subtly in the form of Richard Johnston, who abused Kay Shaughnessy. It was still as yet subtle when the hunter came after Maddie and Kienan."

"It had external forces to control," Eric picked up, "in the form of Nahga who sought to destroy Rayna and Gwyn. It was there as well inside Lorcana Dease."

Kenneth's lashes flinched slightly. "And here we always thought she was just a bitch."

"If she had not been stopped when she had, there are more terrible things she could have done." Something flickered across Gwyn's eyes as a movement of power. "She was judged and punished. I wish I could say she was a tool, Ken, but she was bad to the core to begin with. Take consolation in knowing that there is nothing to mourn."

Rafael gently clapped Kenneth on the shoulder in support and looked at Rhianna. "I will assume that the evil was then in active form when it infused the flesh of Orson Collins and Martin Johns, *sì*? That is why it hated the 3rd District and came after you directly when you came to aid me and Tori. This District represents the happy endings you and Aaron bring."

"Here is not the only place it has had trouble," Aaron offered. "There is another world attached to ours thanks to the Styx being rather sticky."

"The duct tape of magic," Rayna whispered to Gwyn, and her sister giggled.

Aaron ignored them though he briefly smiled. "Mirage has its share of bad magic—curses are vexingly common—but it did not actually manifest true evil until recently." He looked at Rhianna.

"United, we are undefeatable. It could not stand up to our combined power." His left hand slid over hers on the table and their fingers laced together.

"Damn." Mel crossed his arms as he leaned back in his chair. "This is one hell of a mess we've got. Mind if I ask what happened to the rest of the pantheon?"

"Most of them chose to leave this plane when they lost the belief of the people," Rhianna offered, "but they have not left in their entirety. They linger as . . . energies in the ether. Most are near the District. They serve as guardians of sorts now that they are no longer needed. For all intents and purposes, Aaron is the only god that remains."

More than one person at the table didn't entirely agree. Rhianna should have been a goddess as well. Her power certainly rivaled one, and if gods could be made on the basis of 'heroic' deeds and 'good' actions, then she had *entirely* earned it! No one said it out loud, however. There was no knowing where the story might end.

"Alright then." Kenneth nodded firmly. "Where do we stand right now?"

"As of this immediate moment, I am placing several people under active duty. They are the ones who will aid me and Aaron in the final battle." She held up a hand and ticked off the names. "Eric, for obvious reasons. Mel, I want you and Audra alike because I have never seen any combatants as fine as werewolves. Kenneth, I am activating your wife. Her shapeshifting ability gives her a great deal of flexibility. Rafael, I am also activating Theresa."

He visibly bristled. "She is pregnant!"

Aaron inclined his head. "So she is, but she is a powerful healer. She has a completed contract that will protect her, *and* she has the additional defense that evil cannot harm her if it looks her in the eye. If she holds her ground, nothing shall get close to her at all."

Rafael still did not like it, but he knew damned well that no

Enforcer would send Theresa into battle if they thought there may be a chance of her or her child being harmed. "*Scusi,* but I shall worry about her and my niece anyway," he muttered.

Mel held up a hand. "How do we intend to lure out the evil from where it is hiding? I can't imagine it would be dumb enough to come traipsing into our District when it knows there are bigger and meaner things waiting to chomp into it."

"I don't recommend actual chomping," Taylor muttered. "You'd get heartburn."

Rhianna hid a smile. "Mel is correct. It will not come down to us. And 'down' is the operative word." She gestured. "It hides in the invisible realm above our sky. The hidden domain of the gods, Mount Olympus itself. It sealed itself off as soon as Eros departed. He can't get back in without piercing through the barrier with something equally magical."

"Like . . .?"

"Good question." She spread her hands. "That is another thing I must call upon you three to do. Between the resources of your companies, you can surely locate something for us to use. It exists beyond our District at this point, and because I am so directly involved, my ability to see the future is limited. I knew only of this moment happening because I was able to see a vision of the battle to come—through someone else's eyes."

"We'll do whatever we can," Kenneth vowed. "We all owe you, Rhianna. You helped us have our dreams come true, as well as the dreams of our loved ones. The least we can do is try to help you in return."

"Thank you," she said simply. "I will let all of you go now." She smiled. "Take some pastries with you else we eat them all."

Everyone began to slowly file out. Rhianna had a conference call to complete, and Taylor had to go in to his company to work on his game. Gwyn happily commandeered Aaron to show him where Priya had been set up. There was actually an entire unoccupied suite on the first floor that would make an awesome location for a marriage counselor to operate from, but Gwyn kept that to herself. Rhianna did the recruiting stuff.

Rayna had been watching Eric quietly, and she followed him into his office. She shut the door behind herself and leaned against it. "Riku? What were you not saying? I could see the half-truth that left your lips."

He sank into his chair on a heavy sigh. "The contract is In Progress." He put the scroll on the desk and unrolled it. Sure enough, the bright red 'In Progress' was stamped across the middle. "It shouldn't be like this."

She frowned as she moved closer to look. "They have fully reconciled and are entirely one now. That was what they wanted in the past, wasn't it? Then . . . that means one of them still has a dream that has not been fulfilled." Her frown deepened. "There is a clause in this somewhere that has not been met."

"It would be so much better if I could read it," Eric muttered. "I even tried taking it to someone fluent in Ancient Greek, and she said it turned to gibberish the moment she tried to read it." He raked his hands through his hair in agitation and stirred the white streaks that were mark of his power. "How do I Enforce what I can't bloody understand?"

She slid onto his lap and curled close against his chest in an effort to comfort him. His arms went around her fiercely and he buried his face in her hair. It just seemed as if there should somehow be an easy answer. There was almost always something so simple that could guarantee everything would end well. Was the contract blurred because it *wasn't* set in stone yet?

There might still be something terrible yet to happen.

CHAPTER FIFTEEN

The rest of the day went by normally, all things considered for Enforcers. The entire building was smitten with Juno, and she was already learning the lay of the place. Until she was big enough to open doors on her own, boxes were placed beside the doors she might need to come and go from.

Rhianna was finishing up a review of a business proposal from a District member when the clock clicked over to tell her it was quitting time. She would have ignored it and kept on working, as she so often did, but the handle on the office door jiggled. She looked up and then smiled as the door popped open and Juno scampered inside. "Well, look at you!"

Aaron sauntered in behind the puppy. "Quitting time, my love." At her lifted brow, he lifted one back. "You do not think that every person in this building did not inform me that you work more than necessary because there is nothing at home to bring you there? That they have been delighted lately by the way you have taken decent time off—for the first time in centuries? That, maybe, just maybe, they are already putting things into order for Eric to run the place by himself for a month so you and I may take a long honeymoon?"

"I knew they were up to it," she admitted, "and that they were quite happy with my, hmm, *antics* these last few days. I didn't realize I had been tattled on, though." She picked up Juno when she pawed at her leg. "I suppose it makes no difference if I finish this here or at home."

"Speaking of home." He sat on the edge of her desk. "We must discuss this scenario. I do not wish to trade back and forth between our homes. I wish to live here with you in your District."

"Our," she corrected him. "You belong and it therefore belongs to you as well." She sat back in her chair. "I admit that I would rather live here permanently than anywhere else. But I would miss our garden at your home. And we could keep your home as a vacation spot. Eric and Rayna have a castle hidden in the mountains."

"I believe we should then combine our homes. It is the garden from mine that we love most from there." A gold brow lifted arrogantly. "There are many benefits to marrying a god, my beloved. I shall transport the garden down in its entirety into your garden space. There is room enough for it. We shall then merely have another built at our vacation home. Tomos and Belle of Seven Wishes would no doubt love a chance to improve upon their work."

"That plan works perfectly with me." She got to her feet and handed him Juno so that she could gather up her documents and put them in their case. "Where would we go on this honeymoon?"

He studied her for a moment, sensing that she was hiding something. Did she still think there was a chance of not having their happy ending? What had she seen? "I believe I promised someone that I would chase her through my temple. That means a trip home, at the least. We need to replace bad memories with good." His eyes softened. "It must have pained you to return there for what you needed."

"It was a guaranteed burnout for a day or two," she concurred. She smiled. "But that's not a problem now that the past is done. The memories can't overwhelm me anymore." She rose up to kiss him softly. "I love you," she breathed against his lips, and she savored seeing the way sparks flared in his eyes.

His free hand curled around the back of her neck and kept her close for another, hungrier, kiss. By the time he released her, her head was spinning in ways that had nothing to do with the fact that he had transported them home again. He put Juno down where she scampered off and then swept Rhianna up into his arms. She managed a breathless laugh as she clung to his shoulders. "Dinner?"

"Can wait." He strode down the hall. "I have a need to peel that suit off of you and love you most thoroughly. Do you mind?"

"Not at all. Please, carry on."

She later started dinner while he took care of transporting down their beautiful garden. His ability to do things like that was only a small benefit of loving, and being loved, by a god. The biggest benefit would always be the depth of his emotion, something far more profound than most other gods, by nature of who and what he was.

He returned while she was putting down food for Juno as well. "It is done now. We should enjoy it after dinner. You will love how it looks in the night. Perhaps I will love you again."

"Only perhaps?" she teased as she started dishing up their dinner. "I don't think there is much *perhaps* about it. You too thoroughly enjoy what we do to each other. Of course, you're not the only one, so don't take that as a complaint." She handed him a plate before he could grab her. "Food," she scolded lightly. "You can behave yourself at least that long."

"I am making up for lost time." He was smiling as he carried the plate over to the dining table. "No," he chided Juno when she gave him a pitiful look. "You do not get to share. You have your own food."

He and Rhianna were almost done with dinner when her cell phone began to warble. The tune seemed vaguely familiar somehow, and he looked at her in confusion. She grinned. "It's the theme from Disney's *Beauty & The Beast.* Mel's calling me." She hit the speaker button. "Good evening! Working late?"

"So to speak." Humor had warmed Mel's voice. "I might have a lead for you on how to get into Olympus. Kally brought it to my attention this afternoon. You see, we've been working with a new small business owner. He's an organic grocer. He gets in some strange and exotic items you don't always find easily in America." He coughed. "It would seem he got in some, uhm, new beans."

Aaron promptly choked on his tea. Rhianna bit her lip to hide a grin. "Do tell. What happened when he tried to plant them?"

"Weeeell, thankfully he only planted one of them as a test. It seemed to sprout overnight and he ended up with a ten-foot plant that produced no further fruit. He chopped it down for firewood and contacted us to see if we knew any way of helping him get his money back because he was swindled. It kinda tripped Kally's and my sensors." Mel snorted. "Let's face it, Rhi. When it comes to people in the District, even you, sometimes the story is obvious."

"Hard to say fairer than that," she agreed dryly. "Text me his address. Aaron and I will go tomorrow and see if we can't help him get his money back by buying the beans off him."

"With a cow?"

"Oh, very cute." She hung up on him but she was smiling. "And people wonder how these faerie tales become so prevalent. It's because there are certain ways magic can move, and it very rarely bothers to be subtle. I find the story that best works for a situation and let it grow as it naturally will—with a few twists along the way for variety." She picked up their plates and carried them into the kitchen. "Rayna made a peach pie the other day," she called. "Want some for dessert? We can eat by the pool."

"If you insist." He took the plates of pie from her so that she could fetch towels. He sighed as Juno danced at his feet. "Juno! You will trip me. Settle down." He glowered as the command fell on deaf ears. "You need training."

Rhianna arched a brow. "Sit," she ordered firmly.

Juno planted her butt and her tail wagged merrily. Aaron eyed her and then his wife. "I begin to think it is more than merely a talent that no one disobeys you. I strongly suspect you might have the ability to force compulsion."

She just smiled. "Bring the pie, dear."

The first thing they needed to do in the morning was find something valuable that they could use for trade. Why bother altering a plot that was already in their favor? They swung by the District's resident grocer to see what sorts of seeds she had that she used in her massive greenhouse (it was bigger than her actual house), and Aaron could not help but take an appreciative sniff as they walked inside. "Wonderful."

The grocer beamed at him. "I admit, I've been tempted to charge a quarter for people to come in here and just breathe. Or give in to the prodding from Enforcers to build a ventilation system that would let the smells drift over the District. I still say Frankie's bakery should be the first to do that. I wouldn't mind always smelling his cookies and cakes."

"You and me both!" Rhianna agreed. She smiled. "What can you do for us, Kasumi? We need something truly spectacular to offer in trade. Something guaranteed to spark avarice so he thinks he's swindling us."

"Let's see . . ." She flipped through seed packets. "I have some rare stuff in here. I imported this specialty herb from overseas. Gwyn had to help me wrangle it through customs, and I'm still getting calls from other farmers demanding I not monopolize it. I was thinking of letting it spread because it has such wonderful flavors. It goes with most any dish *and* I'd swear it can cure the common cold."

"I have never had a cold," Aaron told Rhianna. "I hear it is terrible."

"I had one. It wasn't that bad. Chicken pox was worse."

Kasumi looked up with wide eyes. "*You* got chicken pox?"

"I'm not a goddess," Rhianna laughed. "And do remember that Eric and I herald from a time before vaccinations and inoculations. We consider ourselves very, very lucky that we have incredibly high resistances, and *anything* we catch, we only catch once. We lucked out in getting vaccines for the truly bad things once they were offered, but we missed on chicken pox." She sighed. "It was about fifteen years ago. He caught it from a child. I babysat him until he was better, and then he had to do the same for me since he gave it to me!"

Aaron snickered softly at the mental image. Kasumi couldn't help but giggle as well. She, and everyone else, had always appreciated the way Rhianna and Eric unashamedly admitted their mistakes and guffaws. It made them real and kept them approachable to their people.

She flipped a few more packets. "Ah ha!" She tugged out the pouch and offered it to Rhianna. "Here you go, Ms. Taber. I've already got this planted, so I can harvest seeds from there to restock myself." Her smile turned impish. "We'll call it a belated wedding gift."

"I never had a wedding, actually. Just a marriage."

"Shame on you," she scolded Aaron.

"There were . . . extenuating circumstances. I do intend to remedy the situation as soon as everything is done."

Rhianna ignored that. She didn't really care one way or another about a ceremony for herself. She was considering it purely for her friends and family who wanted a chance to celebrate her happiness. Perhaps Brian would make her a wedding dress that blended modern Western style and the red *chiton* of Ancient Greece.

Seeds in hand, Aaron used his power to disguise himself and Rhianna as an elderly couple. He took the care to hide anything identifiable about them; it was critical that the grocer not realize he was dealing with Rhianna. Aaron did not have the same reputation yet, and he wasn't sure he ever would. He felt quite fine with that, actually.

It was just early enough that the grocer's shop was not busy yet. The grocer himself was an attractive young man who whistled merrily to himself as he set out the displays for the day. He seemed to sense the couple before they approached and looked up to smile. "Good morning! I'm not quite fully set up, but come in if you like."

"Actually, I wonder if you could help us." Rhianna sighed deeply. "We received this box of goodies from our daughter overseas, and as we have no aptitude for growing things, we're trying to sell or trade off the seeds. We know nothing about gardening."

"Huh. Well, I'm always open to new stuff. Let me see what you have." He took the offered packet and his eyes went wide for a moment as he realized what he held. A shrewd look quickly moved in to replace the surprise. "Hmm, well I guess I could use these. They're somewhat uncommon. Let's consider a trade, how's that?"

Rhianna lightly stepped on Aaron's foot when she sensed his rising amusement. "What did you have in mind?"

"Something that *anyone* can grow!" He disappeared inside and returned shortly with a small sack. He opened it and pulled out a handful of the beans inside. They looked like relatively normal beans in a kidney shape but they were an interesting silvery color not typically found in nature. "See these? Magic beans!"

Aaron obligingly squinted at them. "How are they magic?"

"Results will vary depending on where you plant them. I guarantee that they will produce big and beautiful plants for you to admire without worrying about killing them." He offered the bag. "Do we have a deal?"

"They are magic," Aaron told Rhianna when she pulled a skeptical look. "We cannot kill that."

"Well, since the other won't do us any good, all right." She took the bag of beans and dropped it into the satchel she wore. "Good day to you!"

"And you!" The grocer's whistling had a renewed cheer as he disappeared into his shop to put the seeds away safely.

Aaron and Rhianna left the scene and dropped the disguise

once they were back inside their District. He was chuckling softly. "I am sure he is congratulating himself on a job well done at tricking us into taking these useless things off his hands."

"Some people will notice that they have a role to fill. Others will not. I suppose it depends on how many times the tale will be retold. Those told but once are the ones that are often overlooked until the end. Those that will touch many lives are the ones that often get recognized." She smiled up at him. "I love all of them, but I do admit an additional fondness for the originals. They linger in your memory."

"Or as paintings in the lobby."

"Naturally!" She sighed. "At the risk of a problem, by the way, I was not lying about having no ability to grow things. Eric is the gardener for Enforcers, and he took care of my place too. Said he'd rather put in the effort than see me always killing it. Besides. It keeps him happy and out of my hair."

"Since I have never even tried to grow something—my garden was made to be low maintenance for that very reason—I think we ought to find Eric."

They lucked out. Eric was already in the gardens in front of Enforcers HQ. The lush landscape was a defining feature of the building and lured in passersby as well as employees to sit down for a moment and relax. The warlock was covered in dirt and mulch as he turned over soil for a new section he had plotted. He changed things around once a year in order to keep it always interesting.

Rhianna stopped beside him and smiled. "Riku, got something for you."

"Huh?" He looked up and blinked as she dropped the bag in his hand. "What's this?"

"'Magic' beans."

It took him only a second before he snorted rudely. "Of course. Gee, why didn't *I* think of that? Did you trade a cow for them?"

"Herb seeds, actually. Cows are hard to parade through the

middle of New York, and it's not a drought anyway. Adaptability, dear." She cocked her head. "Can you plant them?"

"Well, better me than you. They'd die within a few hours. You always overwater or smother them."

"We all have our gifts. That just isn't one of mine. I still say that it explains why you can be such a blooming idiot."

"Oh, ha ha. You're just mad that I made your potted plant take over your office as revenge for you teaching Rayna evil things."

"Yes, but they were *good* evil things, and really, every woman should know them if she has a lover stronger than she is. Every man, too, actually. It's the great equalizer for the one without the strength. You haven't heard Taylor complain."

"He's still in the racing clouds over the baby." He started digging a hole for the beans. "So we'll be woken in the middle of the night by this sucker shooting into the sky, yes? I believe that's how it's supposed to go. I'll get to cut it down after and get it out of my orchids, right?"

"You are such a whiny creature sometimes." She knelt down to lean on his shoulder as he dropped in the beans and covered them with soil. "Just replace them with morning glories when we're done."

"Dirty pool," he groused. He knew she knew morning glories were by far his favorite flower since they were the exact same color as Rayna's eyes. Their daughter had even been named for them. "Go on. Get out of my garden. There obviously won't be much time until the fight begins."

Aaron obligingly caught Rhianna's wrist and tugged her away from the scene. She glanced up to see him smiling. "Are you amused at us?" she asked curiously.

"A bit. It is more that I am happy to see the way you two snipe and bicker and love as true siblings do. Your bond is not dissimilar from that between Artemis and Apollo. It makes me feel even happier that we have come to this point in this life." He smoothed a hand down her hair tenderly. "In exchange for enduring two jealous, vain, loathsome sisters who hated you, you have now been given the unwavering love of a nearly twin brother."

"Eric was my sanity too many times to count," she murmured. "I would not have endured as long as I have without him. That's why I made sure that things would fall as needed in order for him to find Rayna. I knew from her birth that she was the right one, but I had not yet deciphered the story until she and Gwyn were given Bloody Checks. As soon as I knew that, I knew what the story would be and what I needed to do in order to ensure it happened."

"Did *he* know his role within it?"

"Nope!" Her grin looked wicked for a moment. "I got to thoroughly enjoy watching him fall in love with Sleeping Beauty and be forced to face facts that he had *always* loved her. It was there right from the beginning. Really, the way he could not stay away from her side while she slept was a *big* clue. It just needed to grow and mature as she did."

He fluttered his lashes. "And then one day she awoke, and he looked into her eyes, and he realized he had found everything he had ever wanted."

It made her laugh outright. "After everything settled and he was sulking at me over him not realizing what had been going on, I reassured him by telling him that at least he did not have to overcome a tower covered in thorny roses or a fire-breathing dragon."

"I would guess he would have rather had the tower than an encounter with the Snake God."

"Can't blame him for that, really. Still, it needed to be done. Letting Nahga escape there would have meant far worse events later."

He smiled. "You sound suspiciously like someone who controls the power of destiny."

"Who, me? I just like to have my own way in things."

The day went by with relative peace though everyone involved in the scenario was on edge. Even as the sun was setting, the first sprouts of the beanstalk had emerged from the land. Nobody was awakened in the middle of the night by any sort of earthshaking growth, but Rhianna awoke just before dawn to a vision rushing across her eyes. The symbolic shattering of a mirror.

"Aaron." She gave him a quick shake before rolling out of bed. "It's time." She dug out her rarely used jeans and a shirt she didn't mind getting grubby. There was no law that said she couldn't be comfortable when heading into what might be her final battle. Besides, she didn't *have* armor, and unlike Eric, she didn't have ritual clothing that denoted her power and bloodline.

On the other hand, she was not at all surprised to see that Aaron had chosen to shift into his familiar *chiton* and sandals. Pieces of armor had been added to the ensemble, and his bow was hooked over his shoulder. In a fight against evil, the arrows he fired would be potentially devastating. Only evil was incapable of feeling love.

They saw the beanstalk as soon as they stepped out into the murky gloom. It had grown in a spiral shape around the HQ building and it continued to spiral up until it seemed to disappear into the sky. Rhianna and Aaron made their way to the garden where it had been planted, and they found Eric standing at the base. The stalk was easily fifteen feet in diameter and would be easy to climb.

The morning wind tugged at Eric's cloak as he watched his sister approach. "I wish to go with you."

"No." Her voice booked no argument. "We need you here, Riku. Someone has to be able to kill the stalk instantly to cut off retreat once we lure the evil down. Aaron can block Olympus. We have to trap the evil here where we can finally destroy it."

He cupped her cheek. "Nothing will keep me here if you need

me."

"I know." She kissed his cheek softly. She turned to start climbing the stalk and then looked back. "Riku? I just want to tell you again how much I love you. You've made my life so much better by being in it."

A little chill went down his back. That sounded suspiciously like a goodbye. "I love you too, Rhi. You know that. I don't think my life would be complete without you and Rayna in it with me."

She smiled at him for a moment and turned back to the stalk. It was not truly a climb thanks to the spiral, but it was an incline and therefore much more difficult than merely climbing stairs. They would not climb all the way to Olympus, though, as that would be silly. They only needed to get high enough in the air that it would not take much power for Aaron to fly them the rest of the way there.

That point was another few hundred feet in the air over the top of the building. The perch gave them a glorious view of the city spread out around them. It never truly slept, but it had not fully awakened for the day either. As Aaron looked out at the scenery, he murmured to Rhianna, "No one will question the beanstalk?"

"Most won't even notice it. It's a part of the magic that even I have never understood. It won't affect air traffic either. Nothing flies over the District. It messes with scanners and instrumentation. I can't imagine why."

He smiled as he lifted her into his arms. "Indeed." He flew up swiftly toward the top of the stalk and power rushed over their bodies as they passed the invisible barrier into Olympus. They emerged on the other side of the clouds, and the beanstalk ended only a few feet higher. It was covered in the bits of puffy debris that showed where it had literally smashed through the blockage.

Olympus was a ruin. It had crumbled and fallen to bits over the last few days as the evil tore it apart in its rage. The sky that always showed Mirage was now dulled and covered with a disgusting filmy substance. The bitter, putrid, stench of evil clung to the air. It smelled of blood and murder, of genocide and the slaughter of innocents.

A low rumble moved on the air as they moved deeper into the forsaken palace. The floor was gouged and cracked apart, and something acidic had burned it through in places. Columns and pillars had collapsed into rubble. The statues of the gods and goddesses had been beheaded entirely. Perhaps most tellingly, the statue of Eros had been smashed into the smallest possible pieces. The others were still partially intact, but not his.

The rumble began to become a hissing as ugly darkness moved in the corners of the place. It started to bubble and ooze out of the cracks like rancid tar, and it slowly crept across the floor. Its mere passage only seared the marble more. Rhianna slowly lifted her hands, and white and silver power began to swirl around her body. Her first strike nipped close enough to burn but not actually strike.

The blob screeched as it surged toward her like the snap of jaws. She danced back gracefully and Aaron let loose an arrow. The blob turned on him instead, and he also danced back. The tempo had been set. The lovers would flick off an attack that taunted rather than damage. They needed it to be on Earth, in the District, where they had the advantage of allies and the very sanctuary of magic.

Both lifted their hands and fired off pure white power that sensually merged halfway and sheared a hole through the blob's body. It went ballistic with rage and started lobbing blasts after blasts of necrotic power as it began to chase them blindly. Aaron grabbed up Rhianna because he could fly faster than they ran, and he plunged down past the barrier once more. The blob could not fly, but it began to creep down the beanstalk like a spreading stain of evil and decay.

"Destroy the stalk!" Aaron shouted at Eric as they approached. "Hurry!"

Eric placed his hands on the base of the stalk and his

command over the element of earth rose. Withering and blackening began to rush upward as he choked the large plant of its very life. It started to dissolve upward as fast as the evil rushed down, and the two met in the middle. The blob seemed to realize what was occurring and started to climb back up the stalk, but it was too late. Power fired off from Aaron's hand and obliterated the entrance to Olympus entirely.

The blob landed on the roof of the headquarters with a splat that shook the entire building. An unnatural scream of rage welled on the air and exploded outward in a blinding rush of evil power that consumed the entire world in silence. All people dropped wherever they were. The only ones spared from the Silence were those who had completed contracts issued by either Rhianna or Aaron, and the entirety of the District itself.

Aaron landed beside Eric and gently placed Rhianna on her feet. They were joined a few moments later by Mel, Audra, Sera, and Theresa. The only outward sign of anyone's uneasiness was the way Theresa's very long hair shifted restlessly in response to her mood. "Let's do this," Sera said briskly. "I have a meeting at ten am, and my boss is a picky bastard sometimes."

The easiest way to get everyone to the roof was to take the elevator inside the building. The last flight to the actual roof was a set of stairs, and Rhianna unlocked the door at the top. The roof beyond was a mess. Broken cement and glass littered the area, and the blob's acidic presence had eaten through other places.

It spotted the small army that had arrived, and a sinister laugh rippled over the air. *You think this is enough?* The words hissed through everyone's minds in a way that made them feel a bit violated. Power flickered over the blob and it began to duplicate into shades of itself that formed into the shape of monsters and demons from lore. *There will be no more happy endings.*

Power rippled over Mel and Audra in turn, and they shifted form entirely. Fur bloomed across their bodies as their nails became claws and their faces elongated into wolf muzzles. Neither got any taller, but they certainly gained more muscle as their natural strength was bolstered. The last time Audra had taken her Battle Wolf self, she had been avenging the deaths of her clan. It seemed fitting to take it now to ensure that kind of thing never happened again. The mated pair rushed across the roof as a blur, and it was impossible to tell who let out the first snarl as they tore into several enemies.

Sera needed to have a rough understanding of whatever shape she shifted into, and she had made sure to read up on potentials the night before. Light swirled around her and replaced her tall figure with the shape of a large grizzly bear. "Cover the ones who can get hurt," she rumbled to Theresa as she lunged into the thick of things.

Theresa hurried to join Aaron and Rhianna, and her protection against evil was evident. Nothing could get close to her at all. If it approached from the front, it would meet her unwavering gaze and be repelled. Approaching from her back encountered her hair rising up as a weapon that could choke and smother.

The shades had their hands full with the lethal beasts, and that left Eric, Rhianna, and Aaron to engage the heart of the evil directly. It became a mess very quick. None of them were designed for close range battle and therefore had to focus on keeping the evil back while still trying to pick it off. They were doing damage, but the two lovers were taking it as well—and faster than Theresa could heal. More shades spilled into the fight and Eric was forced to change targets.

Aaron took the risk of shifting his bow into a sword and lunged toward the blob on the hopes that he was enough his father's son to get by. Rhianna continued to cover him with blasts of power and the bow he had conjured for her. He did well enough at first, but he misjudged a strike and received a sound thump that sent him tumbling head over heels. He cracked his head along the way and lay there for a moment, dazed.

The blob saw an opening and screeched in triumph. It would

render him incapacitated again and obliterate the rest who were there. He would have no choice but to sacrifice his immortal life if he lost the ones he loved most. Like a blur of hate and dripping tar, it fired off spikes with lethal accuracy.

In an ironic twist to history repeating, they were stopped from reaching him when Rhianna leapt in front of him at the last moment. The spikes plowed through her body and blood flew. Everything and everyone froze as a tortured cry ripped from Aaron's lips. The spikes lifted Rhianna off her feet and then dropped her onto the roof with a soft thud.

Eric and Aaron scrambled to her side, and Theresa was right behind them. Tears began to well in her eyes the moment she touched Rhianna. "It's too late," she whispered. Her lips trembled as she bit back a sob. "It . . . it ripped her heart to shreds. I can't heal this! No one can!" She shook her head wildly. "How can this be?! The rest of us can't even be wounded at all, let alone killed!"

Painful understanding filled Eric. "The one person," he whispered hoarsely, "who has saved thousands of lives by issuing contracts formed from the power of love . . . is the one person who is not protected because her contract is not yet complete." He looked up sharply as he felt power rising inside Aaron. "What are you doing?"

Blue eyes faded to a dull gray color, Aaron did not look up from his wife's body resting in his arms. "I am sacrificing myself. I cannot exist without her. I have no power without her. I will follow her on. My sacrifice should be enough to destroy evil." He slowly looked up at Eric. "There will be no more contracts. The happy endings are done."

"Not just yet!" an unfamiliar male voice shouted. Red power blazed as a surge of fire and dropped a man in full ancient Grecian armor on the roof. A sword and shield appeared in his hands as he rushed toward the evil on a shout. "Wolves! Shapeshifter! Aid me! There is still time!"

Mel, Audra, and Sera hurried to join Ares as another swirl of pink and gold light deposited the beautiful figure of Aphrodite. She knelt across from her son and took his shoulders. "Do not sacrifice yourself!" she snapped at him. "It will not be enough! You must avenge your wife before you go! I will transfer my power to you; I have no need for it anymore. Do this last deed, Eros! You must!"

He closed his eyes in acceptance and opened himself to the power she poured into him. It was just barely enough to compensate for the gaping holes torn inside him by Rhianna's death. He eased her body into Eric's care and slowly got to his feet. Power blazed around him with white-hot gold color as he methodically approached the evil blob. The creature seemed to realize what a threat he was, and it tried to scramble for escape. Audra blocked its way. Another route was blocked by Mel. A third by Sera. A fourth by Ares. The only open path was directly at Aaron. The blob screamed in fury and rushed toward him to consume him.

Its scream only lifted more as he began to glow even brighter. Power ripped from his body in a blinding wave, and the blob was completely obliterated. The shockwave spread with the same suddenness as the Silence, and the darkness receded. People stirred and gained their feet as the sun and moon began to shine again upon the world.

A different sort of silence, a pained one, filled the rooftop as Aaron stopped glowing. Nobody had sustained any wounds except for him. The others had been protected by their contracts. Only one person on that roof had been at risk of death, and she had willingly paid that price for her love.

Aaron stiffly returned to her side and knelt to ease her body into his arms. A footstep had him looking up sharply and he saw the unexpected figure of Persephone approaching. Her arms held a wispy, ethereal shape that bore an uncanny resemblance to Rhianna. She knelt and gently released the spirit back into Rhianna's body. "Charon would not ferry her. She was left on the shore until I could get to her and bring her here. I had to do this. It is my atonement for so long ago."

Sunlight fell across Theresa's hands and formed into male hands that guided hers to repair the damage done internally to Rhianna's body. *Like this,* Apollo's voice told her, though in a way all could hear. *It can be done easily enough.*

Rhianna drew a sharp breath as her heart began to beat and her lungs took in air once more. Aphrodite nodded firmly. "There we are. Now. Let us be sure this cannot happen again." She held up her hands, and a crystal chalice filled with shimmering gold liquid appeared on one palm. A piece of what looked like honeycomb yet white in color appeared on her other. "A woman like this really should be a goddess as well, do you not agree?"

Aaron broke the nectar into the ambrosia so that they could be more easily consumed and then gently fed the concoction to Rhianna. Her lashes lifted enough to see what he was doing, and he smiled tremulously. "Drink," he urged her huskily. "You have far earned this right, my beloved."

She drank the entire thing, and a bright glow rippled over her body before sinking into her skin and settling. Theresa found it easier than ever to heal the last of the wounds, even without Apollo's guidance, and soon the only sign of the ordeal was the ragged and ravaged clothes that adorned Rhianna's body. Ares flicked his hand to take care of that problem, and a beautiful *peplos* of the finest linen replaced the last signs of trauma.

Rhianna's eyes opened entirely, and the familiar iridescence of immortality had come to hover in her black gaze. She blinked once before looking up at Aaron and smiling. "I'll be fine now."

"You had better be!" Audra snarled as she and Mel returned to their normal shape. "I could kick your damned ass, Rhianna! Of all the reckless, stupid things! Don't you *dare* scare me like that again!"

"I think I can promise that."

Ares, Aphrodite, and Persephone shared a smile as they got to their feet and began to walk away. "I think our job is done now," Persephone decided with a satisfied nod. "This is how it always should have been."

Ares cocked his head at his lover. "What do you suppose Rhianna is a goddess of? As Athena said, she has to be a goddess of *something*."

A smile tugged at Aphrodite's lips as she glanced back over her shoulder to see their son and daughter-in-law embracing as if they would never let go again. "If Aaron is the God of Love, then I suppose Rhianna must surely be the Goddess of Destiny. They belong perfectly together." She rested her head on his shoulder with a contented sigh. "They are the protectors of lovers. There are plenty more happy endings to be made now. No evil will ever rise to stop them again."

EPILOGUE

Two months later, the resplendent gardens around Enforcers' Headquarters had been attacked by the gleeful designers of Seven Wishes working on provided sketches from Taylor. The entire place felt like a magical garden where dreams could come true. Under an arbor covered in grapes and wild roses, Rhianna and Aaron were finally able to renew their vows before the collected gathering of their friends and family.

Fami*lies*. The entirety of the Shaughnessy, Carmichael, Dease, and Lucino families were present. Priya and Pablo were present. Marina and Markus. Anyone who had ever been helped by either the bride or groom had been sure to put in an appearance.

Rather than exchange wedding bands, for they already wore them, Rhianna and Aaron were finally able to present one another with the custom engagement bands they had promised. Hers was a gold band set with a creamy pearl. His was a silver band set with a small bit of amber holding a very tiny forget-me-not seed inside.

The cheers reached well beyond the District as they finally shared their first kiss in their eternally joined lives. Eric walked up to the arbor where they stood and smiled as he held out a familiar scroll. "I think we need to see what this says. Don't you?"

Rhianna took it from him and slowly unrolled it. Light flickered and the word 'Complete' blazed across the center of the paper with such brilliance that everyone in the audience could see it. The cheers started anew as Rhianna whirled and threw her arms around Aaron's neck. He caught her just as close and buried his face in her hair. This was what he had wanted. His beautiful, *immortal*, lover to be by his side for all time. She would never have dared dream so big, but that was fine with him. They had finally had their dreams come true.

The reception party that followed was merry and joyful. They had foregone the whole bouquet and garter toss, though, since they had *other* ways of setting up the people who needed to be set up. Gwyn couldn't help but tease Rhianna, "I guess you'll need to enchant more file cabinets to have room for all those new contracts you two will be making. Do you have a Taber or a Konstantinos one for yourself?"

"Neither, thank you, but if that's a subtle way of asking, I'm keeping my name." She shook her head wryly. "We decided there would just be too much paperwork to get it changed. On the other hand, he's considering changing his. He says he likes the fact that it has less syllables and people won't misspell it as much."

"I only typoed it once. Sheesh."

Aaron heard the laughter and looked over with a smile. Rhianna had laughed a lot more recently than he had ever heard before. He found himself smiling and laughing more as well. The gift of their completed contract.

Cameron stepped up beside him and asked very solemnly, "So are you going to reopen your business?"

"I think I got recruited," he admitted ruefully. "She started talking about how there was an empty suite and how it would be perfect since it is on the first floor and how there really is nothing open in the District right now and that people who work there have their homes attached and since we live together . . ." He trailed off with a grin. "I did not even try to argue with her. Cupid's Grove is now a division of Enforcers."

"Huh-oh." Cameron grinned. "Taking orders from your lover. That always keeps things interesting, trust me. And since you've got, you know, *Rhianna*? Good luck, friend."

Aaron smiled toward Rhianna and was warmed when she

smiled back. "I would have her no other way," he murmured softly. "She is perfect just as she is."

As the reception finally drew to a close and people began to go home, Aaron and Rhianna were hustled into a carriage that carried them to the Gentle Brook Inn where they had been reserved the largest honeymoon suite. They would spend the weekend there and then transport themselves to Greece for the first part of their month-long honeymoon.

Eric watched them ride off down the street before going into the HQ building. He quietly unfastened his tie as he rode the elevator upstairs to the top floor. Instead of going into his office, however, he went into Rhianna's. He tugged the scroll out of his jacket and unrolled it. Not so surprisingly, it had become legible now that it had been completed. Everything he had wondered about was now spelled out clearly.

He found the space at the bottom and added a few notes. An empty folder sat to the side and he tucked the scroll inside. The folder itself showed the same 'Complete', and he turned to study the as-yet empty drawers in the cabinets. He found one in line of sight to the desk and thought for a moment before writing 'Taber' across the front. He dropped the scroll inside, locked it, and the word 'Finished' appeared beneath the label.

"Riku?" Rayna stood in the doorway with Glory in her arms. She smiled. "Let's go home."

"Yeah." He crossed to her and tucked her safely under his arm as they left the office. He turned off the light and studied the darkness that filled the room. "All this time, we kept saying it. 'She should be a goddess.' 'She's all but a goddess.' 'Her power is godlike,'" he murmured. "I suppose the answer really was right there all along."

Rayna rested her head on his arm as she smiled up at him. "Isn't it always?"

"I suppose it is. What story do you suppose will be next?"

"I don't know, but I *do* know how it will end."

"Yes?"
"Happily ever after."

Status: File Complete
Analysis: The stories that take the longest to get to happy ever after
are the ones with the sweetest endings.

Turn the page to come back to Mirage for one last tale that might just need some double Enforcing . . .

Bonus Folder
ELIZABELLE

CHAPTER ONE

It was that time of year again in Mirage. As surely as the seasons brought rain, flowers, falling leaves, or snow, it brought the rights of passage undertaken by all princes and heroes who sought to prove themselves in the world. Spring season was usually the 'rescue princesses' time. Summer and fall typically held the 'defeat a curse' journeys. And as the first snows began to fall and make the world into wintery wonderlands, the rite du jour was 'slay a dragon.'

The dragons were not wholly keen with the entire thing. Most were quite happy to just find a nice cave and settle in with shiny treasure to admire. The treasures typically came from their own mining and scavenging though there had been occasional raids on kingdoms; it was usually in response to someone in the kingdom doing something stupid first. And, yes, princesses had been kidnapped once in a while, but, well, even dragons got lonely. No princess nabbed by a dragon ever found her captor to be anything except polite, well mannered, and surprisingly adept at card games—and sometimes far more accurate at guessing who her true love might be.

The first snows had begun to fall. Already a few raids had happened. Thankfully, there had only been one casualty thus far, but the numbers were sure to climb. The dragons were simply at the end of their rope. The clan located off the edges of the Montgomery Kingdom had it particularly bad since the kingdom was rife with wizards and sages that drew in heroes and princes seeking advice.

"What if we made alliance?" one elder suggested to the Circle that oversaw the clan.

"You mean send in a delegate to prove we're not the ravaging beasts we're made out to be? Really, it *would* be easier if they accepted us like they do wizards. We have people who go rogue, but you can't write all of us off," another pointed out.

"I think we are in agreement, then." The first nodded his large head briefly. "I suggest we send a younger member of the clan. It's a trivial task, for one thing, and for another, he or she will be small enough to not cause an immediate alarm."

"I recommend Magnus," another offered. She sighed. "He has been driving his family crazy. He won't settle down! We keep trying to tell him that dragons don't go on adventures, but he won't listen. He's always burying his nose in books about travel. 'But why can't a dragon have an adventure? Didn't a prince marry a Good Faerie? Rules can be broken!'" She shook her head. "I remind myself he is but a whelp, but he still vexes me! At least this might make him calm down!"

"Done." The first elder inclined his head. "Coral, would you be so kind as to relay the missive to him?"

Coral rose to her full height and gracefully leapt like a large cat to the window overhead. A flap of her wings sent her soaring into the air around the massive mountain range that the clan called home. She angled down toward a remote, almost hidden, cave that had been cleverly disguised to blend into the surroundings.

She landed lightly and her talons made little clicking noises as she moved into the opening. Around two bends, the cave opened up to reveal a beautiful deposit of precious stones. Magnus was not much of a gold collector. He also did not seem to be present at first, and her eyes narrowed as she swept a quick gaze over the room.

Movement. She turned and spied the tip of a purple tail sticking out of a mound of amethysts. Clever boy. "Hmmm . . . Now wherever could he be . . .?" She moved closer and grabbed onto his tail with her jaws as if he was a pup. Dragon teeth were retractable for just such a thing, much to the gratitude of many parents. She hauled Magnus out and he gave a yelp as he found himself unceremoniously dropped on the ground. "You!" she scolded. "What are you doing, whelp?"

He scowled. "I was trying to avoid all of the antics from next door! Stupid mating season."

Mating season for dragons came about every winter, too. It was partially why it was such a good time to hunt them. Dragons in season were stronger, faster, and more territorial. Perhaps luckily for the race, dragons mated for life. An unmated dragon—like Magnus—was spared the insanity as a whole. Mated dragons really didn't think about much beyond procreation, and therefore made noisy neighbors. Once spring arrived, things would go back to normal and the mated pairs would again remember to be polite. It was the 'until spring' part that drove others nuts.

Coral sighed as she studied Magnus. It really was a shame that he was as-yet unmated himself. He was certainly one of the more handsome males around, and he had strong skills for his age of a hundred. But, since he was only the equivalent of a twenty-five-year-old human, no one was yet pressuring him to think about settling down. That would come in another fifty years. "Just you wait," she scolded him. "You'll get yours!"

"Yes, I know." He clasped a claw to his heart and took on a dramatic tone. "I will happen upon the most beautiful creature in the world—to me—and be instantly consumed with the desire to have her close to me. When mating season comes around once a year, our lives will be put on hold as we while away hours in desperate desire trying to produce a child."

A brow covered in pink scales lifted. "You won't be laughing when you get there. Also? It may be annoying to neighbors, but I've never heard a mated dragon complain about being in season. It is daunting at first until you get used to it. By the third season for a mated pair, they're quite happy for an excuse to stay in their cave together all the time—especially if they already have kids!"

He couldn't dispute that. He was actually amused by how his parents used to dump him off on a cousin or other relative to be babysat for three months. "Why are we discussing this anyway?"

"You brought it up." She sighed. "Magnus. I know you are bored. I think I might be able to help with that a bit. We need a delegate to go to the Montgomery Kingdom and petition them for alliance rather than the current status quo. We need to end this ridiculous 'prove your valor by killing a dragon' thing."

"Can I travel after I talk to them?" he asked hopefully. "I've mastered the ability to disguise myself as a human. The only thing that gives me away is scales on my neck, but a scarf covers it."

She stared at him. It normally took a dragon until at least five centuries to be able to master the ability to disguise as a different race. He was more gifted than she had believed. "Maybe," she hedged. "Why don't we see what happens at the kingdom and go from there?"

"Okay. Done." He flapped his wings and rose up into the air. The light shimmered over his rich purple hued scales and illuminated the silver stripe down his back that was mark of his noble heritage. "I'll do my best to convince them to let it be."

She watched him fly out of the cave and sighed internally again. First a prince marrying his Good Faerie, and now a dragon that didn't want to guard a cave of treasure. What next? A princess that didn't want to be rescued?

The Montgomery Kingdom was relatively normal as far as kingdoms went. It had a king and a queen, a prince that was the heir to the throne, and a princess that was amongst the most beautiful of females in her kingdom. Everything was almost perfect. Idyllic. There was really only one tiny, little problem.

"Elizabelle!!"

Elizabelle Montgomery—Liz to her friends—winced wryly as she heard her mother bellowing her name. She was busted. *Again.* Stifling a sigh, she stopped walking her favorite mare around the corral and dismounted. Those who watched her were forced to hide smiles. The status quo was apparently in shift again, what with this new generation of royalty not sticking to tradition.

Liz assuredly had the ladylike manners, gracious demeanor, and ability to make small talk with the best of her ilk. She also rode better than the masters, was better with a sword than even her brother, and she had picked up various forms of other combat by mere observation from her tower window.

Every suitor that had come by over the last six years since her sixteenth birthday had been treated to the same polite yet firm response: no way, no how. Liz was holding out for true love (which no one argued with) but the fact that true love for her meant someone willing to overlook her less than princess-ly charms implied that her search might take a while.

She ducked into the secret room near the stables to quickly change out of her leggings and tunic. She yanked on her royal dress again and hastily coiled her hair to hide all the tangles. A quick scrub of a cloth over her face removed sweat and dirt. She nearly forgot to replace her headband with her coronet and was trying to pin it into place as she hurried toward the drawing room inside the castle.

Her mother was inside and, as always, looked like she was getting ready for a ball. Liz knew some people genuinely enjoyed dressing up and being pampered, but she just wasn't one of them. In the same way some commoners were really meant to be royalty, she was one of the members of royalty meant to be common. Everyone had their own happy zone. A castle wasn't hers.

She sketched an elegant curtsey. "Yes, Mother?"

Her mother scowled at her. "Oh, don't try that sweetness thing! And don't widen your eyes so innocently, Elizabelle! I saw you from the window. I know damned well you were out in the corral again. We encouraged your wish to learn to ride because all

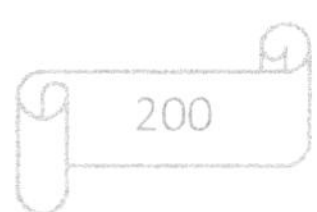

princesses should, but you should be riding *sidesaddle*."

"It's not as easy to control a horse that way," Liz sighed. "And it's uncomfortable."

"It's more proper." That was met with a roll of the eyes, and the queen stifled a long sigh. She loved her daughter, she truly did, but she often wished she could simply understand her better. "We have tried to be lenient with you, Elizabelle, but your father and I are putting our foot down. No more riding. No more leggings. Your brother has been instructed not to teach you anything else. You will start again on the etiquette and housekeeping lessons you have shunned for so many years."

"No."

"They will—" She broke off and her eyes widened. "I'm sorry?"

"No." Liz crossed her arms. "As in 'no, I will not.' Like it or not, I'm twenty-two years old. I'm an adult. There is nothing stopping me from simply leaving home."

Her mother's eyes narrowed. "I think we disagree. We will not have our daughter off traipsing around the world without an escort!"

Hopefully, Liz asked, "If I have an escort, would you let me go?"

"Guards!" The queen turned as the door opened and two wary guards looked inside. "Escort the princess to her tower and lock her inside. She shall remain there until she comes to her senses over this ridiculous nonsense!"

With obvious reluctance, the guards moved to flank Liz. The guards and ladies-in-waiting alike adored Liz and very much wanted her to be happy—something she would never be inside the castle. Liz said nothing as the guards took her back to her tower that overlooked the barracks. They obligingly locked the door before shutting her inside, but one of them slipped her an extra master castle key *just* in case she decided she wanted to run away. They knew their princess better than her mother did.

The benefit to being 'locked' in her tower was that she could wear whatever she wanted. She bathed and changed into the tunic-dress and leggings that one of the maids had snuck in to her. She then perched in her large window to watch the courtyard on the other side of the barracks to see who was coming and going. She liked to people watch. It was fun.

Her brother, Solomon, was going through the courtyard, and he glanced up to see her. "Liz!" he scolded when he saw what she was wearing. "You'll get yourself kidnapped by a dragon if you keep being so willful!"

"I'd rather be kidnapped by a dragon than stuck here to await some idiot trying to rescue me!" she retorted. "And what are you still doing here? I thought you were leaving to go rescue some other princess."

"I got delayed by the weather and missed out." He shrugged and grinned. "No big loss. I have an adventure coming in my near future. I can feel it."

"Lucky you," she muttered.

Magnus had a healthy sense of self-preservation. He had no intentions of flying up to the castle and risking being shot down. He instead landed out of sight and changed into his human form before beginning his approach. As a human, he was just as surprisingly handsome as the dragons found him in his natural shape. His purple scales had turned into purple eyes, and his silver stripe had become silver hair. There was a slightly silver hue to his pale skin as well, and the shimmer of scales over his neck were iridescent purple.

The hue to his skin could be dismissed as a result of magical bloodlines, either faerie or mage, but the scales were a dead giveaway. He wouldn't bother with a scarf until he was trying to be incognito. For this meeting, he needed to be clear who and what he represented. There was no way this would be easy.

One thing was easy, though: getting inside. Nobody stopped him from entering the city around the castle, and he only got a few curious looks rather than outright hostility. He got even luckier when he approached the actual castle and spoke with a guard. Though obviously astonished at a dragon arriving to talk diplomacy, the guard nonetheless went to talk to the king and queen. Five minutes later, Magnus was being escorted to the throne room.

The sheer opulence of the place made his nose wrinkle slightly. He lived in a cave stuffed with treasure, and this *still* felt ostentatious. Seeing the number of robes and massive crowns that the ruling couple wore didn't make him feel any better. He could barely stand normal clothes. Weren't they smothering?

"Well!" The king's brows shot up as he beheld Magnus. "I have to admit you surprised us, er, sir. We don't often get dragons requesting audiences with us. What brings you here?"

"The ritual slaughter of my people every winter?" Magnus countered politely. "Your majesties, with all due respect, the dragons are getting quite fed up with this 'slay a dragon to prove your valor' thing. We're not all bloodthirsty, ravaging beasts. We're a civilized society. We have the occasional bad apple, but, who doesn't? We would ask for an alliance in an effort to call off this ridiculous annual hunt."

"Don't be ridiculous!" the king chided. "How else is a man supposed to prove his worth? Hunting ogres? They're not intelligent enough to be a threat."

It was almost a compliment. "Sire. Really. Look at it through our eyes. With the way your kind comes tromping through just because we're dragons, *you* come across as the bloodthirsty and brutal creatures. Tell me truly. How many times can you recall a dragon attacking a kingdom *without being slighted first*?"

"Uhm. Once or twice. Maybe three times." The king waved it aside. "The status stays where it is. We have no reason to change tradition at this time. Dragons are beasts, and beasts are for hunting and killing. An alliance is ridiculous."

A puff of smoke emerged from Magnus' nose as he snorted rudely. Before he said something in anger that he might regret, he turned and left the throne room entirely. The king had just been confronted with manners and intelligent conversation, and a request for alliance, and still had the gall to call dragons beasts?

He was partway across the courtyard when he heard someone whistle at him. He looked around quickly and then upward. A young woman was waving at him from a tower window and gesturing for him to join her. He looked around again, and a passing guard shrugged. "The princess. You can visit her. She's locked up right now. She's probably bored. We won't tell if you want to say hi."

Well, at least not *everyone* was rude. He looked up again, shrugged, and used his magic to fly himself up to the window. Dragons in human form could still fly though it did take a bit more power than normal. He landed delicately on the windowsill and stepped down into the room. "You called?" he started to ask dryly, only to break off and stare.

Delicate strands of onyx hair framed a striking face set with deep emerald eyes and ruby lips. A lithe and lovely figure matched with ivory skin made his fingers suddenly itch to touch. This gemstone princess was practically a creature of his deepest fantasy. A deep and powerful desire to mate rose hard and fast. A brief panicky thought fluttered through his mind, *She can't be my mate!*

But, really, how else was he supposed to explain his desire? It was not merely to make love to her; he very, very, *very* badly wanted to get her pregnant and see her carrying a child. That could mean only one thing. It was mating season, and he had accidentally found his mate. Trying to tell his hormones that dragons and humans probably could *not* breed kids didn't seem to do much to shut them up—and why would it, when it never worked for the same-gender pairs either? They would keep going nuts he got his mate pregnant *or* until the season ended. Of all the rotten luck!

Liz was almost not breathing as he stared at her with burning purple eyes. She didn't think it was her imagination that he was contemplating ravishing her on the floor, and the fact that she entirely didn't mind the threat told her she might be in trouble. "Hi." It came out breathless against her will. "Uhm, I'm Elizabelle Montgomery. Liz for short." She offered a hand for a handshake.

He caught her hand in his but brought it to his lips as he bowed deeply. "Magnus Silverback." A slightly deeper note to his voice was as telling as the breathless note in hers. "It's a pleasure."

Not yet it wasn't, but it probably would be! Why hadn't the princess guidebook come with a chapter on 'lusting after the wrong species'? Being a practical princess, she knew damned well the way her world worked. That much unexpected desire out of nowhere was a big damn clue that Love with a capital L was probably not far behind. She really couldn't imagine there was any other reason she had an urge to blurt, 'I'm single! I want your babies!' What the hell had brought *that* on? The desire was surprising enough without throwing in the urge to have eggs with the guy!

Rather than continue to stare into her darkened eyes, he glanced around the tower room. A smile tugged at his lips as he saw the practical décor and rather plain style of living. This was one princess who had no real care for the fancy things in life. The only gems he could spot at all were chunks of stone in the raw, like the ones he mined. "You're not normal."

She had to grin. "You have no idea." She huffed out a breath. "Magnus, you're a dragon, right?"

"Right."

"I have a big, *big* favor to ask."

"Okay . . ."

"I need you to kidnap me."

He stared at her for long moments. "I beg pardon?"

She caught his arm urgently. He stood many inches taller than her five-four frame, and he was much more powerfully built than most human men, yet she felt nothing but safe. "Please," she begged, "I can't STAND it here anymore! All they want is for me to sit around docilely and wait for some stupid hero to come save me! I want to travel, or, at the least, find some place I can live where people don't care if I use a sword and ride astride or want to wear normal clothes other than ball gowns!"

Empathy moved through him. It seemed a bit like finding a kindred spirit. "I know the feeling," he admitted softly. "All my people want me to do is settle down and guard a cave of treasure. I want adventure. To travel as well. What good are my treasures if I don't spend them on stuff?"

She took both of his hands with hers. "We could travel together. I wouldn't mind spending time with you." She grinned a bit. "I'd be lying if I tried to pretend I don't find you attractive and fascinating, and that I would absolutely not mind if you had decided to carry me away of your own will rather than me asking you to."

If she didn't stop looking at him like that, he was going to pounce on her and probably get himself shot by the guards. He felt a bit desperate to taste her. How long would he manage to keep his hands off her? She was a *princess*. Princesses did *not* become the mates of dragons, damn it! "Ground rules," he heard himself saying. "One, I think it's fair to clear the air and state that I'm badly attracted to you *but* you can trust me to protect your virtue."

She watched him from under her lashes. He should be more worried about *his* virtue. If true love came along, then she would have him. It was that simple. "Okay. And two?"

"Honesty. We have to mutually decide where we're going and what we do. We should be equals. I'd rather a friend than just a companion. I don't have many friends," he admitted.

"Me neither." She smiled. "I can agree to both, and I will be honest enough to admit I'm pretty badly attracted to you as well—as if I hadn't already implied it. Let's start with friends. Deal?"

"Deal." Though he would do his best to *keep* it as friendship until he was absolutely sure that she was his mate and he wasn't just being deviant. The only way to know for certain would be if she had the same urge to mate that he did. Considering you couldn't just *ask,* 'hey, you want to have babies?', it would be best to just see what developed. "Ready to get kidnapped?"

"Am I ever!" She rushed over to her closet and hastily threw several items into a backpack. She slipped it on and followed him over to the window. Fascinated, she watched as he jumped out and turned into his natural form before he dropped more than a foot.

He was a surprisingly handsome dragon to even her eyes. She had no way to define what his race considered beautiful, but she really liked how he looked. She kinda wanted to pet him; his scales looked really soft and shiny. He was not much bigger than ten feet overall, and he flew close enough to the window for her to climb out onto his back. The years of riding astride paid off, and she was perfectly comfortable as he flew over the courtyard wall.

A yelp rose on the air as they were spotted, and guards rushed into the throne room. "The princess was kidnapped by the dragon!" they blurted

The king shot to his feet. "So much for civilized!" he snapped. "Send out the word! Any able-bodied prince and hero in the vicinity who brings my daughter home safely may have her hand in marriage and a piece of my kingdom!" He scowled darkly as the guards ran out again. "I always knew she would get herself into trouble if she kept up being so willful! Kidnapped by a dragon!" He threw himself down into his chair with a huff. "Well, at least she'll get married and settle down after this!"

"And hopefully find true love," his wife sighed.

CHAPTER TWO

It took an hour of flight before Magnus felt it was safe to land. He touched down gently and angled a wing to help Liz slide safely to the ground. He shifted back into human form and shook his head for a moment to clear the disorienting sensation. It was always an oddity to go from ten feet to slightly less than six.

Liz grinned a bit. "Vertigo?"

"A little." He grinned back. "First time I managed this form, I tripped over my own feet because I had no idea how to get my legs to function. It was a completely new way of balancing myself. I still get kinda clumsy, just as a warning. I lose my sense of depth or forget I have longer legs relative to the placement of my knees."

She tried to bite back a snicker. "Maybe we should stop and have you watch some toddlers to see how they do it." She stretched happily and looked around. "Even just being outside the palace has made me feel better. I was getting choked in there. Apparently royals forget that being royal does not make one any less an adult once of the proper age."

"How old are you?" he asked curiously as he fell into step beside her.

"Twenty-two. You?"

"Literally one hundred, but I'm about the equivalent of a twenty-five-year-old human. We grow roughly four years for every one of yours."

"Not immortal though."

"We average about four hundred or so. We technically live as

long as humans do but we just live it longer."

She blinked. "I actually understood that. Can you do that thing that faeries do where you can choose to grow old faster?"

"Sure! Any magical creature can do that." He bumped her shoulder companionably with his. "Tell me about the princess I kidnapped. Are you the heir to the throne?"

"*No,* thankfully." She shook her head. "I have an elder brother named Solomon. He's slightly younger than your mental age. He's done a few low-key type adventures, routed some ogres and the like, but nothing big yet. Keeps trying to set out and always gets waylaid. He thinks his grand adventure is coming soon. I would *happily* go on his adventures for him."

"No suitors?" It was asked casually though he felt anything but casual at the idea of competition. He might have to start eating people, and that would suck for the dragons' reputation. Also, he had heard that princes were a bit on the chewy side.

"None that have stuck!" she answered cheerfully. "First one came along when I was just sixteen." She fluttered her lashes. "How handsome he was! Fair haired and charming with blue eyes, and a nice figure of a body. He swung a dashing sword and brought me roses. He vowed to sweep me off my feet and place me in the lap of luxury."

He coughed. "And?"

"He happened to be vain as the sun will rise. I think he coiffed his hair more than a legion of princesses. He also had too high an opinion of himself. I chucked him out on his ass. Last I heard he had pissed off some witch and gotten turned into a frog. Good luck to him finding true love like *that.*"

"Hmm." He was trying not to laugh. "After that?"

"Every spring, rain or shine, the line tromps through the castle. 'Be mine and I'll make you a queen!'" She clasped a hand to her heart dramatically. "'Marry me and you will never work a day!' 'Give me your hand and I will shower you in gold and silk!'" Her mocking smile softened. "There was one, though. A plain man. He was the fourth in line to inherit his kingdom. He told me he had nothing to offer except a promise to be faithful and caring. I wish I could have loved him. I couldn't, so I did the next best thing. I arranged for him to deliver a gift to a friend of mine on his way home."

"Did he find true love with her?" he asked softly.

"He did! It made me happy." She sighed. "Anyway, this coming year promises to be the worst yet. With each passing year, I've been slipping further down on the list of marriage material. Not that I'm *complaining*, but it does mean I'm scraping the bottom of the barrel. I just want to be loved. That's all." She shrugged it off. "What about you? Tell me about the dragons. Do you get the 'settle down and marry' thing, too?"

"Not until we hit the age of one-fifty. I have fifty years left before they start nagging the hell out of me. I *have* had offers, and I *have* had some lifted brows, though. Dragons mate for life," he explained, "and we have the capacity to recognize our mate on sight. I've met everyone in my clan, so everyone knows my mate isn't there yet."

She *really* wanted to ask him if he had recognized her and that was why they had both reacted as they had, but she didn't quite have the nerve for it. She didn't want to scare him off. He seemed kind of skittish. "Dragons lay eggs, right?"

"Actually, no." He smiled. "We're mammals, too. We birth live children. We only *look* like reptiles. Did you know we once had fur?" Her eyes widened and his smile deepened. "Seriously! Once we evolved to live in places other than the coldest mountains, we developed scales instead. They protect us from the changes in season. You can still see the evidence of fur in our whelps: newborn dragons have fur until they're about, hmm, one year old. The fur then falls off and scales grow in."

"I want to see a furry dragon," she sighed wistfully. "At the risk of being potentially insensitive, it sounds so cute!"

"Nope, not insensitive. It *is* cute. Seriously, if people realized

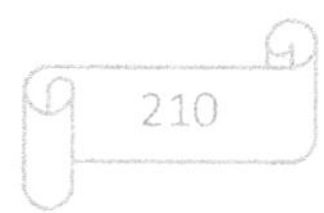

how adorable baby dragons are, they wouldn't be so quick to hunt us." He scowled. "Speaking of. Your father's an ass."

"Preaching to the choir there, Magnus. Why were you here anyway?"

"We're tired of the hunting season. We thought we'd offer an alliance. But noooo. A man can only prove his valor by slaying such intelligent and powerful beasts as dragons. Never mind that we don't attack without provocation or that what few princesses were captured were usually just grabbed because the dragon was bored and wanted a friend. We make good companions."

"So far I'm happy with it," she teased him. Her breath caught anew as he looked down at her with another of those laughing smiles, and his purple eyes glowed softly. The glow shifted abruptly, and hunger tightened his face. She was definitely not mistaken about the threat of being ravished. It seemed as if he was having to exert careful control over himself for some reason. Maybe he *had* recognized her as his mate. "Magnus?"

He let out a long breath. Rather than give the whole truth, he hedged around the edges. "Winter is dragon breeding season."

"Oh." She blinked, and it dawned. "*Oh.*" She winced. "And heroes *hunt* you during this time? I would not want to go near temperamental and hormonal creatures with sharp teeth unless I was bringing snacks and peace offerings!" Did that mean, then, that his desire for her would have happened for any female of any species? That was disheartening, but not entirely discouraging. "Can dragons breed with humans?" she asked skeptically. "It seems unlikely you'd be eyeing me as breeding potential if we weren't compatible. I would think nature had ways of preventing that from happening."

"I honestly don't know," he admitted, "though I concur with your assessment. You caught me off-guard. I had never wanted a human before, and I have seen a few females in my time despite being relatively cave-locked. I never saw them with more than the sort of admiration you might feel for a pretty bird." His smile turned wry. "Let's just say that my first reaction to seeing you involved things that, if I said them out loud, would get my face slapped." His sharp ears caught sound and he looked down the road to see a town not far ahead. "Ah. There we are. Resting spot!"

She would have rather found out what he had been thinking; it sounded promising. She followed his gaze down the road and sighed happily to see the town. A chance to be normal! "Do I look like a princess?"

"Hmm." He critically eyed her. "Not really. The clothes mostly hide it, and you don't have coloring that screams some specific royal bloodline. I think you'd at most be mistaken for the type of girl who could marry a prince to become a princess."

"Perfect!" She eyed his neck where the scales were visible. It was highly tempting to put her lips there. "You need a scarf." She stopped and took off her backpack to dig inside. She emerged shortly with a scarf and offered it to him. "Here you go." After he put it on, she nodded decisively. "Now you just look like a wizard who has been imbued with magic."

"As you said, perfect!" He impulsively caught her hand and held on as they continued down the road. The noise got louder as they approached, and his brows lifted as he saw the massive commotion. It looked like a bunch of people were preparing for a journey all at once. "What's going on?"

She winced as she saw the half a dozen young men in various types of armor and weaponry. "Heroes. You can't miss them. They have 'valorous type' etched into their foreheads!"

He cleared his throat and stopped an old man who was going by. "What's going on?"

The old man shook his head. "The princess of the Montgomery Kingdom was kidnapped by a dragon. The king has said that returning her safely will net her hand and a piece of the kingdom."

Liz's jaw dropped, and Magnus hastily clamped his hand over her mouth. "Don't mind her!" he blurted. "We just came from there and we didn't see anything like that at all. Are they sure she was actually kidnapped?"

"Well, the king says so, and you know how heroes are. They probably wouldn't care if she was a willing kidnappee. Throw in a beautiful princess, money, *and* dragon slaying, and you'll have every hero or prince worth his salt wanting to prove his stuff in the hopes of finding true love." The old man continued to shuffle along on his way.

Liz had a very un-princesslike urge to smack her father very hard. She could understand him misinterpreting the situation. The 'rescue my daughter and marry her' part was what bothered her. Kidnapping was completely different from curses where only true love would wake you. For all he knew, some adept guy would rescue her and not at all be her true love. Couldn't he have left it at a gold reward?

Magnus held her elbow more tightly and looked around quickly. He spotted a building with a sign that had a bed on it and hurried her that direction. He had luckily thought to bring gems with him for money, and he booked two rooms for at least the night. He urged Liz up the stairs with him and into her room. He shut the door behind himself and let out a breath. "Phew. Alright. You can let your temper loose now."

"I can't believe this!" she exploded as she threw down her backpack. "Am I the only princess in the world who thinks this is getting out of hand?"

He held up his hands soothingly. "Believe it or not, things are changing right now. You and I are proof of it. It happens in cycles. Give it another decade or two, and we'll see where the cycle is really heading. If you have a daughter someday, *she* might be the one to go on adventures and rescue silly princes who don't know better."

It made her snort with humor as he had intended. She threw herself down onto a chair with a huff. "I vote for staying here until tomorrow. They'll have all left by then. And since they'll be looking for us to be heading to ground somewhere, we're not likely to have to worry about them no matter where we go."

"Too true." He sat down across from her and grinned. "May I assume from your ire that you don't want to be rescued?"

"Meh." She made a 'maybe' gesture. "I'm not saying it wouldn't be romantic to be rescued in a time of need, but my need for rescue is a small one. Magic would be my only downfall. I'm quite skilled with a sword, and I can fight with my hands and feet as well."

"Really?" He brightened. "I'm the opposite. Magic is my thing, and if I'm in my natural form, I can claw stuff, but I lack any real physical training, *especially* with this body. Y'think you could teach me some stuff? Just some basics?"

"Sure!" She hopped to her feet. "Scarf off. I don't want to accidentally choke you." She removed the cloak she had thrown on and heeled off her shoes. "Okay. Grab me like this." She put his hands where they needed to be. "Hold on really tight." His grip tightened and she lithely twisted her body in a strange way. She promptly got free.

His eyes slowly widened. "I can't even figure out how you did that. Also, my fingers feel funny."

"Let me show you." She patiently went over the exact movements needed and how to make his human body use them. It didn't matter that he was physically stronger; if he broke free of her grip the right way, it would work on anyone of any strength. The effectiveness lay in the brief numbing of the captor's fingers.

His first attempt did nothing except make him stumble. He got free only because she lacked the strength to keep a grip. They reset and tried again, and he tried to twist himself as she had shown him. He misjudged his ratio of space, however, and threw himself off balance entirely. She tried to catch him this time and only ended up going onto the floor with him. She landed with a thump on his chest. "Ooph!" She blew locks of hair out of her eyes and smiled wryly. "Well, that's a sign of 'almost right' if ever I saw it. A little more balance and you'd have it."

There was no response and she looked down to see him staring at her with a heat that seared her to her toes. Something clenched hard and hot low inside her body with a wild rush of eager desire. She slowly reached out to touch his lips, craving the sensation of them pressed to hers. "Do dragons kiss?" she asked huskily.

His answer was to fist his hands in her hair and drag her down for a wild kiss. She shuddered in his grip and moaned softly as his tongue tangled hotly with hers. The room spun around her head as he rolled over to pin her to the cool wood floor. Her fingers found the silk of his hair and she twisted upward to fight fire with fire. Dragons not only kissed, they were also *really* good at it.

The wicked potency of the pleasure surging inside her body was stunning in its power. Nothing mattered except his taste and his touch. Nothing mattered except making love with him until she finally carried his child inside.

Child. Breeding season. Through the haze in her brain, she realized that it had gotten them both. She *had* to be his mate. She could get the whole 'he needed to mate' thing on his side. A normal desire on her side could be relatively understood, despite the crossed species thing. The fact that all *she* could think about was reproducing—where she had *never* before had the urge in more than a 'meh, someday' kind of way—was a big damn clue that they had to be mates.

She broke out of the kiss to gulp in air, and it was flavored with the oddly sweet scent of his skin. It was addicting. "Magnus." She framed his face in her hands and stared into his seething purple eyes. She did not have to look for the answer. It had been there from the beginning just as she had suspected. Love. How could she not love him? He was everything perfect for her. "If we're going to make love," she warned him thickly, "can we relocate to the bed?"

Shock pierced the intensity of his eyes as he realized how close he was to ripping off her clothes and having her right there.

He released her as if burned and scooted away quickly. He averted his eyes as peach color stained his silvery cheeks. "Liz." His voice was rougher and deeper than normally possible for human voices. "I'm sorry."

"Did I look or sound like I was complaining?" She carefully sat up and looked at her hands. They were trembling as hard as her internal organs. She felt achy, frustrated, and more than a bit irked that he had stopped. "I asked for a relocation, not a ceasefire." She slid closer to him. "I've wanted you to touch me since I saw you."

His entire body quivered as she moved closer and the ripe scent of her skin gouged into his lungs. Nothing was as powerful an aphrodisiac to a dragon as the smell of his or her mate, especially at this time of year. His fingers bit into the floor hard enough to make small dents in the wood. "Move back." It came out as almost a growl.

"Magnus, am I your mate?" It was asked calmly.

His breath hissed out as her fingers trailed down his arm. Every inch of his body felt sensitized unbearably. "Yes," he bit out. "You have to be. Mating season doesn't affect a dragon unless they're mated." Fingers skimmed over the scales on his neck and he whirled to grab her arms. Wild magic poured through his eyes. "I don't think you comprehend, Elizabelle!" he snapped. "If I start to make love to you, I won't let you out of bed again until at least spring, or until you were pregnant!"

She pursed her lips as she thought about things. "Is that the only time we'd be setting the sheets on fire?"

He stared at her. "Well, no. Our relationships are always tempestuous with our mates. Breeding season just kicks it into overdrive."

"So . . . we get three months out of a year to completely indulge in desire and not worry about anyone bothering us?"

"Yes . . ."

". . . You're complaining *why*?" She eased up to nibble on his lower lip. "Not that I think we want to spend three months in this inn, beautiful as it is, but I am entirely not opposed to the concept of being your mate and, if we were so lucky, having your child." His hands fell off her arms in shock and she caught his face in her hands. A smile tugged at her lips. "Magnus. This is *Mirage*. True love comes where it chooses to come. We are part of the changing cycle, and I couldn't be happier. My true love needed to be kind of quirky, kind of different, and willing to let me be me. Also? I kind of like the whole flying thing."

He could only stare at her. A dangerous blend of love and desire tangled inside him too powerfully to be borne. "Where did you come from?" he managed to ask.

"A tower."

He couldn't help but laugh though it sounded rough. He buried his fingers in her hair and dragged her up for another hungry kiss. "I do love you," he admitted against her lips. "My true love needed to be adventurous and fun and not expect me to know everything." He rested his forehead against hers, and a hint of peach again climbed his cheeks. "I don't want to make love to you here."

"Three months would be a bit much, lovely as the place is."

"No, not that." His eyes shifted away shyly. "You'll laugh at me."

"No, I won't." She tugged him back. "What is it, Magnus?"

"I just . . . ." He huffed out a breath. "I want us to be in my cave. And . . . I . . . ." Much softer, he admitted, "I want to be married first. A new life. For us. Together. If we're married, then no one can take us away from each other. Even your dad would have to concede."

She took a long breath. "Okay, you're going to make me cry, and that's not fair because I'm not the crying type. Does it have to be a big ceremony?" she asked warily. "I'm not the ceremonial type."

"I'd settle for finding a judge willing to perform it," he confessed. "The problem is . . . dragons aren't governed by human laws. We would need to find someone with authority that both of our species obey. That might take a while, and the longer we go without consummating our relationship, the closer to insanity we're going to get."

She drummed her fingers on her arm as she thought quickly. "Okay. Here's what we'll do. Let's skip the kissing and cuddling thing—because even tame sparks can become infernos *fast*—and focus on finding someone that can marry us. We'll hit the road back toward the dragon lands, and once we're married, we'll hide away in your cave and hope that we get lucky enough to make our own furry baby dragon. I'll send a letter to my parents to tell them they'll be grandparents and then we can live happy ever after, right?"

He grinned. "Right."

CHAPTER THREE

It was just as well they decided to wait before becoming lovers. Both were quite famished from the trip and needed to refuel. They set out into the town once more and were relieved to notice most of the heroes had departed. Boy, were *they* in for a surprise! The tavern was open and merry, and the couple headed there for lunch.

Neither had ever been in a tavern before, and the onslaught of sounds and voices and bodies was momentarily disorienting. Both shortly adapted and grabbed seats at the only vacant table. A cheerful waitress dropped off a menu for them, and Liz contentedly studied the offerings. "What do dragons eat anyway?"

"Mostly veggies and fruit but we like bread," he answered absently.

She slowly looked up. "Dragons are *herbivores*? Then why the heck do you have those sharp teeth?"

"Fighting. They're weapons, not tools." He grinned as he perused the salad options. "Of course, we big, mighty, terrible beasts must be meat-eaters since we obviously devour whole the foolish princes who dare test our might. We even snack on princesses." He shot her a decidedly sensual look over the top of the menu. "I'm looking forward to snacking on mine."

She hastily drank her water. "You have to admit it *is* unexpected for you to be veggie eaters." She pouted. "I like red meat. Would I have to give it up?"

"Nah. We can adapt for you omnivore types. We don't eat

meat because we can't digest it. It's not that we're bothered by it." He held up a hand to get their waitress' attention. When she hurried over, he smiled. "One large Veggie Lover salad for me, and a beer."

"Ale," Liz requested. She handed over the menu with a smile as well. "And the rare cut of the day."

"Sure thing. Give us 'bout half an hour for the meals." She headed behind the bar and returned shortly with their drinks. "Here you go. Enjoy."

Liz sipped her ale happily. She very rarely got to indulge in drinking anything except wine. It was such a delicate and refined drink that royalty pretty much drank nothing else. It was considered one of the reasons most royals couldn't match the endurance of peasants in a drinking contest.

She and Magnus enjoyed people-watching while they waited for their meals, and both dug in happily once they were served. They debated over dessert and then decided to split a piece of decadent chocolate cake. Dragons were herbivores, but they loved sweets in all shapes and sizes.

They were lingering over the last few bites when a conversation from the next table drifted close. "Did you hear the first set of heroes can't find the kidnapped princess?" the one woman asked her companion. "The king is getting vexed. I think I heard from someone that he might be trying to make a deal with the Wizard Rovan."

"Ugh." Her husband sat back on a scowl. "That's asking for further trouble. Isn't Rovan the one who uses all of that shady magic? The king is only going to make things worse for himself."

Liz scowled and pushed away the plate. "Well, there went my appetite."

"Mine too." Magnus got to his feet. "I'll pay for our meal and we can rest for the remainder of the day. We'll set out first thing tomorrow morning to head for the dragon settlement. We'll still be safer there than anywhere. Deals with shady wizards? That sounds like the makings of some serious trouble."

"Agreed."

They spent the rest of the afternoon relaxing at the inn. It wasn't entirely restful though. They had to keep at least a foot of space between themselves, and even that didn't help much. It seemed that the harder they fought, the worst it got. Liz had the mental impression of a piece of rubber pulled too far apart; eventually it would reach its max and yank them together without care or regard for whatever else was going on.

They set out onto the road again right after dawn the following day. Liz was armed with a sword this time thanks to a stop at a shop. "Will you protect my virtue?" Magnus teased her lightly.

She shot him a heated look. "As if you don't know that I'm the biggest danger to your virtue. Will this be easier to handle once we're lovers?"

"Not really. This is pretty much how we're going to be all season." He winced wryly. "Guess I owe an apology to some friends and neighbors for complaining about the noise they make. I have a whole new sympathy." He couldn't resist tangling his fingers into her hair for a moment. "And I think I understand what my elder was saying when she mentioned it was daunting at first but enjoyable once you got used to it."

"I do feel strangely happy," she concurred. "I mean, I'm slightly insane, half tempted to rip off your clothes, and on the point of discovering self-combustion, but I'm actually *happy*. Maybe because it feels good to want someone and be wanted that much." She shot him an impish grin. "Not to mention we both know we're *really* going to enjoy working off the frustration part. I do believe you're going to make it worth waiting for, Magnus."

"I would agree."

She lifted a brow. "Is that because you've never, hmm, *tested* this form, or because you've never mated in any sense of the word?"

He smiled. "We mate for life, remember?" He gave a gusty

sigh. "Too bad you can't take a dragon form. Then we would have two ways to *test*, as you put it."

"And make enough noise to get revenge on your neighbors?"

"I'm not admitting it if it's true."

The teasing came to an abrupt halt when bushes rustled around them. Before they could move, a band of men leapt out of hiding. All were armed with enchanted weapons sure to do a lot of damage to any magical creature, even a dragon. "Ah ha!" one exclaimed. "You must be the princess we're looking for! Come with us and you'll get home safely, Your Highness."

Liz covered her face with a hand. "Uh, gentlemen, I do hate to break the bad news, but I wasn't kidnapped. I went willingly. We're on a journey." Among other things. "Do I *look* like I've been kidnapped? I mean, if *you* were going to kidnap a princess, wouldn't you lock her up somewhere?"

"That's not how it works, dear." One of the men propped his sword on his shoulder. "Rovan hired us to return you at all costs, and the dragon is to become steaks for the banquet. You're coming with us whether you like it or not." He smirked rudely when she drew her sword. "Really? What do you know about weapons?"

She calmly aimed the tip under his chin and watched him warily ease back. "A lot more than you might be comfortable admitting." She slipped the backpack off her shoulder with her free hand and held it out to Magnus. "Hold this."

"Yes, dear."

Having the element of surprise on her side allowed her to knock two of the slayers flat before the other two realized what she was doing. She competently kept the two still standing at bay before finally finding a place where she could kick one hard enough to plant him on his butt in the dirt. The last was the leader, and he was both skilled and strong. They went back and forth several times before he finally barked out something that sounded like a foreign language.

One of the downed men held up his hand and a large ball of

magic formed. Magnus gave a shout as he lunged forward, but he wasn't quick enough. The blast smashed into Liz's blade and sent it reeling out of her hands. The backwash of the attack knocked her back several steps where she tripped over a stump and landed on the ground.

One of the other men had gained his feet and he grabbed Magnus. The leader reached down and hauled Liz up to her feet by her arm. Fury blazed out of his eyes. "Not bad," he grit out. "They said you were an odd one, and now I see what they mean. You should have played nice, princess. We have no reason to bring you home in one piece. They'll blame your buddy there."

She leaned back as he leaned in and nearly gagged at the stench of his breath. "I'll scream from here until next year what really happened. You can't intimidate me into anything!" Her free hand shot up and smashed into his chest with a force that made his internal organs feel strangely gooey for a moment. He staggered and she tore herself out of his grip. It tore her sleeve in the process, and the ugly bruises forming on her skin became visible.

Magnus saw red. He had been pushing the edge of his temper already with threats to his mate, but her calm handling of the ordeal had kept him tame. Seeing marks on her skin ripped aside every shred of civility. Nothing and no one *dared* harm a dragon's mate. With a quick application of the technique he had been taught, he got free of the one holding him.

A surge of bright magic changed him back into dragon shape. A snarl locked in his throat as he pounced on the first offender and broke several bones. A second barely managed a scream before claws tore him apart. Two others managed to escape. The leader grabbed up his sword and rushed in to attack, but Magnus smacked the blade away. Smoke puffed from his nose as he grabbed the man in a painful vise made from sharp claws. "Do humans fly?" he rumbled. "Let's find out!" He whirled around and hurled the man through the air with casual and almost brutal strength. He had no care for where he landed or if he would survive.

Liz had a feeling her jaw was hanging open. She had almost forgotten that her playful, sexy, would-be lover was actually a very big, very easily provoked, beast with claws and teeth. "Uhm." Her eyes widened as he moved closer, and her heart began to race. Not with fear. Strangely, she was feeling a little bit thrilled. She kind of had the feeling that only his current shape kept him from tumbling her into the bushes. "May I retract an earlier statement?" she asked breathlessly.

"Which one?" He lowered his head, and fresh rage flared as he saw the splotches of black and blue on her arm.

"I have changed my mind and I entirely don't mind being rescued, if you're doing it. It was really amazing."

A low laugh rumbled in his chest. "I didn't rescue you. I just cleaned up what you started." He delicately began to use a claw to rip her sleeve away from the shoulder entirely. That done, he softly nuzzled her arm and then began to gently lick the bruises.

Pink flushed her face. "Dare I ask?" She turned her head in surprise as she felt magic tingling through her arm. Her eyes widened slightly as she saw the bruises disappearing and felt the dull ache fading. "You can *heal*? With a *lick*?"

"Gift of a mated dragon." He watched in satisfaction as the marks faded. "I'm sure there's some rational explanation that has something to do with the chemistry that makes us mates at all, but we dragons just say that love heals and call it a gift from the God of Love." He gently closed his claws around her body. It was hard to believe that much strength was packed inside such a delicate frame. "We're getting out of here. We'll stop long enough in a town for supplies and then fly non-stop for my cave and safety."

She still wasn't wholly breathing as he flew up into the air and effectively carried her off. Marriage or no marriage, she was absolutely going to seduce him as soon as they were in his cave. It would still be a new life. Or, maybe, they might get *really* lucky and find someone to help them in the next town.

He landed just out of sight of the town and put her down. He shifted back to human, but his head hadn't stopped spinning before she leapt into his arms and kissed him wildly. He growled softly and dragged her even closer. He whirled and pinned her against the nearest tree in order to have the freedom of his hands. His fingers rushed open the laces of her tunic to find the heated flesh beneath. It never occurred to either of them that they were a hundred yards from a town and hardly somewhere private. The season had consumed them.

Perhaps luckily, a pair of doves flying by happened to coo loudly enough that it brought back a moment of cognizance. Magnus cursed ripely under his breath as he tried to lace Liz's tunic again but his shaking fingers kept interfering. Her entire body quivered violently against his, and her dazed emerald eyes looked like dark gems. "We won't survive three months," she managed to say huskily.

"Oh, we will," he muttered, "but we won't be walking after. Also? If you get pregnant early on, the season will lessen its grip because, hey, we succeeded at what it wanted."

She held up a trembling finger. "I would like to state that I wouldn't mind a month of mindless passion before we conceive and go back to the normal mindless-yet-endurable version."

"So noted." He managed to put her tunic back to rights and tucked her cloak around her shoulders again to hide her torn sleeve. "You said no kissing," he scolded her.

"It's not my fault that getting rescued by you got to me like that." She couldn't resist snuggling up against his side as they walked into the town. His skin always seemed a bit on the cool side but felt really delicious against hers. He warmed up pretty quickly, too, if she was kissing him. It would be fun to see how warm he got if she started petting him.

"Stop smiling like that," he grumbled. "You're not making my life easier, Liz." He firmly extricated his arm and poked her in the nose. "Stay here and be good. I'll buy what we need. We should reach my cave by nightfall."

"Okay." She watched him walk away and looked around curiously. The town was much like any other of its size, she supposed, since it had all the same amenities of the last one they had seen. It felt kind of boring, so maybe she wasn't cut out to travel after all. At least, not to the small places. It might be fun to visit other large cities. There was always more to do.

An elderly hand holding a red rose lowered in front of her. She turned her head quickly and discovered an old man had come up behind her silently. His was a wizened face set with surprisingly youthful blue eyes. She took the rose and smiled. "Thank you. What's this for?"

"You look a bit lost." He cocked his head slightly. "What has you troubled, my dear?

"Well . . ." She had never been the type to dump her problems on other people, yet something about this stranger just made her trust him. "I'm in a bit of a bind." She gestured to where Magnus was haggling price on bread with a baker. "We want to get married. Start a life together."

He shrewdly eyed Magnus. "Dragon, yes?"

"Yes."

"You worry that the laws of the land will not govern your union." He tugged lightly on his beard. "A fair worry, but perhaps time for a change. Now, I have a fondness for true love." Humor filled his eyes. "I imagine it is quite . . . tempestuous for you two this time of year."

"Good word for it," she muttered.

"Indeed. I think perhaps I may be able to assist you, Elizabelle." He rummaged in the pack slung across his body and emerged with a scroll. "Behold! A creation of the purest magic in the land and the force of raw love energy. A contract forged by the hands of Eros and Psyche themselves."

Her eyes slowly widened. "The God of Love?"

"And the Goddess of Destiny. They seem to be fond of you." He offered the contract.

She unrolled it and began to read. Delight slowly rose inside as she realized what she held. There, in plain language, was a marriage agreement. The seal located in the upper corner was unfamiliar somehow, yet she felt she ought to know it. "If Magnus and I sign this, we are married?" she asked eagerly. "And it says here it will be enforced. Will it?"

"You can be sure it will be Enforced to the highest degree," he promised softly.

She rolled it back up again and tucked it into a pocket inside her cloak. She rose on her toes to quickly brush a kiss over the wrinkled cheek before her. "Thank you so much!" She turned to hurry away but something made her glance back. Perhaps unsurprisingly, the old man had disappeared. She just smiled. Good spirits came in all kinds.

Magnus walked up with a large sack slung over his shoulder. "Phew! We're good to go. We'll have enough to wait out the storm likely to hit just after we get home. It's promising to be one hell of a blizzard." He winced. "We'll see if we manage to stick to our promise when we're closed in with no outside forces for a few days."

She bit back a smile. "I think we'll be fine. Let's go now. I want to see your cave!" She paused. "Uhm, not to be too *human* on you, but . . . do you have furniture? Like a bed . . . chairs . . . things other than just a cave floor and copious piles of gemstones? Blankets?"

"Blankets, yes. Furniture will have to come later. I'm sorry. I *can* promise a mattress though. I have one for my dragon form. Big and fluffy with down feathers. We might get lost in it for now, but it won't be a floor."

"That works for me."

They left town to where there was room to shift, and the storm clouds were indeed moving in overhead. This part of Mirage always got heavy snowfall when winter arrived. Magnus turned back to dragon form, and Liz climbed up onto his back. She held onto their packs as he flew low through the trees. They didn't want to fly high enough to be spotted. The storm would also buy them a few more days, thankfully.

It was hard to determine the passage of time thanks to the heavy cover, and the gloom thickened as the air got colder and colder. They circled into the mountains as the first fat flakes began to fall, and they were both lightly dusted by the time they arrived at his hidden cave. He uncovered the entrance and ushered her inside, and then closed it tightly behind himself before he shrank down to human again.

She was surprised to discover it felt warm inside the cave. "How is that possible?" she asked curiously.

"There's a vein of hot springs running under the mountains. We figured out ages ago how to divert them to warm our homes during winter times. It's especially useful since half the clan is mated and doesn't emerge during those months." He slung the packs over his shoulder and took her hand. "Come with me," he urged. "I don't know if my treasure will suit a princess, but I will share it with you gladly."

She caught her breath as he brought her around the last corner and revealed the heaps upon heaps of stone in the raw that he had mined. Torches filled the place with flickering warm light, and proudly displayed the bounty. "They're beautiful!" She reverently reached out to touch a huge deposit of emerald that was eerily like her eye color. "You mine these yourself?"

"I do." He put the packs down. Her delight at seeing his collection made him happy. "I like them, but I'd be happy to spend them. I don't have a need to hoard when I can find more. We could use them to pay for more travels. Or not." He shrugged with a wry smile. "I didn't enjoy it as much as I thought."

"I was thinking the same. Maybe I'd want to see big cities and then come home to a base. Like here." She picked up a piece of ruby and admired it. "I could make a necklace from this," she noted wistfully. Realizing what she had said, she turned with wide eyes. "I mean . . ."

"Ah ha!" He grinned. "I was wondering if you had any other talents you hadn't shared. The princess who should be adorned in jewels would rather be *making* them."

She winced wryly. "I had to do it on the sly. I always wished I could be common so I could open a trade."

He spread his hands. "Here you go," he said simply. "What I have is yours to use. If you need gold or silver, we can trade with other dragons. You can make your jewelry and then we can travel and sell it. The best of all worlds." Peach climbed his cheeks. "And, you know, if we have a baby someday. I could watch over him or her if you were working hard. Travel as a family."

She took a deep breath. It seemed like such an impossible dream that he offered her. There was no recrimination for her less than ladylike skills and graces. He loved everything about her the way she loved everything about him. If they were the new cycle, then the new cycle would be wonderful. "Magnus." She slowly drew the scroll out of her cloak. "This was given to me."

He took it and opened it. His eyes began to widen as he read. "What?" he breathed. "We're married if we sign this?"

"It is overseen and Enforced by the highest of powers. The very protectors of lovers themselves. They're real. They're not a faerie tale. All species abide by the laws of love. Neither your clan nor my family could dare argue." She held up a pen. "I don't need a ceremony. Maybe a party eventually, if anyone wants to celebrate. Will the dragons like me?" she asked hesitantly. "We've assumed they would accept us."

"It's not an assumption. They might be surprised since it's unexpected, but if we're mates, then we're mates. They'll just throw a party to celebrate and probably kidnap a human doctor so our doctors can learn what they need to take care of you as needed." He took the pen from her and signed on the line above his name. "What's the line? 'I thee wed.'"

She signed as well and smiled. "I thee wed." She thought about things for a moment. "I want to make our rings."

"Done." He dropped the scroll on the ground and pounced on her to scoop her up into his arms. Her shriek of laughter made him grin as he swung around and strode past the piles of jewels. "I have a very big bed. It has blankets. We can make a nest and not emerge for a day." The wailing of the storm overhead seemed to thicken and he slowly smiled. "Maybe three days, even."

She spotted the large and definitely fluffy bed they approached. It wasn't *too* big. He was only ten feet long, and the bed was only two feet bigger than that. She laughed again as he tossed her onto it and she sank in. "I like it!" She closed her eyes and spread her arms wide for a moment. Movement made her open her eyes once more and she looked up to see her husband kneeling beside her.

The hunger on his face stirred up every primal urge. Any hope of maintaining the lighthearted mood simply evaporated. She rose up to her knees to face him and buried her hands in his hair to drag him down for the kisses she needed more than air. His hands clenched hard around her waist as he fed from her mouth, and that wonderful low growl came from his chest.

A small gasp was all she could manage as he literally tore away her cloak and what remained of her tunic-dress. She yanked wildly at his tunic in turn and he ripped it off quickly. She tried to reach for him, but he caught her around the waist and lifted her with effortless strength to bury his face between her breasts. "I like human-type mammals," he rumbled. His teeth scraped deliciously. "So soft. Silky. Hot."

Hot? She was burning alive with the need to touch and be touched. She could feel her womb clenching and unclenching in greedy demand, and every pulse in her body throbbed with wild pleasure. "Tease later," she managed to say. "Not now. I can't stand it."

He had waited too damn long to rush that much. He ripped away her bra so that he could feast upon her damp flesh with hungry kisses. She moaned softly and another growl answered her.

He yanked and tore away the rest of her clothes until she was finally naked in his arms. A bit dazed, he stared at her. He had found no treasure more beautiful than the creature in his arms. Maybe he would become a hoarder after all.

Their lips met in another desperate kiss and his breath whooshed out as she tumbled him over. She could not strip him as quickly as he had stripped her, but she was surprisingly strong and efficient. As soon as he was naked, he wrapped her within his arms and held on. The sensation of bare skin against bare skin made them both shudder.

He rolled over again and pinned her to the bed as he kissed her greedily. His freed hand slid between her legs only to find her more than ready for him. The first stroke of his fingers made her cry out. The second had her arching. It was such an erotic sight that he fought for control long enough to stroke her again.

"Hurry *up*!" she demanded breathlessly. Fingers stroked again and her breath broke on a sob. "I'm getting you back for this!"

He dragged her closer and braced himself over her. She fiercely wrapped her legs around his waist as he plunged deep into her body, and all she could manage was a strangled gasp as she felt him pulsing deep inside her body.

Nothing else mattered but the driving urge to live. To celebrate life. To create life. He drove into her again and again until her nails bit into his shoulders in desperation. When ecstasy finally arrived, it boiled up from some hidden place inside until it consumed them both in fire. Somehow, blessedly, the searing heat of his release deep inside her body seemed to help ease the demand of the season. Whether it would last or not, she didn't know, but it was enough to simply savor the lingering throb inside her entire body. She had no energy or desire to be anywhere else but there in his arms.

He had enough presence of mind to catch his weight on his arms to not smother her, but that was the extent of his ability. A little shift of her body allowed him to relax fully and they could both focus on catching their breath.

"Umph." She found the strength to wrap her arms around his shoulders. "So very worth waiting for," she sighed contentedly.

"Agreed." He turned his head to nuzzle her neck. Just the scent of her sweaty skin was enough to bring fresh desire rushing back in. She might or might not be pregnant yet. He wouldn't be sure for another few days when her body chemistry began to change and affect her scent. Only then would the season ease. In the meantime, they had a storm to enjoy. "Again?" he asked huskily as he tasted her pulse.

"If you insist," she murmured breathlessly. "But I'd recommend feeding me and letting me bathe after else I be too sore and tired for anything else."

"Feeding I can do." He slowly stroked in and out and savored the way her eyes deepened and darkened with arousal. "I can even offer a bath. Don't worry about being sore, though." He pressed deeper and caught her around the waist when she arched in reflex. "Remember what we dragons can do for our mates."

"I think I like being a dragon's mate." She was still going to have to get her revenge on him, though. Turnabout was assuredly fair play.

CHAPTER FOUR

Three blissful days passed in quiet solitude. Magnus showed Liz his portion of the hot spring that he used as a bath, and many playful moments were spent splashing each other mercilessly. They explored the stacks of gems for the best ones for their rings and finally found the ones they wanted. They could get her some tools later. They ate their meals wherever they liked, and he winced wryly when she revealed her spare clothes that she had no intention of wearing until they left the cave. It was best to not risk getting these ones ripped off too.

They made love as often as their bodies would let them. Intimacy infused the entire cave until there wasn't any place that they couldn't look at without one of them getting the giggles. Neither had ever spent that much time alone with another person let alone expected to enjoy it so deeply. It was more than just the frenzy of the season. It was the quiet moments in between where they talked, and laughed, and shared secrets.

Only one sobering moment came, and it was when she finally asked softly, "Will you age with me, Magnus?"

His fingers buried in her tangled hair. They were snuggling together under the blankets, contentedly entwined after the most recent wave of passion. "Of course," he answered simply. "I've already adjusted my aging process. All creatures with longevity are born knowing how to abandon it if needed. For as long as we are given, we will be together."

The storm had finally lessened its fury. Being as sane as they might be for the time, they reluctantly got out of bed. She got dressed in her spare clothes, and she grinned as she watched him turn to dragon and back. The process recreated clothes for him. "At least until I can get more of my own," he assured her.

"You don't need to stay in this form all the time," she noted reasonably. "I think you're quite handsome as a dragon."

"I've found I'm strangely comfortable on two legs." He grinned sheepishly. "And the longer I maintain it, the better I get at it. I might be less likely to trip you onto the floor."

"On *accident* anyway." Her brows lifted as she heard a loud scratching noise at the entrance. "Is that the equivalent of a knock?"

"It is. The one sound we can't ignore is a claw on stone." He shifted into dragon again and reached down to offer her a claw. He lifted her up to sit on his shoulder and called, "You may enter!"

A few moments later, Coral walked cautiously into the cave. "Magnus?" she asked skeptically. "We hadn't heard from you after you left, and someone said they saw you return right before the storm. Why didn't you . . ." She trailed off as she spotted Liz sitting on Magnus' shoulder. "Oh. You have a guest." It dawned and she groaned. "Tell me you didn't kidnap her from the kingdom!"

"I asked him to," Liz assured her hastily. "I'm the one who called to him. I didn't expect my father to misunderstand and overreact."

Coral eyed her knowingly and then Magnus. "I'm sure that wasn't all you two didn't expect."

Magnus eyed her back. "You sound entirely unsurprised."

"I admit I'm not." Coral shrugged with a smile. "It happens infrequently. Once or twice every few generations. It's just not talked about because the humans get so damned pissy about the silliest things. Oh, sure, half-faeries are just fine, but the gods forbid there be half-dragons running around."

Delight brightened Liz's face. "Then we *might* have a child?"

"Truth told, you two have better odds than most dragon

couples. That's why we have breeding seasons, young ones. Dragons are not exceptionally fertile. Humans, however, are. We shall have to see if you have been blessed after the last few days." She smirked at Magnus. "Better sympathy now for your neighbors?"

"And then some," he grumbled. He huffed out a breath. "Liz and I are married."

Scaly brows lifted. "How is that possible?" She spotted the scroll that Liz held up, and she recognized its type immediately. She had seen one or two in her long life. "Ah. Of course. In a way, that does not surprise me either. Well then. Come along, whelps. We should go to the council and explain what has occurred."

Liz felt curiously unafraid and not nervous at all as she rode Magnus' back while he flew toward the meeting area. Coral's reaction alone had told her that she would find far more understanding here than among her own kind. As she looked around at the series of caves and cliffs scattered across the mountains that made up the clan's settlement, she decided she very much liked it there. If they could only get an alliance going! Humans and dragons would work together really well. After all, any hero worth his salt would probably be more effective with a dragon for an ally rather than an enemy.

The elders were a bit nonplussed by the wiling arrival of a human princess within the settlement, but they listened intently as Magnus candidly recounted the events up to and including the realization that Liz was his mate and their marriage contract overseen by the God of Love and Goddess of Destiny. He finished the tale by saying, "We would have checked in sooner, but, well, the storm was convenient."

"There isn't a mated dragon on grounds that would begrudge you that," one elder noted dryly. He sighed gustily. "I miss those days."

Liz bit her lip to hide a smile. She had asked about what would happen when she was past her childbearing years, and Magnus had cheerfully told her that dragons had the same thing happen around the same equivalent age. Male and female alike were unable to produce children once they were more than halfway through their lifespan. It ensured that any children born to a couple would keep their parents until they were adults themselves (barring outside factors, of course).

"Well!" Another elder bent down to peer closer at Liz. "Welcome to the settlement, Liz. I think we should name you an honorary dragon and have a celebratory party to commemorate your marriage to our Magnus." She winked roguishly. "We'll then leave you two mates alone to hopefully produce our first half-dragon baby in two centuries." She patted Liz gently on the head. "You need not worry about your care during such a time. We have skilled healers, and one is old enough to have tended the last birth. You are in good claws, little dragon."

Liz looked at Magnus with a smile. "I *really* like it here. I think I finally have somewhere to fit in!"

Dragons were a resourceful lot who loved a good party. Word spread rapidly about the events and food was hastily assembled for the celebration. One of the cooks even graciously made a dish with meat in it just for Liz; breeding season was murder on energy levels, and they didn't want her to miss out on her needed nutrients just because they were herbivores. The sheer level of their consideration for her made Liz begin to realize that dragons might just be the more civilized of the two races. And she was just fine with that, really.

Those who could take a human form did so as well to help make more room for those who couldn't. They played music, laughed, danced, and had a grand time celebrating the new couple's union. Magnus introduced Liz to his parents, and she could only laugh when they both enthusiastically hugged her and thanked her for taming Magnus' adventurous spirit. Taming, nothing! They fully intended to share and enjoy it.

The party was brought to an abrupt and crashing halt by the sudden explosion of magical fireballs against the side of the mountain. "Raid!" someone shouted. "There's a raid attacking! They bear the colors of the Montgomery Kingdom and the Wizard Rovan!"

"Someone must've been watching the settlement," Coral said grimly. "To arms!" she shouted. "Drive them out but avoid bloodshed if possible! This is merely a misunderstanding!"

It was hard to call it a mere misunderstanding when Rovan was leading a small army of heroes and princes desperate to prove their valor. Liz scowled and looked around. "Alright! Who here hoards weaponry as treasure?" A few claws went up. "I need a sword and a shield. I can't promise they'll be intact when I return them. I might be bashing heads in."

Almost collectively, the entire clan fell in love. One dragon hurried off to his cave and shortly returned with a polished sword and jewel-covered shield. Liz took them gratefully and ran over to where Magnus was standing in dragon form with Coral. The fight had already started outside. More than one hero looked slightly surprised at having his life spared if he was knocked down. A rising tide of confusion began to move through some of the army.

The doors burst open and the fight poured into the celebration hall. Dragons might have been bigger targets, but they could throw magic and breathe fire. Liz darted fearlessly around legs and tails to knock back any enemy that threatened to do more permanent injury to her new family.

One prince in particular caught her eye as he dueled Coral. He was by far the most skilled of the bunch and he had already done a great deal of damage. Liz gave a little snarl and hurled her sword at him like a spear. It struck his blade with enough force to knock it out of his hand. Before he could turn, she was on him. The next thing he knew, he was flat on the stone and his head was reeling around on his shoulders.

He shook his head to clear the stars and looked up to see who had defeated him. Shock made his jaw drop. "*Elizabelle*?!"

Liz stared at him in turn. "Solomon? What are you *doing*

here?" She knelt beside her brother and scowled. "Are you insane? Why didn't you or Mother and Father think to *check* before assuming I was kidnapped? This is *me*, remember? As if I would be kidnapped by anyone! *You* taught me to defend myself, and *I* invited Magnus up to my tower! Any guard would confirm it!"

He slowly sat up. "What the hell is going on?" he asked warily.

She grabbed his head and jerked it around to stare at the fight. "See that? The dragons aren't playing nice because they think you're cute. They don't want to fight! Damn it, Solomon, I'm *married* to Magnus! We're mates, and dragons mate for life. The dragons consider me one of their own now!"

His head swung back to her. "Are you serious?" he demanded.

"After three days of trying to conceive a half-dragon baby? I'm damned serious."

That was not a mental image he had needed, though he was kind of tickled at the idea of his sister as a mother. A half-dragon baby also sounded, well, really adorable. "You're happy here? Really happy?"

"Happier than I ever have been," she confirmed softly. "Solomon . . . everything we've ever thought about dragons is wrong. Magnus proved the truth of it when he tried to offer alliance. And what did our Father do? Brushed him off and called him a beast. There's so much we could learn from each other. This entire fight is pointless."

He took a long breath. "Well. I feel foolish." He let her tug him up to his feet, and he looked at Coral shamefully. "My sincerest apologies. I sought only to save my sister."

"You are forgiven," the elder assured him. "We have never held a grudge against your kind. To mark all of you as blind, bloodthirsty beasts would be to treat you no better than you have treated us." She winced. "My mate will tend to my wounds, young ones. Hurry and end this madness."

Solomon and Liz rushed into the crowd, and both began to grab as many of the humans as they could to spread the word that

Liz was willing, the dragons were not evil, and this entire fight was only going to make things worse. Blessedly, heroes and princes alike were quite susceptible to the pleas of a beautiful maiden. Liz knew it, and she played it for all it was worth by sprinkling a few tears and begging for a chance to be happy with her dragon.

The fight ended swiftly thereafter and turned into an almost eerie silence. Wounds dotted both sides but there had been no casualties. Liz looked around quickly but did not spot her husband. She could see his clan mates, but not him. A cold wind touched her skin and she looked quickly toward the entrance to see it was still open. She ran swiftly toward the opening. The sound of magic made her heart skip a beat with fear. "Magnus!"

She could see the bloodstained ground where a particularly vicious fight had occurred. Snow was disturbed and shoved aside as if something large had been dragged through. She scrambled down the cliffs as fast as possible and ran to the edge where she could see the road below. Her heart stopped entirely.

A very large cage was being hauled away by oxen, and her mate was inside the cage. He looked bloody though somewhat whole overall, and he had been chained and muzzled. A man in the familiar clothes of a wizard rode at the front of the cage, and any time that Magnus tried to break free, the wizard fired off a magical blast that just did more damage.

"Rovan." Solomon had come up beside Liz. Anger darkened his face. "I didn't like it from the beginning when Father reached out to him to assist the men trying to rescue you. There were plenty of other good wizards and witches to seek aid from, and he chose the one who did nothing but bad magic."

"What would taking Magnus back to Father without me hope to accomplish?" Liz demanded sharply.

"Quite simply," an unfamiliar woman's voice said behind them, "Rovan intends to claim Magnus murdered you and should be killed. If Magnus dies, you will die as well. Mated pairs simply can't exist apart any more than lovebirds could. A failure to save you would in no way stop Rovan from claiming his reward for capturing the beast that slayed you."

The siblings turned to discover that an old woman had somehow joined them. She seemed quite beautiful especially in her advanced age, and iridescent black eyes held little bits of sparks that could only be evidence of temper. "Who are you?" Liz asked slowly.

"That is not important." She held out an interesting mask that shimmered with magic. "This is called the Mask of Illusions. It will change your appearance to suit your needs. It will serve you well in rescuing your dragon, Liz. Consider it a . . . prop on loan to you while your contract is still in progress."

Liz took the mask and studied it for a moment before turning to her brother. "I need an enchanted sword and the mantle of a dragon slayer."

"Let's see if the dragons can help." He ran back toward the hall, and she was right on his heels.

The old woman smiled to herself as she watched them go and then sighed as the old man stepped up beside her. "You didn't think to give it to her sooner."

"I assumed you would need something to do, beloved." He scowled down at her, since she stood many inches shorter. "You *should* be resting, though."

She merely snorted at him.

Upon reaching the kingdom, Magnus evaluated his options and decided to change into his human form. His wounds protested the shift, but at least they weren't spread over as large a surface. They even healed to some extent since some couldn't transfer. The muzzle also went away, but his magical chains just shrank down and continued to hold onto his wrists and ankles.

He was pissed, he was scared, and he was confused. The

confusion came from much the same wonderings as Liz, but there was an additional confusion for the fact that he was pissed but not *enraged*. The breeding season had made him far more temperamental overall, yet he felt relatively normal in his anger. Maybe because Liz wasn't there? He couldn't really say. The entire thing was new to him.

Rovan eventually stopped the cage outside the castle, and guards came to escort Magnus into the throne room where the king and queen awaited. The wizard walked with a distinct swagger that made Magnus barely refrain from rolling his eyes.

The king glared intently at Magnus. "You have a lot of nerve! Coming here professing to be after alliance, and you take my daughter from me when I refuse! How can you claim to be civilized? Where is my daughter?" he demanded.

Magnus opened his mouth, and Rovan cut in with a falsely sincere tone, "I am sorry, my liege. There was nothing to be done. She has already been slain."

Magnus stared at him. He knew it was a lie. It had to be a lie. He would have felt if he had lost his mate. He would have protested the entire thing, but people in the room were already beginning to cry and wail. The queen dissolved into sobs, and the king seemed pale and sick. It was unlikely anyone would listen to the accused murderer if he tried to protest or explain reality. He needed an outsider to plead his case!

One promptly arrived in an unlikely form. The crown prince burst in the doors and demanded furiously, "Will you all cease this ridiculousness?" He stalked across the room and aligned himself beside Magnus. "Elizabelle is *alive*. Rovan is lying through his teeth in order to secure his reward! Liz was with Magnus in the settlement, certainly, but she was there *willingly*."

"Solomon, are you mad?" his father snapped.

"I am more sane than you!" He gestured at the bound dragon. "I stand by my brother-in-law! He and Liz are married, and their contract is governed by the highest of powers!"

A murmur of disgust began to run through the crowd. Several people looked ill. Vicious whispers of 'unnatural', 'immoral', and 'disgusting' began to be heard. Solomon looked around at all the people who had proclaimed to be civilized, to want their princess' happiness, and he saw finally what his sister already had. He was beginning to prefer the dragons as well.

"Enough!" the king roared as he leapt to his feet. "Fetch me a dragon slayer! This creature's head will roll!" He glared at Solomon. "And you, son, will spend a few days in the dungeon for your foolishness!"

"Why not the tower?" Solomon muttered so low only Magnus heard. "Why do we get the dungeons?"

"You don't cry," his brother-in-law muttered back.

The throne room doors opened and a figure strode inside. A cloak covered him from head to toe, and a mask under the hood kept his face hidden from view. No one who looked at him could seem to put a finger on his height or frame. Solomon and Magnus saw with eyes that loved, however, and could easily see the shorter stature and delicate frame that would not normally belong to any slayer. There was no mistaking that the person in the cloak was a woman.

The slayer stopped beside Magnus, and he barely kept the shock off his face as a familiar scent curled into his lungs. *Liz.* A second shock rippled through his heart and was followed shortly by blinding joy as he smelled something else and realized why his temper had leveled off. Their season had ended.

"You called for a slayer?" The voice that came from within the cloak was impossible for anyone to recognize, except for Solomon and Magnus. "What does he stand accused of?"

"Kidnapping and murder." The king glared malevolently at Magnus. "Your end is here, dragon! You will rue the day you met my daughter!"

"The one thing I will never do," Magnus countered softly, "is ever regret that."

The slayer drew an enchanted sword from a sheath and aimed the tip under Magnus' chin. With shocking speed and accuracy, the blade flashed through the air. It did not go for the dragon's neck, however. It shot downward and cleanly ripped through the magical binds. Shocked gasps and cries rose as Magnus was freed and turned to attack Rovan. The wizard darted away like a coward.

"What is the meaning of this?" the queen snapped.

The slayer reached up to pull down her hood and revealed ebony hair. She calmly removed the sculpted mask she wore, and everyone was immediately able to recognize her. Her armor disappeared to reveal a common tunic and leggings. She casually dropped the cloak on the floor though she retained her weapon. "Rumors of my death were highly exaggerated."

Her father and mother stared at her for long moments. "Elizabelle?" her mother asked in a trembling voice.

Liz turned a narrow look toward Rovan. "You are a lying, cheating, filthy sack of deceit and viciousness." She swung around to her parents. "Read my lips: I was not kidnapped. I was not murdered. The *closest* I have come to being in any danger was when this vile beast," she gestured at the wizard, "sent thugs after me and Magnus that threatened to assault me if I didn't return willingly."

"Then where have you been the last few days?" her father demanded.

A hint of a feminine smirk touched her lips. "Enjoying my honeymoon and dragon breeding season."

Silence fell sharply for long moments. Then, finally, the king sighed. "You are truly in love?"

"Very truly. I am happy, Father. I found where I belong."

He said nothing as he digested that. He reached a decision at last and gave a quick nod. "So be it. From this day forward, let there be al—"

"I don't think so!" Rovan snarled furiously. Magic coalesced around his hands and body. "I was promised a king's fortune, and I will have it!" He gave a bellow of rage as he hurled the blasts right at the thrones where the ruling couple sat.

It never reached them. Magnus shot across the floor and shifted to dragon form just as he reached them. The transformation created a surge of magic that repelled the attack entirely. He spread his wings wide to protect the two humans. "You won't harm my wife's parents!" he snarled. "Though they probably deserve a knock or two," he added under his breath.

A bit shakily, the queen admitted, "I begin to think you're right!"

Solomon drew the sword he wore, and he and his sister went after Rovan as one. The wizard could only fend off one of them at a time. If he tried to blast one of them, the other got in a strike with a sword. The enchanted blade did the most damage, and Rovan realized almost too late that he was outnumbered. He rushed away in a terror and scrambled out of the palace. He made it out into the city before he noticed the shadows moving in. Slowly he looked up and found several dragons hovering in the air.

His terrified shriek cut off abruptly as one of them landed directly on his back and flattened him to the ground with a bone-crunching force. His hand twitched once and then ceased to move at all. The dragon looked around at the astonished gathering of citizens and asked politely, "Oh, sorry. Was this seat taken?"

Inside the throne room, Magnus moved back to Liz's side though he did not leave his natural form. He curled a claw tenderly around her body to keep her close. Everyone watched the absolute trust with which Liz cuddled against his leg, and they at last began to see that there really was true love present.

The king slowly straightened to his full height. "As I was saying before we were interrupted . . . I am sorry." His gaze lowered. "Magnus, I ask your forgiveness. Elizabelle—Liz—my beautiful daughter, I am sorry to you as well." His chin lifted. "Let it be known that the princess has married her chosen suitor, and there is a new prince claimed by this kingdom. Let it be known also that no more will the Montgomery Kingdom condone the senseless hunting of dragons. From this day forward, there will be alliance, and we will do all within our power to bring our fellow kingdoms onboard as well!"

A resounding cheer rose, and Magnus shifted into human form. He promptly laughed as Liz leapt into his arms and kissed him quite soundly in front of the entire court. He swung her in a happy circle before tenderly lowering her to the ground. He pressed his forehead to hers. "How do you feel?" he whispered.

"I feel normal enough," she whispered back. "Should I feel odd?"

"Maybe not yet, but you will soon enough. Did you notice we didn't go nuts from that kiss?"

Delight lit her face. "Really?" A happy laugh bubbled up as she threw her arms around his neck. She turned her head and there was no mistaking the glow in her eyes as she looked at her family. "Mother, you need to learn to knit!"

Well, that called for another celebration. The kingdom threw open its doors to as many dragons as could fit, and a new party was launched. As the dragons had adapted for Liz, so did the humans adapt for the dragons, though there *was* a bit of bemused humor at the realization that dragons were vegetable eaters. The party lasted until the early hours and only broke as dawn approached and it was time for the dragons to return home.

Liz bid a tearful goodbye with her parents with the promise to visit, and for them to visit as well. She turned to hug her brother as well only to realize he had changed into durable clothes for traveling. "Are you leaving now?" she asked curiously.

"I think I am." He smiled. "I think I have a bit more to learn about our world." He kissed her cheek. "Send me word when I'm about to be an uncle, and I'll rush back. Be happy, little sister."

She kissed him in turn. "And you."

They traveled partway together before he turned go down a

different road that led the opposite direction of the mountains. Magnus turned to a dragon and Liz started to climb onto his back when she spotted a familiar old man watching them with a smile. "Well, hello!" She walked over to him and held out the contract and mask. "I think I need to give these back to you, don't I? Have we fulfilled the terms?"

He opened the scroll and smiled as the word 'Complete' appeared in red across the middle. "Indeed. It was an honor to aid you." He bowed with more grace than his age implied. He tucked the scroll into his bag once more and headed down the road to where the old woman waited. Their fingers entwined with a nearly sensual sort of belonging, and they simply dissolved into the sunrise within a few steps.

"Who were they?" Magnus murmured.

Liz smiled up at him. "The protectors of lovers." She swung up onto his back gracefully. "Let's go home." She hugged him tight around the neck and sighed contentedly as his wings folded back to hug her in return. "I think we finally have our happy ending."

EPILOGUE

The 3rd District in New York City on Earth was overseen by the company known as Enforcers. The co-owners were Rhianna Taber and Eric Mason; one covered the day-to-day operations and the other worked behind-the-scenes. They had also recently added a sub-partner in order to have someone keeping a more steady watch on the world of Mirage; the two worlds were somewhat glued together, so Enforcers kept an eye on both.

Aaron Taber sauntered into his wife's office and boasted, "I knew all along that they would be perfect."

Rhianna did not look up from where she had been adding notes to their latest scroll. "You wouldn't have even noticed them if I hadn't pointed out where their paths converged."

"Hmph." He leaned on the edge of the desk and watched her put the scroll into a folder that also reflected its completion. "You would not have shared that vision if I had not said that I was intrigued by them."

"And you would not have been intrigued if I had not suggested peeking in on the current events." She opened the drawer where she kept Mirage contracts and slid the folder inside. She closed the drawer with a little snap of satisfaction. Another job well done.

When she got to her feet, she was halted from advancing around the desk by her husband's hands curling warmly around her rapidly expanding waistline. He tugged her closer and smoothed his palm tenderly over the large swell of her belly. "You should be resting. You are carrying twins, my beloved."

"I can't even break a nail without someone fretting," she complained. "The next thing I know, you're going to try to hide me away in some secret palace again!"

"He's not suicidal," came a mutter from the office beside hers, followed by a giggle from another voice.

"You two hush!" Rhianna scolded, but she was smiling. She slid her arms up around Aaron's neck and tugged him down for a lingering kiss. In the last few months, every memory of every painful moment had almost ceased to exist inside their happiness. "We do good work," she murmured.

"We do." He trailed his fingers down her cheek. "Do you suppose Solomon has a story to tell?"

"Don't we all? I suppose we'll just have to see what will happen."

"So sayeth the Goddess of Destiny?"

She just smiled. There would be hundreds of thousands of stories to be told in the future, and each would earn a special place within their files. Until the very force of love itself stopped, there would *always* be a tale to be told that would begin once upon a time, and end happily ever after.

Who could ask for more?

Status: File Complete
Analysis: Sometimes it's the dragon that wins the princess, if the dragon is the one who loves her with all his heart.

Author Notes

And that's all she wrote—almost literally. The District Series has finally come to an end. And here, at the end, I can finally say with sincerity that all along it told Rhianna's story. From the day I set out to write THE SHAUGHNESSY FILE, I knew that this book was where we would end. I hope you loved your journey through my magical District, and I equally hope it is one you will return to again and again.

What's next? Glad you asked! In 2018, look for THE TWO KINGDOMS, the first book in the Kingdoms Series, where a universe far away from our own lays out worlds like flowers in a garden, and only the ones known as Cultivators can keep the weeds of evil at bay. Be they Ruler or Defender, the Cultivators tend their worlds and the universe beyond—but always at a high price, for history is stained with their blood.

If you loved this story, or any of my stories, please leave me a review on Amazon! Reviews are the bread and butter of an author's life, and even a simple "More, please!" will keep us going.

You can keep up with me on www.facebook.com/stacyjgarrett or www.stacyjgarrett.com or follow my blog at stacyjgarrett.wordpress.com. I sometimes lurk on Twitter (@stacyjgarrett), and Tumblr as well (stacyjgarrett.tumblr.com).

I can't wait to see you again within my magical District! Until then, keep looking for those happy ever afters!

Stacy J Garrett

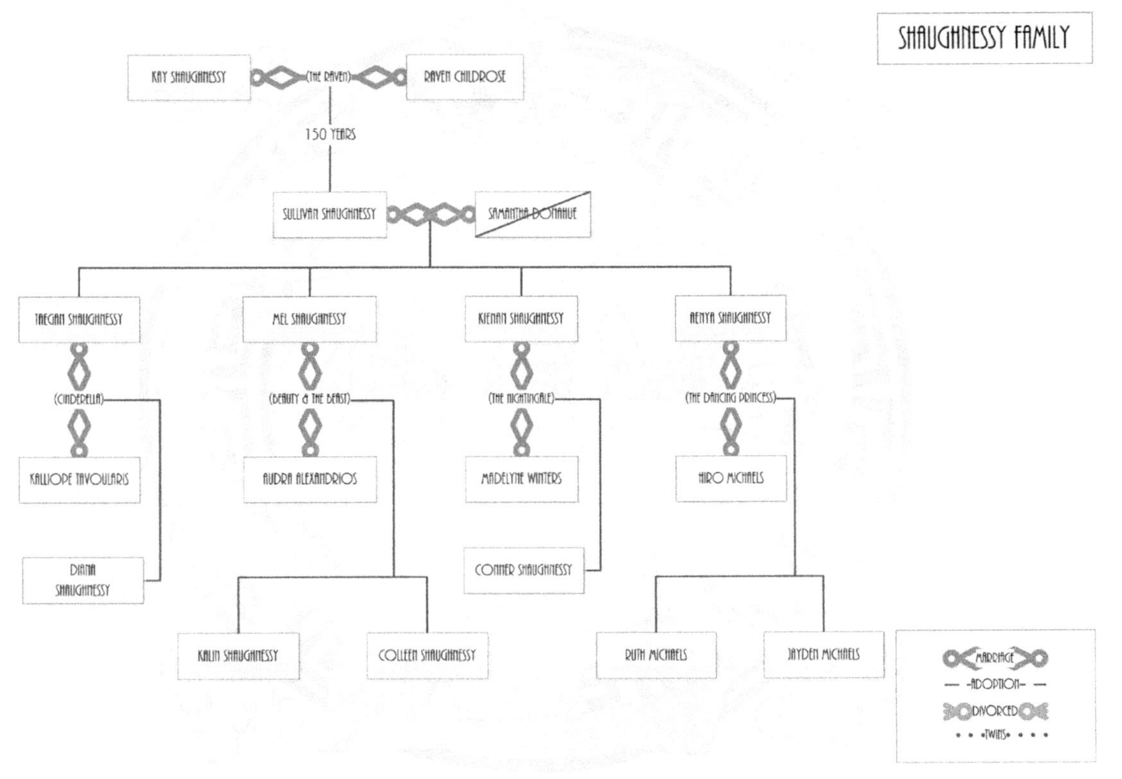

SHAUGHNESSY FAMILY
KAY SHAUGHNESSY
(THE RAVEN)
RAVEN CHILDROSE
150 YEARS
SULLIVAN SHAUGHNESSY
SAMANTHA BONAHUE
TAEGAN SHAUGHNESSY
MEL SHAUGHNESSY
KIENAN SHAUGHNESSY
AENYA SHAUGHNESSY
(CINDERELLA)
(BEAUTY & THE BEAST)
(THE NIGHTINGALE)
(THE DANCING PRINCESS)
KALLIOPE TAVOULARIS
AUDRA ALEXANDRIOS
MADELYNE WINTERS
HIRO MICHAELS
DIANA SHAUGHNESSY
CONNER SHAUGHNESSY
KALIN SHAUGHNESSY
COLLEEN SHAUGHNESSY
RUTH MICHAELS
JAYDEN MICHAELS
MARRIAGE
ADOPTION
DIVORCED
TWINS

THE TABER FILE

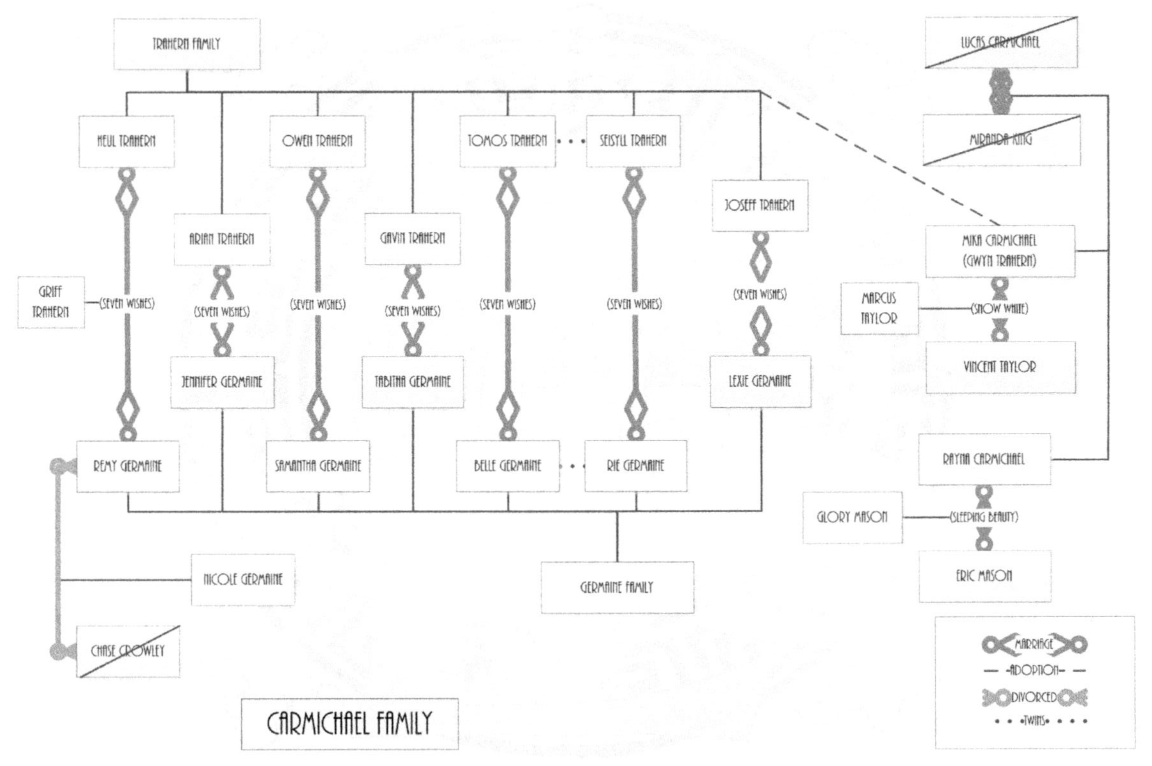

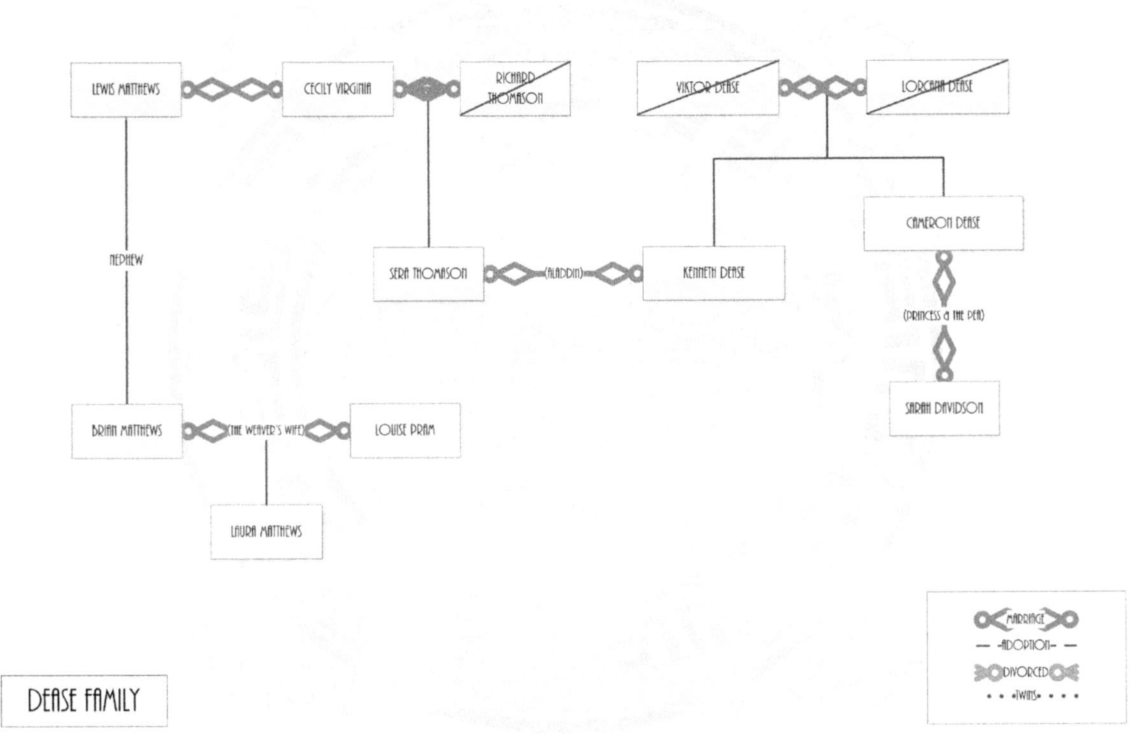
LEWIS MATTHEWS
CECILY VIRGINIA
RICHARD THOMASON
VIKTOR DEASE
LORCAN DEASE
NEPHEW
SERA THOMASON
(ALADDIN)
KENNETH DEASE
CAMERON DEASE
(PRINCESS & THE PEA)
SARAH DAVIDSON
BRIAN MATTHEWS
(THE WEAVER'S WIFE)
LOUISE PRAM
LAURA MATTHEWS
MARRIAGE
ADOPTION
DIVORCED
TWINS
DEASE FAMILY

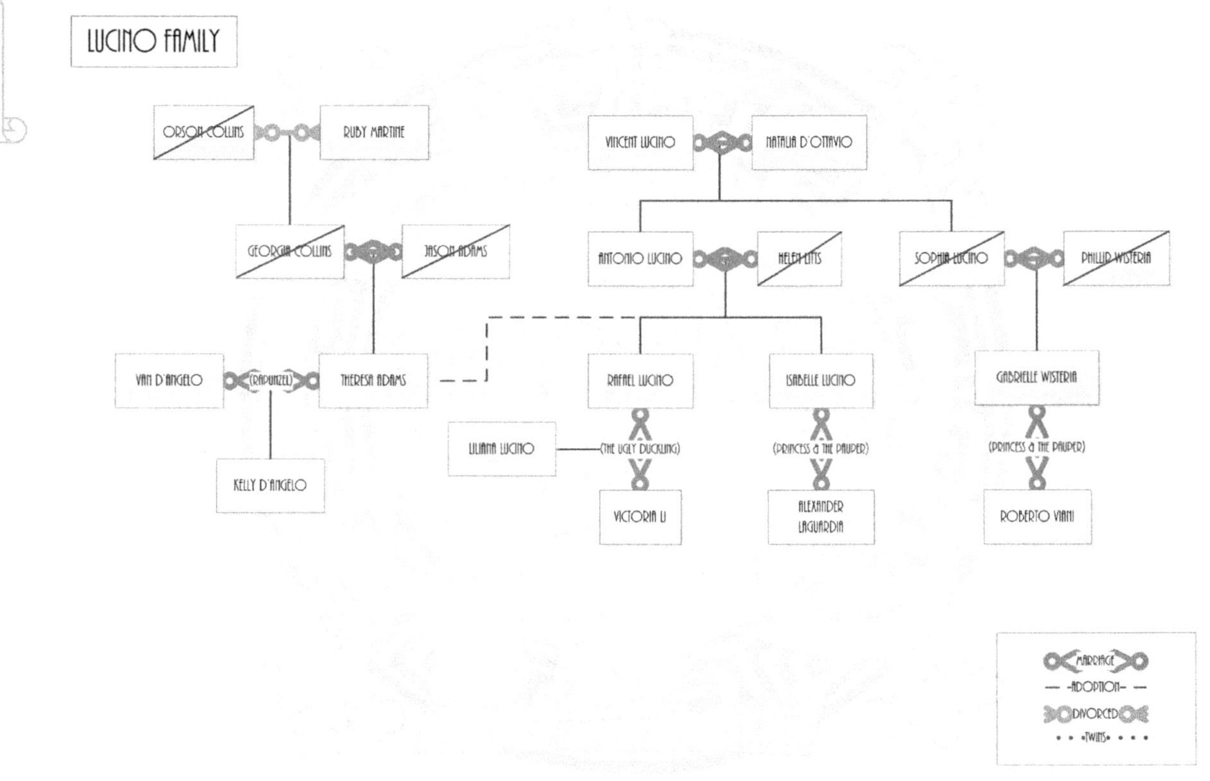

LUCINO FAMILY
ORSON COLLINS
RUBY MARTINE
VINCENT LUCINO
NATALIA D'OTTAVIO
GEORGIA COLLINS
JASON ADAMS
ANTONIO LUCINO
HELEN PITTS
SOPHIA LUCINO
PHILLIP WISTERIA
VAN D'ANGELO
(RAPUNZEL)
THERESA ADAMS
RAFAEL LUCINO
ISABELLE LUCINO
GABRIELLE WISTERIA
KELLY D'ANGELO
LILIANA LUCINO
(THE UGLY DUCKLING)
(PRINCESS & THE PAUPER)
(PRINCESS & THE PAUPER)
VICTORIA LI
ALEXANDER LAGUARDIA
ROBERTO VIANI
MARRIAGE
ADOPTION
DIVORCED
TWINS

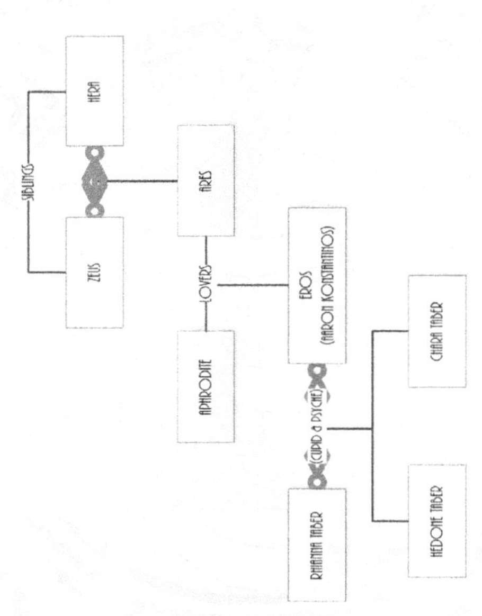

TABER FAMILY

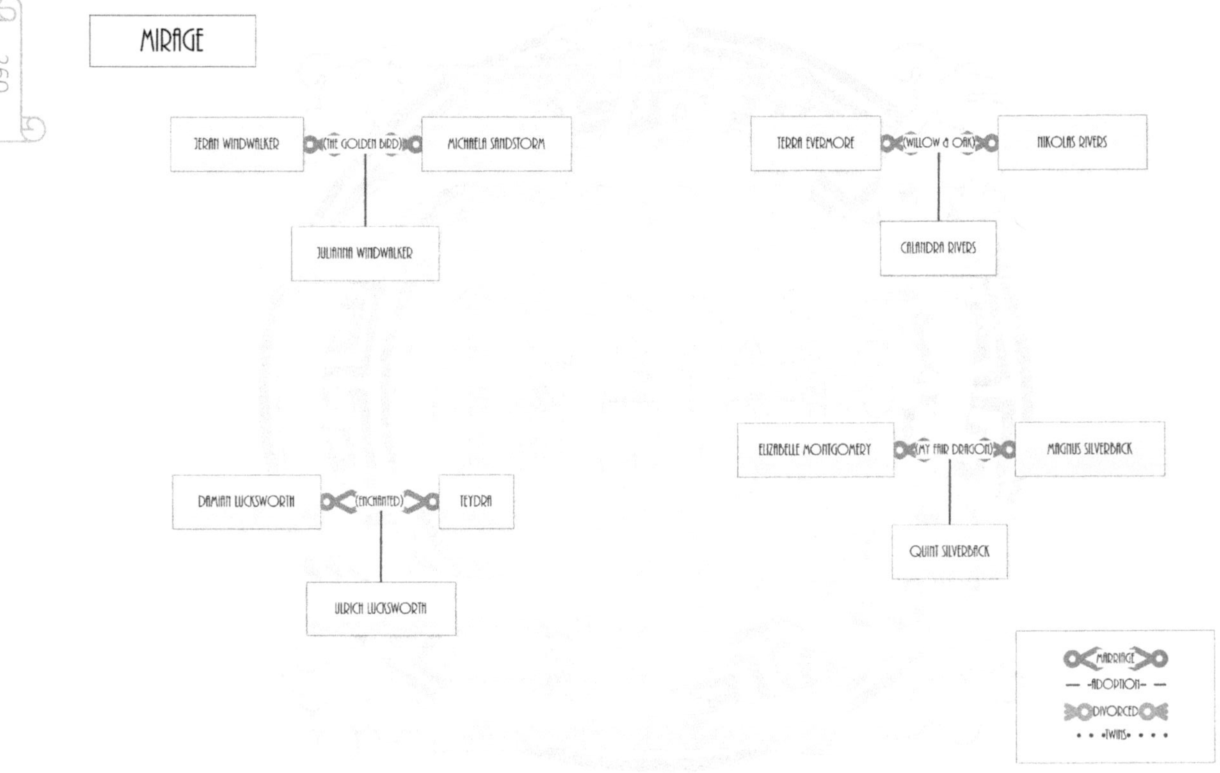
MIRAGE
JERAN WINDWALKER
(THE GOLDEN BIRD)
MICHAELA SANDSTORM
JULIANNA WINDWALKER
TERRA EVERMORE
(WILLOW & OAK)
NIKOLAS RIVERS
CALANDRA RIVERS
DAMIAN LUCKSWORTH
(ENCHANTED)
TEYDRA
ULRICH LUCKSWORTH
ELIZABELLE MONTGOMERY
(MY FAIR DRAGON)
MAGNUS SILVERBACK
QUINT SILVERBACK
MARRIAGE
ADOPTION
DIVORCED
TWINS

Stacy J. Garrett was made in England but born in Sacramento, California, and like the redwoods of the state, her roots have dug deep. Her destiny as a bard was somewhat inevitable. Little else can explain how she constantly told her mother tall tales so outlandish that she couldn't even get grounded for them. Her mother and grandmother had her reading by age three, and that love of a good story propelled her through so many books that Scholastic Books gave her a medal. A love of worlds created by others eventually brought out the desire to create her own, and she has never looked back.

Stacy has seen both good and evil in her life, and her stories, like life, have no half measures. Even in a fantasy world of dragons and faeries, even in a modern city where magic abounds, she knows that the constants of real emotion never change. Dreams come true, love can be found at first sight, princesses can rescue their princes, and maybe there really can be happily ever after. Her happy endings never come without cost, though, for she truly believes we can't appreciate the good and the joy without the bad and the pain along the way.

Her current haunt is a comfy house in her beloved Sacramento where she wrangles four feline fur-kids and consumes peppermints like mana in order to balance a calendar filled with more creative venues than a sane person should realistically undertake. If she's not chained to her desk, she's stomping through the scenery in search of equally fantastical photographs.

www.ingramcontent.com/pod-product-compliance
Lightning Source LLC
Chambersburg PA
CBHW061026120726
47910CB00006B/2125